THE
MONET
MURDERS

THE
MONET
MURDERS

TERRY MORT

PEGASUS CRIME
NEW YORK LONDON

THE MONET MURDERS

Pegasus Books LLC
80 Broad Street, 5th Floor
New York, NY 10004

First Pegasus Books edition September 2015

Interior design by Maria Fernandez

Library of Congress Cataloging-in-Publication Data is available.

ISBN: 978-1-60598-697-5

10 9 8 7 6 5 4 3 2 1

Printed in the United States of America
Distributed by W. W. Norton & Company

For Izabella and Brooks.
Someday I may tell you the circumstances that led
to your coming to be. On the other hand, maybe I won't.
A little mystery is good for the imagination.

THE
MONET
MURDERS

CHAPTER ONE

I t was through Ethel Welkin's influence that I found myself calling on Manny Stairs. Ethel was the pint-sized ardent admirer of one Riley Fitzhugh, although she didn't know that was my real name. She was married to a big-shot producer, and she was the cousin of this Manny Stairs, himself probably the second most powerful man in Hollywood after Thalberg. I had shaken hands with Stairs at a party at the Thalbergs' a few months ago. I had been there with Ethel. When I sat down opposite him in his office, Stairs was nice enough to pretend that he remembered meeting me. It was a cream-colored affair with polished stainless-steel accents and glass bookshelves filled with knickknacks, awards, and photographs—and no books. That was not surprising. I had learned by then that producers in Hollywood didn't read; they listened—to pitches, arguments, whining, tantrums, and yes-men. What's more, to put it delicately, they had not come from a tradition of reading and literature. They had come from a tradition of schmatta, which is their word for the garment business. Samuel Goldwyn had started out selling ladies' gloves, or something. That was back when he was still Shmuel Goldfish.

"What do you think?" asked Stairs. "Nice layout, eh?"

"Very nice." Why this guy would need or want affirmation from me tells you something about the town.

"If you can't get a good setup in Hollywood, where can you?"

He was just an inch or so above being able to ride the roller coaster. Maybe five-two. He was wearing a double-breasted gray pinstriped suit cut beautifully and expensively and most likely designed to make him look a little taller. He wore a yellow silk tie any tap-dancer from Harlem would have been proud of. He had receding black hair, a sallow complexion that reminded you of old putty, and thick glasses that magnified his eyes and gave him the look of a walleye on a bed of ice. He was smoking a cigar just a shade smaller than a barber pole. The air in the room was a light blue and smelled Cuban. There weren't the usual potted rubber plants anywhere to be seen; maybe the acrid cigar smoke had killed them off. The carpet was white, although there were cigar-ash blemishes here and there. No doubt they would be gone tomorrow, soon to be replaced by new ones. Aside from the office and his expensive clothes, it was hard to believe that

Manny Stairs was one of the movers and shakers out here, but he was. He and cousin Ethel had been neighbors as immigrant kids back in Brooklyn. They grew them short in that family. But they grew them aggressive.

"So. Ethel tells me you're a private detective."

"That's right."

"You look a little young."

"I'm older than I look." In some ways, that was actually true.

"Like that guy in the story who stays young while his picture gets older up in the attic? We're thinking of doing that one."

"I'm familiar with the original."

"Original? What original?"

"It was a book."

"No kidding?" He seemed genuinely surprised, although he could have been stringing me along. It was hard to tell with some of these guys. "You a college man?"

"No. Self-taught. I read a lot."

"Lots of time to read when you're on a stakeout." It was not a question, so I let it ride.

He studied me for a minute, just the way he had no doubt studied a couple of thousand would-be's. "I'm surprised you don't want to be in pictures. You got the looks. And Ethel could give you a hand in more ways than how she's giving you the hand now."

"I tried it. But I like being my own boss."

"Too many phonies and jerkoffs in the business?"

"That's one way to put it."

"Tell me about it. How much do you make a week?"

"My standard fee is twenty-five dollars a day plus expenses. Some weeks are better than others."

"Twenty-five a day ain't much."

"I don't eat much. Besides, it's the going rate, and I'm the new boy in town."

"You could make a lot more in pictures."

"I could make a lot more robbing banks, too."

This brought a laugh.

"How about a drink?" he asked me.

"Sure."

"Bourbon suit you?"

"Like a custom-made suit."

"This one's custom," he said, fingering his lapel lovingly. "Had it made in London. Savile Row."

"I've heard of it."

"Have you been there? London?"

"No. But I read a lot."

"So you said. I been there lots of times. I go over there to hire writers and directors. You can't hit a nine-iron in any direction without beaning a writer in London. And if you miss a writer, you hit a director. Same with New York. A lot of them are pansies, but we don't care much about that out here. The only pansies we can't tolerate are the ones on the screen—if the word gets out. Otherwise, who cares? Besides, word almost never gets out. The news boys like money as much as the next guy."

"So I've heard." The sleazier the magazine, the happier they were to take a bribe to hush up a sordid story. Some of those rags were really just blackmail operations masquerading as sensational journalism—out to make news and then suppress it, for payoffs. One or two of them had approached me to do a little work for them—tailing some star into a bathhouse where he wanted to be but shouldn't be—but I didn't want that kind of work. It helped that I also didn't need it.

"These English and New York writers are all pains in the ass," said Manny. "We give them a contract for more money than they ever imagined, bring them to Hollywood, put them in an office at the studio, and tell them to write. Nine to five. We want to hear those typewriters clacking. It's piecework, like the old days in the ILGWU [the International Ladies' Garment Workers' Union], only putting down words instead of sewing on sleeves. The system bewilders the hell out of most of them, especially when we introduce them to their collaborators. None of these guys ever worked with a collaborator before or been put on a schedule like a normal worker, and, to be honest, most of them can't ever get used to it. Hurts their pride. Can you believe that?"

"If you say so." I wondered why he was explaining all this to me; maybe he just liked to talk. Or maybe it had something to do with the reason I was here. I assumed he'd get to it sooner or later; I wasn't doing anything else.

"I do say so. And we generally put another and different team of writers on the same picture at the same time, and they turn out some more bullshit, and then we have meetings and argue and paste all the pieces together and somehow it comes out all right. But the writers from New York and London never quite get used to the system. They think they're making art. We think we're making raincoats. And when we're finished, what do we have?"

"Raincoats."

"Right. With dreams attached on a tag. A combination that always sells in Peoria. Sometimes they're artistic raincoats with nice linings, but that's secondary. It's a business, not the Sistine Chapel. Am I right?"

"I've seen my share of movies."

"Ha! So you know I'm right. And you know the funny thing is, most of these creative schmucks are Reds, while the producers here, most of whom have actually done some real labor, are all good Republicans. We understand sweatshops."

"You'd think it'd be the other way around."

"You can say that about a lot of things in this town. They're only Reds because they hate the guys who control the money, meaning us. It fits with a simple-minded system of thought. Us versus them. Try to cut their salaries, though, and see what happens. They're all for the proletariat unless they have to be one. You want ice?"

"No, thanks. Bruises the flavor."

"Good. Private detectives are supposed to be hard-drinking cynical guys, quick with their fists and a rod. Right? At least that's how we show them in the pictures. Which means it must be true." He smiled in ironic appreciation.

"Well, I'm not that cynical." Nor did I carry a rod. I did have a thirty-eight police special in the glove box of my car, but carrying it around seemed a little melodramatic. Plus the thing was heavy, especially when it was loaded, and it was uncomfortable to wear no matter where you put it. If you wore it on your belt, it dragged your pants down; if you wore it in a shoulder holster, it spoiled the cut of your jacket. As for fighting, the last one I'd had was in high school during a football game against Boardman High, and I won't say who won, though I will say a sharp kick in the shins is enough to discourage the average scrawny quarterback.

But I didn't tell Stairs any of that. Let him think what he liked.

Stairs grinned and poured out a couple of man-sized slugs of bourbon, slid one to me, and then tossed his off without a wince.

Then he studied me some more.

"You don't look like a Bruno Feldspar."

"That's because I'm not. I'm not even *the* Bruno Feldspar, except during office hours."

"I didn't think so. You look like a nice Presbyterian kid from the Midwest."

"Right on all accounts except one."

"Which one?"

"I'm no kid. The name was Ethel's idea. She thought it would go over better with the powers that be. And I had reasons to go along with it." I said this in a way that made him think I had something to hide, which was nothing more than the truth. He seemed to buy it. Ethel thought my real name was Thomas Parke D'Invilliers, although it wasn't.

"No big deal. Everyone in this town has a different name than they were born with. Even me. I used to be a Shlomo Rabinowitz. You believe that?"

"Yes." It made me wonder, though, why he'd chosen "Manny Stairs." Maybe it was a secret joke to himself—the idea of upward mobility in his adopted country. If so, it was harmless enough. Of course, "stairs" go both ways. Maybe that was the dark side of his secret joke. These guys played for high stakes and knew it. And when they lost, it was back to the bottom, with a long climb out again. A lot of times, they didn't make it.

"Let's get down to business," he said. "I got a problem."

"I figured," I said.

"Of course. Why else would the second-most important producer in this town call a twenty-five-dollar-a-day private dick?"

It was a rhetorical question, so I didn't answer, just shrugged.

He got up and went to the bookshelves and grabbed an eight-by-ten photo in a silver frame.

"Take a look at that," he said.

It was a platinum blonde. No surprise there. She had a sultry look that almost seemed genuine, and I recognized her as an actress who'd made a few movies a couple of years back. For a moment, the name didn't come to me. Then it did.

"Minnie David, isn't it?" Then I remembered why she hadn't made any pictures lately. She had died two or three years ago in a cheap motor court out in Joshua Tree. Some said it was an overdose, but it had been reported at the time as a heart attack. The guy she was with phoned it in and then took off.

"Minnie David was my wife."

"I didn't know. Sorry."

"We were Hollywood's second couple," he said wistfully, "after Thalberg and Norma. Minnie and Manny, Hollywood royalty. But then she died. It's been three years now. And two months. And fourteen days."

If I'd been as hardboiled as private dicks are supposed to be, I'd have smiled at this bald-headed midget, as handsome as a vacuum cleaner, lamenting a lost love who was beautiful beyond words, with emerald eyes and breasts most men would risk hell for. And, although the word was that her brains had barely qualified her for licking stamps in a post office, that was irrelevant. Beauty may not be truth, but it's a good substitute. And a lot easier to recognize.

But I didn't smile, because I understood. I'd been there too. Still was, really, though my lost love was alive and married, more or less, and spending her days at the country club and being photographed by the local newspaper. Her being alive and well and living in Ohio made losing her all that much harder to live with, because it held out false hopes that were hard to dismiss. So I understood Manny. It didn't matter what a man looked like on the outside; we were the same sad fools on the inside.

"But that ain't Minnie David," said Manny Stairs. "*This* is Minnie David." He showed me another photo in another silver frame, and it looked to me like it was just another shot of that same woman in a slightly different pose.

"I don't understand."

"Amazing, isn't it? They could be identical twins," he said. "But they weren't. This one is named Catherine Moore. She's the problem."

The story went like this—one day about three weeks ago, Manny Stairs had been idly looking out his office window just as some tourists were being ushered through the lot. There were maybe twenty of them, all the predictable kind from somewhere in Middle America, snapping pictures of the exotic sets with Kodak box cameras or looking with wide eyes at the pirates and cowboys and other assorted extras who were lounging outside the commissary, complaining about their agents. But then Manny had noticed one girl who was bringing up the rear, walking by herself, kind of aloof but obviously fascinated by the entire scene. Manny had almost keeled over from shock, because the girl was a near-perfect duplicate of Minnie David, his dead wife. After he got a grip on himself, he ran downstairs; but by the time he got there, the group had boarded their tour bus and left.

So Manny called studio security and set them on her trail. It wasn't hard to find her again, because the studio had a list of the tourists who came through each day. She was a local, living in a small week-by-week apartment in Santa Monica and working as a secretary in an insurance company. Manny called her up and introduced himself and asked for a date, and she agreed. And from there, things took off in a romantic whirl. Manny suddenly found himself being really happy again, swept away for the first time in the years since his wife had died. They went dancing at the Trocadero (he bought her the evening gowns), had lunch at the Brown Derby, dinner at Romanov's, drinks at the Coconut Grove; and in between he showed her around the studio and they watched movies being made and sets being built, and they walked around the lot, moving easily from the OK Corral to the Great Wall of China and through the canals of Venice that had been drained recently to allow some leaks to be repaired, and it was all a wonderland to her, and he hoped that she was being swept off her feet by the glamour of the place. As they moved between sets and sound stages, he made sure to have a few angry confrontations with nervous directors, just to show her who was running the show. He also gave her a few baubles along the way—nothing that she could pawn and live happily ever after on, but shiny enough to indicate that the gravy train was gathering steam in the station.

And Manny was no fool: he never introduced her to the male stars who might be dumb enough to make a pass at her. He knew the ones who were capable of that level of clueless narcissism and the others who were aware of who paid the bills. He restricted her access to these latter fellows. He also knew that all this glamour reflected on him and to some extent blinded her, and that if not for that glamour, she would probably not be so interested in a five-foot-two goggle-eyed producer originally from Brooklyn whose accents and inflections had come there via Minsk.

But that was nothing new to him. It had been the same with his first wife, and that had worked out fine until she killed herself, accidentally, most likely. It was almost like she had come back to life, because this girl, Catherine Moore, was just as beautiful and just as dim-witted as Minnie had been. The crowning moment of the relationship had been when Manny took Catherine out to his beach house in Malibu—a house that was only just then being built and was only half finished—and they stayed there through the night and watched the waves rolling up onto the beach and the stars shining and the moon setting, while they talked of this and that and drank chilled champagne and ate cold lobster, until they got down to what Manny described as some really prime schtupping.

This went on for three weeks and Manny was deliriously happy, until one day he got a letter from Catherine saying that her fiancé from St. Paul was coming to town and they were running away to get married. She was sorry, but she felt she owed it to him, her fiancé, because she had given her promise and although she had loved every minute of her time with Manny and especially going to the beach and the schtupping (which she misspelled, not being conversant with Yiddish), she felt it was her duty to marry this other guy, and so, wishing Manny the best of luck and hoping that he would always think of her fondly and hoping that one day they might even be friends, she told him good-bye.

In short, she gave him the mitten.

"So, what would you like me to do?" I asked when Manny had finished his story. To tell you the truth, I felt a little sorry for him, even though incongruity is the soul of comedy and there was nothing more incongruous than the thought of Manny and this beautiful airhead. He had met this woman in a dream, and he had dreamed it a while, and now had awakened to find that the dream girl had vanished. I understood.

"I want you to find them. Her, I mean. I had the studio security boys look around, but she's left her job and left her apartment, so they drew a blank. Besides, this is in the nature of a confidential assignment. It wouldn't do for the story to get around that I was what you might call obsessed with this broad. The security boys are used to arranging quickies, but it's gotten past the stage where I can use them safely without spreading gossip."

"What about the cops? The missing persons."

"They'd say she ain't missing. Just gone. And then they'd give me the horselaugh, and it would spread. I can't afford to get the horselaugh. Not in this town. The horselaugh in this town is like blood in the water."

"And if I find her, then what?"

"Don't say 'if.' Say 'when.'"

"All right—when."

"I'll worry about that later. Maybe I'll have the guy bumped off." He grinned as if to indicate he was kidding. But it made me wonder. "And maybe they haven't gone through with it yet. Maybe there's still time to get her to come to her senses."

It occurred to me that, maybe, that's exactly what had already happened. She'd figured out that being the wife of an insurance salesman in St. Paul, dull as it would ultimately and very quickly become, was better than being schtupped by Manny Stairs. After a very quick while, seeing movie stars in person isn't all that different from seeing regular people on a downtown bus. The glamour wears off pretty fast. It's all imagery, after all, with nothing behind it. And that goes double and triple for producers. Stripped of his Savile Row suit, Manny would probably not be a sight to make the female heart beat faster, except maybe in panic. You wouldn't want to imagine him in his shorts.

"When did you get this letter?"

"Last Friday. So you see, they even might not be married yet."

"So all you want from me is to find out where she is?"

"More or less. First things first. There might be something else after that. We'll have to play that one by ear. But, you understand, there is some sense of urgency about this."

Well, so far as I could see, the only urgency was in this guy's imagination. He wanted her back and he wanted her now. I understood what he was thinking. In the long run, it wouldn't matter to him whether she was married or not; divorces were easy to come by in Hollywood. Mexico was only a couple of hours away, and divorces there were cheap and, more importantly, quick. No, he was longing for her, plain and simple. It was eating at him, hurting, and he wanted it to stop. Well, as I said, I understood.

"Can I have this picture?"

"No, but I have another one." He pulled open his desk drawer and gave me a snapshot of the two of them standing in front of the Great Wall of China, Hollywood version. He was grinning from ear to ear, and she was staring at the camera like the proverbial deer in the headlights. From her expression, I figured it was a recent photo; she had second thoughts written all over her face. Even so, she did look gorgeous.

My business card said "Bruno Feldspar, Private Detective to the Stars." The name wasn't my idea. Ethel Welkin had dreamed it up when I was out here last year trying half-heartedly to get into the movies. (I'd met her at the Polo Lounge one day, and we'd struck up an acquaintance. Which, after I gave up on the movies, turned into her giving me a hand in getting set up as a detective.) I say "trying half-heartedly" because it didn't take me long to figure out that the movie business wasn't meant for me, or I for it. I mean, you don't have to go to more than one audition and sit around with fifty other guys trying to look like some version of Douglas Fairbanks and waiting to be called into a room with a couple of gnomes who give you thirty seconds to make an impression to understand that this business is not for grown-ups. I did that once and it was enough. I did end up with one bit part, a wagon driver in *Cimarron*, but that was it for me.

Of course, I liked California and the good weather and all the beautiful women. There's nothing not to like about that. But the business itself seemed not worth doing, like being the head chef for Hostess Twinkies. There were too many people pulling you this way and that and no one really knowing what was going on, because the people who controlled the money were a bunch of rag merchants from the east, and most of the people who made the films and considered themselves artistes were just guessing about what they were doing and what would appeal to the masses.

So there was a lot of screaming and temper tantrums and silliness and posing, and underneath it all was a vast and abiding insecurity. Almost all of those people were worried that someday they would be found out. Someone would shout from the sidewalk that the emperor was buck naked, and it would all be over. That made them chronically nervous, and worse, and consequently not fit to be around. There might be some places in California where not everyone was on the make, but it wasn't Hollywood. The money was great, of course, if you were a hit, but that was a long shot under the best of circumstances. The few who did make it were pretty much just lucky, and I never liked relying on luck. It came and went without reason. Luck was for gamblers, and most gamblers were losers.

Then there was that little matter of those capers back East last year, before I came out here, and it seemed to me that putting my rugged features on the silver screen was not the smartest thing to do just then. There wasn't much chance that anyone in either Detroit or Youngstown would recognize me or connect me to that hijacking in Detroit or the money-laundering scheme in Youngstown. But even so, I figured it would be the better part of valor to lie a little low for a while and keep in touch with my friend from the FBI.

I explained some of this to Ethel, though not the part about the capers, and she more or less understood. After all, she didn't care whether I was a big star or a carnival barker. To her, movie stars were so many head of mostly beautiful cattle. She was only interested in one thing; and when I told her I was thinking of becoming a private detective because I had been reading some novels that made it sound at least interesting, she let loose one of her hundred-decibel cackles and said "That's perfect. A private dick. Yum."

Well, she was not what you'd call a lady.

But she was useful and not even that bad a bed partner, though you wouldn't think it to look at her, dressed. Nothing you would want as an exclusive arrangement, of course, because she more or less resembled a fire hydrant in both length and shape, and her fondness for garlic bagels, pickles, and pastrami was a definite drawback. But she was a jolly soul and made no demands other than the one, which was something quickly taken care of in a couple of afternoons a week—she was generally pretty efficient. The rest of the time, I was on my own.

And as an example of her helpful nature, she had introduced me around to some big shots in the business, all of whom at one time or another needed a private detective either to get the goods on a wandering wife or mistress, or to get the wife's private detective off his, meaning the producer's, trail as he merrily cut a swath through fields of beautiful hopefuls from Dubuque and such places. These were the girls who hadn't yet, and probably never would, become a star, or even starlet. But they stayed, still dreaming. Going back home a failure was too sad to think about. They knew they'd get the sly, oh-so-satisfied smiles from the homely girls they'd always behaved condescendingly to. So they hung on in Hollywood and worked the lunch counter at Schwab's or found jobs as secretaries and spent their free time reluctantly in the sack with some guy named Herman who had come out from the Bronx to work for his uncle Isadore as an assistant producer, which let Herman tell all the girls he could get them a screen test. Then they'd send their folks back home a postcard showing the Santa Monica pier in color and saying that they had a big break coming next week, some time. Hopefulness is as addictive as any other drug and, in this town, almost as toxic.

I did like the idea of being a private detective—at least until something else came along that was more interesting. I'd found that I had a talent of sorts for the business when I was back in Youngstown and working undercover with the FBI to set up a money-laundering scheme for the local Mafiosi. What the FBI didn't know was that I was intending to make off with a major chunk of the money, but things didn't work out as planned, and the end result was that I had actually helped the FBI build a case on the local hoodlums, which in turn made the feds grateful to the point of greasing the skids for me to get a license out in L.A. to operate as a private investigator under a fictitious name.

And when I say things didn't work out as planned, I mean I didn't make any money from that deal. But that was all right with me. I only needed a lot of money because my girl Lily was the kind who needed to be kept in the style to which she had become accustomed, as the saying goes. But when she decided she'd better stay with her husband there in her mansion by a lake in Ohio and not run away with me back to California (I had gone back to Ohio to pry her away from him), well, I didn't need big money anymore. It was something of a relief because, had I gone through with my plan, there was a distinct possibility that the FBI or the local Youngstown mob or maybe even both would have figured out what I was up to. They both have long memories, especially when they've been conned. The other thing was, I'd gotten kind of fond of the mobsters I was dealing with. I was even flattered when the local boss offered me a job working with them. I saw it for what it was—a compliment, because he knew I wasn't Italian, let alone Sicilian—and I appreciated the offer, sincerely. So I felt bad about setting them up.

I also liked my contact in the FBI. And he was in no hurry to make the pinch, as far as I knew, and nothing had really happened. Not yet, anyway. For all I knew, my friend in the FBI was currently enjoying a payoff from the Youngstown branch of the Sons of Sicily. Just because a guy wears a crew cut doesn't mean you can't get to him. Well, that was their business. I suppose my ambivalence says something about me. Well, of course it does. But as it turned out, that was all behind me.

The truth was, it was much better this way, although I still missed Lily. She would have been worth the risks involved in the money-laundering caper. But she was settled into her new life and couldn't see how being with me would work. To be honest, she didn't really trust me as a long-term arrangement. I understood, although I didn't like it. She came from a wealthy family and had married a wealthy man, and I had to admit to myself that she was fairly conventional—if you put aside her enthusiastic cuckolding of her husband with her old high school flame, meaning me. But conventionality aside, she also had a new baby, which was a complication. I could imagine her leaving her husband, but not her baby. Well, no mother would. Or at least not many.

I wouldn't have minded bringing the kid along; it wouldn't have been right for her to leave the baby—I knew that. I can take babies or leave them, but more or less adopting the kid would have been worth it to have Lily. But in the end she chose the well-trodden path. It's always the easier route, and I came to California alone.

So I found myself in California without Lily, and with Ethel's help and contacts I quickly got into the swing of the detective business and pretty soon was doing confidential work for clients whose talent for getting into trouble far exceeded their talent for making movies. I even had a little office in the Cahuenga Building on Hollywood Boulevard, complete with a secretary named Della who answered the phone and typed proposals and invoices with a perpetual Pall Mall hanging from the side of her mouth and her right eye squinting and watering from the smoke. She was a sharp middle-aged lady with artificially red hair and a smoker's cough.

Her husband, Perry, ran a water taxi in Santa Monica, taking sports out to the gambling ships anchored just beyond the three-mile limit. He was a former first-class petty officer in the Navy, so he'd run lots of liberty boats and knew how to handle a boatful of drunks, rough seas or smooth. There were a bunch of these gambling ships out there, so Della's husband did a pretty good business, although he worked mostly from seven in the evening till three or four in the morning, hauling high-spirited high rollers out and bringing sodden losers back a few hours later. I guess that didn't leave Della and her husband much domestic time together—and, from what I could interpret, that suited them both. They had reached that stage when it was useful to be married but not so useful as to need time together. Della only came in to the office three days a week, but she added the right kind of hardboiled accent when she was there, and, besides, Perry did a little bootlegging on the side and so was a source of Scotch at a discount. Bourbon, too. Even though Prohibition was over, finally, there were still lots of people who liked to get booze on the cheap. I never asked where he got his supplies.

Della ran an escort service the rest of the week. At least, that's what she called it. The fact that she wanted to work for me part-time made me wonder about the quality of her stable. But I didn't look into that. That was her business.

My benefactor, Ethel, had put up the cash for this office setup, although the truth was I didn't need it. I still had the bulk of the money from that hijacking in Detroit a year or so ago, or should I say that undercover operation that we pulled off and thereby relieved the Purple Gang (a mob of bootleggers and hijackers who operated out of Detroit) of one of their illegal shipments of booze. It was a big score (though hardly enough to keep Lily in style)—twenty grand, which is something people in the heartland could live on pretty comfortably for twenty years, though not in Hollywood. I figured twenty grand could last me a good ten years, if I was careful, so I wasn't worried. I was not extravagant. You grow up in Ohio where most people either farm or work in the steel mills, and you learn the value of money. And the fact was, that Detroit caper led to some gangland executions among the Purples, which in turn led to some arrests and the virtual breakup of the gang. So part of me felt that I had done a good deed for society, while the rest of me was satisfied to keep the cash we'd gotten from selling the booze to Capone in Chicago.

I was staying at the Garden of Allah Hotel on Sunset Boulevard, just across the street from Schwab's Drug Store, lunch counter to the stars, the maybe's, the hopefuls, and the never-will-be's. The hotel had formerly been the home of an aging silent film star, Alla Nazinova, who'd fallen on hard times when the talkies came in because her voice sounded like a dump truck unloading gravel, and so she'd transformed her palatial home into a hotel and augmented the main building with twenty-five bungalows surrounding a swimming pool. There were flower gardens and winding, uneven brick paths among the bungalows and the usual birds tweeting and hibiscus smelling, and it was really a very pleasant place.

But Alla must not have been any better at hotel management than she'd been at acting in talkies, because she soon went broke and had to sell the place, whereupon she moved into one of the bungalows and no doubt began brooding and muttering "sic transit gloria" or its equivalent in Russian. The original name of the place had been the Garden of Alla, after its first owner, but the new management added an H to the Alla in order to give it an exotic touch.

Ethel had suggested the place, because she said it was the favorite of writers from back east who were living there in semi-permanent exile from all things they cherished most, meaning the bars and restaurants of New York and London. The hotel was also a favorite of movie stars who were just passing through for a few weeks, so the atmosphere was in general something along the lines of a fraternity house.

Ethel had some notion that I was a kind of minor gangster trying to reform, more or less, and so thought I would appreciate the free spirits that roamed around the grounds or sat beside the swimming pool. Granted, during the day some of these free spirits were steeped in gloom because of a Homeric hangover or because of the inherent absurdity of being a writer in Hollywood—an absurdity that they all complained about or whined about or damned. They wrote words, but movies were pictures, and therein lay their dilemma. That plus the fact that they had bosses who thought nothing of firing them from a project or bringing in another team of writers to work on the same project. But every evening like clockwork, the gloom and the hangovers would fade away like the San Pedro fog and the bottles would come out and the parties would begin, and after a while some astonishing-looking starlet would take off her clothes and go swimming in the pool, while a half dozen swaying writers, all at some stage of physical collapse, looked on and leered happily, until inevitably one of them fell into the pool too. And in the background, someone's victrola would be playing "Bolero" or "Tea for Two" or "What'll I Do When You Are Far Away," a tune that always made me feel a little depressed because it reminded me of Lily.

And even farther in the background, you could hear the sounds of bouncing bedsprings and the usual groaning or unconvincing screaming from a starlet who was essentially auditioning, for the walls were not thick in these bungalows. Even though they looked like stucco, they weren't. Like much of Hollywood, they were something less than they appeared. There was a story going around about some writer who was asleep and heard a female asking for a glass of water, and so, still half-stewed and thinking it was his bedmate, he got up to get it, only to discover that he was alone and the thirsty woman was next door.

There were women writers living there, too, and they weren't about to be left behind in the dissipation sweepstakes. One time I overheard some guy asking a dumpy-looking brunette with bangs why she looked so tired, and she replied "I'm too fucking busy. And vice versa." It made me wonder how drunk someone would have to be to take her on. But there was more than enough booze available at The Garden to turn even a sagging, past-her-prime Eastern writer into an object of desire. I guess. She had a big contract to write for the movies and, like all the exiles from New York, she hated herself for staying, and said so. But, you see, the money was just too good. Integrity comes high, but it comes.

Ethel thought I would like this place. I don't know whether that was a compliment or not. But I have to be honest, I did. Like it, I mean. It made me think that once I got tired of being a private detective, I might try my hand at writing for the movies. If these people could do it, I figured anyone could. I could drink as well as any of them, and there didn't seem to be much more involved in the business. Besides, what better way of picking up story ideas than digging around in the Hollywood dirt as a private dick? It was not a noble idea, but noble ideas were thin on the ground just then. At least on my ground.

I was living in one of the bungalows with Myrtle George, whose name had been changed by some genius in studio publicity to Yvonne Adore. I had brought Myrtle to California (after Lily had turned me down) and introduced her to Ethel as soon as we got to Hollywood, and, true to Ethel's nose for potential, she'd gotten Myrtle a screen test immediately. Ethel recognized a quality in Myrtle that would come through on the screen—a kind of Garbo-esque melancholy that went with Myrtle's quite stunning physical beauty.

Myrtle was Croatian and had worked hard on her English, so that she had just enough of an accent to sound interesting.

The hint of sadness about her was genuine and had been well developed long before she came to this country as a kind of mail-order bride, and she'd refined it through three years of marriage to the broken-down owner of a diner in the steel-mill town of Youngstown, Ohio, which is where I'd met her. She was also the mistress of my Lily's husband, who was a lout and a boor, but a rich man who could offer Myrtle at least a little diversion and a glimpse of something better than serving up blue plate specials, even though he would never do anything to improve her lot in life beyond a cheap bracelet or two. In her heart, she knew that as well as I did.

And so when I came along with a counteroffer to come with me to California, she had no trouble making up her mind. This was just after her pathetic husband had gotten himself run over by a bus. Whether he meant to do it or not didn't seem to matter in the long run. Myrtle was free to go, and freely she went, after selling the diner to an Italian who was connected and therefore understood the advantages of a legitimate business when it came time to launder money from other sources. I have to confess, if that's the word, that I'd been involved in this particular deal. It had worked out well, because Myrtle didn't want much beyond getting out, and the buyers knew a bargain when they saw it. I even got a commission. I knew more than a few of those boys, and they liked me. They liked me because the old guy who ran the town liked me. There's no sense going into why; suffice it to say that he did, and that gave me a pass with all the local goombahs. Had they known what I was trying to do in partnership with the FBI, it would have been very different. But they didn't. Not so far, anyway.

There was a definite upside to the whole experience, though—I have to admit I enjoyed taking Myrtle away from the cartoon character Lily had married. It came close to evening the score. They say revenge is a dish best served cold, but I say it's like good Scotch—hot or cold, it satisfies. Besides, I could tell myself I was doing Lily a last favor by whisking her husband's girlfriend away so that he could then pay more attention to his wife. Maybe they could work out their little problems and settle into domestic contentment. Or, as they used to say, felicity. I could tell myself that, but I try never to lie—to myself. I didn't want to think of Lily thirty years on, a little heavier and chairwoman of the country-club flower committee. But I knew that's where she would be if I needed to find her. There was comfort, and its opposite, in that thought.

I was only a little in love with Myrtle, and I think she felt the same way. You couldn't really tell about her, because she had a natural reserve, a kind of protectiveness that she'd developed long before I met her. Part of it was the tentativeness that many immigrants feel when they come to this country, especially those coming from poor countries where tomorrow was not a sure thing for most folks. Part of it was the constant knowledge of being an alien, someone apart; I suppose that's why she worked so hard on her accent.

In any event, for whatever reason, there was always something Myrtle kept hidden, even from me. So even though she was a warm and passionate bed partner, there was no way of knowing whether it was just pure animal spirit or something deeper. The best I could figure was that our relationship wasn't exactly a business arrangement, and it wasn't exactly true romance: it was somewhere in between. Maybe we were just friends. The French—who else?—have an expression for this: "amie amoreuse." A friend/lover. That about summed it up, I guess. In any case, I'd wanted to help her, and introducing her to Ethel had been the fastest way to do that.

You might think that Ethel would get jealous, and for a moment I worried about that too. But I should have known better. Ethel was only interested in the schtupping, to borrow Manny Stairs's Yiddish dictionary. She liked me, but that was as far as it went. It wouldn't have mattered to her if I'd been married and had a mistress to boot. She just wanted her afternoon diversions, and in exchange she was only too happy to help me or mine get along in the business. I admired her for that. It was unselfish of her. And that kind of unselfishness was rare in Hollywood. Or anywhere else.

So Myrtle got a screen test and they offered her a contract then and there. It was three years at five hundred a week, with bonus possibilities if she hit it big. It was more money than she'd ever dreamed of, and the evening after she signed it I could hear her in the bedroom weeping. I didn't try to comfort her. I just let her alone. She was getting rid of some heavy things. God most likely knew what they were. I could only guess.

CHAPTER TWO

I wasn't in any particular hurry to find Catherine Moore. I knew when I found her and told her Manny's tragic story, she'd laugh in my face, while her new husband from St. Paul, who was probably an ex-lumberjack or left tackle, would offer to break my jaw for me, and I'd have to talk him out of it or kick him where it'd do the most good before hustling away with dignity intact, more or less.

Besides, I was on a daily retainer. I didn't feel guilty about taking my time. Manny didn't need the money. I didn't either, but I liked it. Besides, I wanted to think the situation through. There was no sense running off half-cocked with no plan. In the end, a good plan of action would be more professional and would probably save Manny money. Was I rationalizing? Could be.

By the time I'd finished my meeting with Manny, I was ready to go back to the Garden of Allah. It was cocktail hour and the starlets were just starting to think about going for a swim. I was still feeling a little glow from Manny's bourbon, and, of course, that's precisely the condition you're in when you're sure another drink is a good idea.

When I got back to my bungalow at the Garden, I was surprised to see that Myrtle was packing her suitcase. Her eyes were red and a little swollen and her nose was running. Even so, she was stunning. She was wearing shorts and a thin top with nothing underneath. That was obvious.

"Hi, honey. Was it something I said?"

She came over and put her arms around me. The smell of her perfume was faint but arousing. So was the feel of her body. She could have been an athlete—and in some ways, she was.

"Oh, Riley. I am so sad."

"I figured that when I noticed you were crying. You forget, I'm a detective. Or at least my alter ego is."

"Don't make a joke. It's true. You see, the studio people came to me today and said my contract has a morals clause and that living with you like this was not a good thing."

"*I* think it's a good thing."

"I do too." She snuffled on my shoulder. "But. . . ."

Well, I wasn't surprised. Living in sin, as some people call it, was okay for the anonymous Myrtle George, but not for Yvonne Adore, a potential star. The studio was going to remake her into some kind of mystery woman from a faraway country—which was not much of a stretch, really—but that image would be incompatible with cohabiting at the Garden of Allah with a private detective going by the name of Bruno Feldspar. The studio boys would concoct some improbable story about her—that she was a Greek virgin who had just left the convent or something along those lines; but if she was still living with me, the tabloids would soon sniff out the truth and go into exposé mode, and everyone would get the horselaugh, which, as Manny Stairs explained, was career cyanide. Some people say there's no such thing as bad publicity, but they're wrong. Consider Fatty Arbuckle as Exhibit A.

Then, once the studio had established her exotic story in the public's mind, they would arrange a romance for her with one of their other contract stars in order to boost the publicity for both of them. It was a well-oiled process. It wouldn't be a real romance and the guy could in all probability be a beautiful pansy, so that the story would do double duty, providing cover for the pansy and publicity for them both. The two of them would look good together on the covers of the magazines. Funny thing was, though, Myrtle's actual story was a lot more interesting than anything the studio flacks would ever dream up. But they wouldn't see it that way. For the time being, her virginity had to be restored.

"What can I do?" she asked tearfully.

"Well, for starters you can stop crying and wipe your nose. I understand why they're doing this, and you—we—have no choice. One of the downsides of signing a fat contract is that you're expected to live up to the terms. And besides, they're not sending you to Mongolia."

"No. Mabilu, I think they said it was. There is a house there."

"That's probably more likely to be 'Malibu.' And it's just a few miles up the coast. There's no reason why we can't still see each other. I do have a car, you know." It was a two-toned cream-and-tan Packard convertible that was my proverbial pride and joy. The leather seats could have come from the Bel Air club. "If anyone gets wind of the fact that we're meeting now and then, the publicity department could put out the word that I'm a private detective working for you on some mysterious case. That'd be a fireproof story, since anyone checking on it would run into actual facts—something most of the tabloids don't know what to do with. After all, I really am a private detective."

"Yes. Your hat gives you away."

"To say nothing of the trench coat when it rains. All part of the image. People expect it. And remember, private detectives are honor-bound to keep their assignments confidential. So my hanging around may actually suit the fairy tale the studio boys are concocting for you."

"They said I'm supposed to be a White Russian princess."

"I'm not surprised."

"I don't like the Russians. They are hairy."

"Well, they're fashionable these days, although the Whites less so than the Reds. Sort of like wine. But the story has to play in Middle America, and most of those good people have more sense than to identify with the bolshies."

"But I don't know Russian."

"Don't worry. Half the people out here don't know English, let alone a foreign language. The whole point is to make you seem mysterious; so the less you say about your made-up past, the better. Let the studio hacks speak for you. They'll know much more about your biography than you will. If anyone asks you about yourself, just look sad and say 'I'd rather not talk about it.' Or 'I vant to forget.'"

She smiled at the absurdity of it all but then grew thoughtful again. She kissed me in a very tender way. She had the softest lips.

"But what about us?" she asked.

That touched me and surprised me. She understood, as I did, that things would probably never again be quite the same between us. It was the end of a chapter, and neither of us could predict what the next one would bring. Or even if there *would* be a next one. It made me sad, which surprised me, so naturally I replied with a joke.

"Well, we'll always have the Garden of Allah."

"You're making fun again."

"Maybe a little. But you know I have always been sort of half in love with you, and I think you feel pretty much the same. No?"

I hoped like hell right then that she didn't disagree. Otherwise, it was the two of us forever. I'd never be able to resist her if she said no, that in fact she was completely in love with me, especially now that she was on the verge of leaving, wearing no underwear.

"Just half in love?" I asked, just to frame the issue again.

"Yes. I think so." She smiled. She had one eyetooth that was slightly crooked; it was her only imperfection, and I liked it. But the studio would no doubt have it straightened. They had an adolescent concept of female beauty.

"So if we see each other half the time, we'll be in love all those half hours, or half days. Does that make sense?" Of course it didn't, but I thought it might fly.

"Maybe."

"And who knows, maybe someday soon you'll meet the man of your dreams—someone you're not just half, but completely in love with—and you'll live happily ever after."

"Would you come to the wedding?"

I began to think we had reached safe ground when she made this joke. She didn't make them often.

"Yes, but don't expect an expensive gift. I only get twenty-five dollars a day, plus expenses."

She looked at me seductively. She smoldered better than Garbo, which no doubt the screen test had revealed. Take my word, she could really smolder.

"How do you know you're not the man of my dreams? Maybe I'm more than half in love."

"I doubt it. I may be the man of your daydreams, but not the important kind. They come at night." For a moment I wished I was wrong about that, but I didn't think I was. I knew she was just feeling vulnerable. We had come west together, and now she was turning herself over to some corporation with its publicity-making machine, and she was nervous. Anyone with any sense would be; her life was spinning out of her control. Hell, she had just lost her own biography. At that moment, I think I could have talked her out of the whole deal, told her to give the studio the back of her hand and come with me . . . somewhere. But it wouldn't have been right. She was too beautiful, and she deserved a chance. There was a real possibility that she could make it. She had that proverbial "something."

Besides, I wasn't going anywhere. I'd keep an eye on her. If someone did her wrong, they'd have to answer for it. I made that pact with myself as I held her.

"I owe you so much," she said, tearing up again. She had the most gorgeous blue eyes, almost lavender.

"Get me a ticket to your first premiere, and we'll call it square. I'll rent a tuxedo. And there are other ways. As I said, I know the way to Malibu, and gas is cheap. How soon do you have to go?"

"The studio is sending a car. They should be here in an hour."

It was my turn to render a seductive look. Now and then I can get one right. "That gives us just enough time."

For the first few minutes after Myrtle left, I have to admit I was a little depressed. The bed seemed empty even though I was still in it. The scent of her perfume, most of it natural, was lingering on the pillow and sheets where moments ago we had said a temporary good-bye. It was depressing to think that it might not have been just temporary. Things seemed to spiral out of control in life. What's the second law of thermodynamics? Things move from stasis to chaos, or something like that. Lives did that too, sometimes. And wouldn't my high-school science teacher be proud of me for remembering that. He was an odd character, with only two neckties and one shiny suit. There'd been an acid burn in one of the ties, but he still wore it. Times had been tough then, just like now. You didn't give up on a tie just because it had a hole in it.

I got up finally, put on my bathing suit, and poured myself the long-delayed drink and drank it. Maybe the starlets were swimming by now. As anyone who has thought about it knows, the only antidotes to booze and women are booze and women. I went out to the pool to see what was happening.

They said the pool was shaped like the Black Sea because when Alla built it, she had wanted to be reminded of her homeland, which was somewhere in the Crimea. Maybe so. But it was certainly big enough. There were the usual collections of stunning young women in scanty bathing suits holding frosted glasses of something and the usual group of writers, most of them overweight and unfit. They, too, were holding frosted glasses. The sun was just about to go down, so the air was cool and the palm trees were not troubled by any breeze. I threw my towel on one of the pool chairs and dived into the water. It felt wonderful, cool and cleansing— not that I needed cleansing after being with Myrtle; she was cleansing of a higher sort.

I swam underwater across the pool toward a group of writers who were just beginning to have trouble balancing on two feet. I assumed there would be some gin and tonic available close by, and I was right. I had gotten to know quite a few of the writers by now, and, as I pulled myself out of the pool on the far side, they welcomed me like a fraternity brother. They all knew I was a detective, not a writer, so I was no threat to them; and they did not expect any witty ripostes from me that they'd have to top, so they could relax. Besides, I might potentially be a source of good stories. One or two might have been slightly worried that I might be on their case. But my boyish charm more or less disarmed even the ones who had something to hide.

"Bruno Feldspar, ace detective, rises from the sea like Venus on a clamshell," said one of them.

"Venus? What are you suggesting?"

"Nothing, my boy. Nothing at all. Come and have a drink." He was a pudgy character with a pencil moustache and thinning hair that he slicked back. He had a receding double chin that went perfectly with a potbelly that had taken years of self-indulgence to create. He was considered the presiding wit of the place. Like most of these characters he had come here from New York, so he had an air of guilt mixed with tired yet amused self-loathing. He was here for the money and made no bones about it; but he was, like the rest of them, fundamentally uncomfortable and out of place, and it showed in his manner and expression. He wanted to be back in Manhattan, exchanging witticisms with people like himself, with everyone seated around a round lunch table and everyone understanding the references and jokes. In Hollywood, if you happened to mention *Ulysses*, people would think you were talking about a proposed sword-and-sandal epic starring Douglas Fairbanks, with Mary Pickford playing Ulysses's girlfriend Lola and Wallace Beery as Ulysses's sidekick Fuzzy.

You might think that the writers would have enough comradeship among themselves, and to some extent they did. But theirs was a brotherhood of despair. They all were constantly depressed by the nature of their assignments, and that got in the way of the kind of sophisticated banter they nostalgically longed for. They wanted a salon but were in a saloon, and they knew it. They wanted to write books and sell them and live on the royalties, but they couldn't make nearly the amount of money doing that that they made here, so they sold out.

I lifted myself out of the water, feeling childishly good about the condition of my body in contrast to the creative types, who collectively had the muscle tone of a dumpling. I noticed a few approving glances from the naked-starlets-volunteer-un-synchronized-swimming show. Maybe they thought I was "somebody." Maybe not. It didn't matter. For the time being, I was merely a starlet aficionado, because that hour with Myrtle had been sufficient. For the time being. But I made a mental note of the more interested glances.

"How many criminals did you catch today, my beamish boy?" asked the head man, whose name was Bob something. I suppose a private detective should be alert to names, but I have always operated under the theory that the best way to approach life is to edit it carefully. I have no trouble remembering useful information. The rest, I sift through quickly and discard most of it. I had no interest in cataloging the wreckage at the Garden. And in the great wide world, there was plenty of bad news to ignore.

"Criminals? I only saw one, and he hired me."

"A producer, in other words."

"My lips are sealed. Professional confidence."

"Perhaps they will unseal once you've had one of these." He handed me a tall frosted glass. It was a gin and tonic. Or at least there may have been some tonic clinging desperately to one or two of the ice cubes, but if so the gin didn't seem to notice it, nor did I.

I blinked a time or two as I swallowed, thinking that a gin and tonic without the tonic ought to be called something else. And then I noticed yet another writer emerging from his bungalow. He was coming down the Spanish-tiled steps from one of the upstairs apartments. He was a recent arrival to the Garden, but I recognized him: I had met him several months ago at Thalberg's party—the same party where I'd met Manny Stairs. At that party, he'd been playing the piano and singing a comic song about a dog and believing that he was entertaining the crowd when in fact he was annoying them so thoroughly that when he finished, they booed him. The air had gone out of him in an instant and he'd seemed to shrink right there, and he wasn't that big a man to begin with—maybe five-seven or so in his shoes. I remember asking Ethel who he was, and she said "Him? Nobody. Just a writer."

As an aside, Ethel's attitude was pervasive among the producing class, and that was yet another reason why the overpaid writers hated themselves for staying. In New York or London, a writer was "somebody"; not here, though. One big-time producer called them "schmucks with Underwoods." Anyway, I'd felt sorry for the guy for making such a fool of himself, and when the disapproving crowd had dispersed I'd gone up and introduced myself and said I'd enjoyed his song, although I hadn't, particularly. He'd smiled sort of wanly and told me his name. Turned out he'd been a famous writer back in the twenties—made all sorts of money, but then lost most of it through too many parties, too much travel, and the other usual culprits. He'd thought the party would never end, but it had for him, around the time of the Crash. Now, a few years later, he was here trying to repair his fortunes in the movie business. He didn't seem all that old: possibly not even forty, maybe a bit older, although it was hard to tell. His wife, apparently, was difficult. That was not a unique situation in this town.

More importantly, he was the one who had given me the idea that I'd used with the Youngstown money-laundering sting operation. He had worked the whole thing out as a scenario in one of his books; and at that party, when I'd told him I had actually *read* his books, he became very chummy.

No surprise there. When I asked him what he was working on just then, he spilled his whole story—after learning that I was not a writer, aspiring or otherwise.

Some months had passed since that party, and I felt pretty sure he wouldn't remember me, but I was wrong. He came straight up to me, smiling, and held out his hand.

"You're the actor with the funny name. We met at Thalberg's."

"Actually, now I'm the private detective with the funny name. My acting career died shortly after birth, unlamented by all."

He nodded. "Wise decision. This business is no place for adults, unless you're on the money side. How about a drink?"

"Sure." Mine was about gone by then. We went over to the bar and poured two more gins and then sat down at one of the poolside tables.

"Did you ever make that movie about the money-laundering scheme?" I asked.

He grimaced. "You remember that, eh? No. It never got past the treatment stage. Too bad. I thought it could work."

I was tempted to tell him that it did work—so tempted, in fact, that I *did* tell him. I just gave him the broad strokes, leaving out locations and names, but positioning myself as an undercover operative for the FBI, which was nothing more than the truth, although not the whole truth. His eyes grew wider and wider as I explained some of what had happened.

"I'll be damned," he said when I had finished. He was almost giddy with pleasure. "I knew it was a good idea." He looked at me with increased respect. "So all the time that you were out here posing as an aspiring actor, you were really a G-man."

"More or less."

"But now you're in private practice."

"Yes. The FBI was too big an organization. I like being my own boss better." Once again, something close to the truth.

He nodded ruefully. "I understand." He gestured over to the lineup of swaying writers. "All of us out here are used to being our own bosses. If we put something on paper that we like, it stays there. Not here. Here you get a committee looking over your shoulders every minute. Do you realize that they actually expect us to keep regular office hours?"

"I've heard." We were silent for a while, puzzling sadly over the indignities you had to endure in exchange for a thousand a week. "What are you working on now?" I asked finally.

"Between projects. That's why I came to the Garden—to relax and unwind. I just got fired from an epic called *The Redheaded Woman*. They gave it to some woman from New York to finish. They said my approach was too serious. And guess who is set to star in the picture? Jean Harlow! Ha! I guess they'll put a wig on her. Either that or hope the public doesn't notice that the redheaded woman is a platinum blonde."

"You don't seem too upset about being fired."

"It happens. As long as the checks keep coming, I can put up with just about anything." He looked as though that was almost true. But not quite. He sighed without melodrama. He seemed more depressed than he wanted to admit.

"Do you ever get tired of being yourself?" he asked.

"I guess everyone does, now and then."

"Some more than others. You know who I'd like to be? Hobey Baker. Ever hear of him?"

"No."

"Before your time, I suppose. He was a little before me, too, at Princeton, but we all knew about him. He was like a blond god on the football field. And in the hockey rink, too. He was handsome and gifted and celebrated in the newspapers. He played football without a helmet, and his blond hair was always visible even in the most terrible scrums. We all idolized him."

"What happened to him?"

"He was killed in the war. Actually it was just days after the war ended, I think. He was taking his Spad out for a test run and crashed. An athlete dying young. Do you know that poem?"

"I don't think I do."

"*Smart lad, to slip betimes away / From fields where glory does not stay / And early though the laurel grows / It withers quicker than the rose.* I sometimes think that sentiment applies to writers, too. The ones who have early success. Far better to get it over with early than to wither away on Hollywood and Vine. Ha! A good pun."

He was silent for more than a few moments, obviously remembering something he didn't want to share.

"Shall I call you Hobey from now on?" I asked, after a while. The idea appealed to him, and he perked up and grinned.

"Yes! By god, I can kill two birds with one stone—lose myself and become my hero. Good idea. How about a drink?"

"Suits me."

"So tell me. What are you doing out here? Working on anything interesting?"

"More or less. Not government business, of course. Private."

"And? Anything juicy? A story idea is always welcome."

"Well, kind of."

"Well? I'm always interested. Don't worry. I won't say anything."

That seemed unlikely. I'd heard he was famous for taking notes during a conversation—a habit that irritated almost everyone he met. But I figured I owed him something, and besides the gin had made me a little incautious—that, plus I was still miffed about the studio's moving Myrtle out; so I gave him the broad outlines of the Manny Stairs story, mentioning no names. I suppose he could put two and two together if he wanted to. Truth to tell, I didn't care.

"Interesting," he said, when I finished. "The woman was an exact double. Yes. Very interesting."

"I'd appreciate it if you didn't do a treatment on it and shop it around."

"No, no. Of course not. But it might make a good basis for a novel some day."

Well, that was all right. Novels take a while to write and by the time he finished, if he ever did, I'd most likely be on to something new.

Catherine Moore had been a secretary in an insurance office in Santa Monica. Manny Stairs had given me the address, and even though his studio cops had checked the place and turned up nothing, I figured it was at least worth double-checking. The office was in a five-story commercial building on Santa Monica Boulevard, not far from the pier. The exterior of the building had a crack running up the side from the first floor to the second, maybe the result of the last earthquake. Based on that, I didn't like taking the elevator, but I did anyway, to the third floor.

The elevator operator was an ancient character with a nasty squint. He wore a shiny maroon uniform topped off with a bellman's cap. The brass buttons had lost their shine back during the Spanish-American War. He smelled strongly of cigars and misanthropy. Well, I couldn't blame him much; what kind of life would it be, spending all day in that windowless cell, going nowhere but up and down—a metaphor that even the meanest intelligence would appreciate? I mean, when you think about it, you have to wonder how some people, most people, probably, manage to make it through the day. Who was it that said most people live lives of quiet desperation? Thoreau? Yes. Well, he had it right. And wouldn't my old English teacher, Granny Graves, be proud of me. Truth is, though, I didn't care much for Thoreau. I like a little style with my philosophy.

I got off on the third floor after giving the elevator operator a quarter. The office was halfway down the hall. The door was one of those half-wood, half-frosted-glass standard office doors. The letters on the frosted glass said HARVEY MILES, LIFE INSURANCE AGENT TO THE STARS. That was not surprising. Everyone was something to the stars in this town—wiener maker to the stars, trash collector to the stars, periodontist, undertaker, toupee maker, you name it. Even my card said that Bruno Feldspar was private detective to the stars. They have a similar thing in England where every purveyor of anything wants to get a royal warrant. "By appointment to His Royal Highness, chamber-pot maker." Well, the stars in Hollywood are this country's royalty—everyone knows that, and in my view they're lots more useful; they entertain and they can't start wars, two things that put them ahead of any king and his family.

Of course, most of the stars are preening dimwits and worse, but that just makes them less dangerous. Just think what might happen if they got involved in politics. I remembered Manny's comment about most of them being Reds, but I put that down to fashion and the herd instinct, which I guess are essentially the same thing. They were all for the masses because they didn't have to associate with them.

The receptionist looked up and smiled when I walked in, which you would think should be standard procedure, but I've walked into plenty of offices where they don't pay any attention to you until they're good and ready. It's a way of pretending to be in charge.

The receptionist was about as homely a creature as I had ever laid eyes on, so maybe that's why she was pleasant. She was wearing a blue polka-dot dress of the kind you remember your grandmother wearing, and her hair was pulled back into a tight bun. She had a single eyebrow and a Cyrano nose. And she was as thin as Olive Oyl.

I returned her smile without any effort.

"May I help you?" she asked.

"I hope so." I gave her a business card.

"Oh," she said, visibly impressed, a sign that she'd seen too many movies or had too many fantasies.

"Is Mr. Miles in? I'd like to have a quick chat with him. Won't take long."

"Oh, I'm afraid he's not in today. There's a big convention of general agents in San Diego. He's down there all this week."

"So you're holding down the fort."

"Yes. There's no one else in the office. Mr. Miles works alone. Is there anything . . . I can help you with?"

The usual way of handling this question from a woman is to smile roguishly and see what develops, but in this case she was being utterly sincere in a professionally friendly way. She had looked in enough mirrors to understand that flirtatiousness wouldn't be her strong suit.

"I hope so. I'm on a private case trying to trace a woman who used to work here—Catherine Moore."

"Oh, yes. She left last week. She said she was going to get married. But you know, there were some police earlier this week looking for her, too. Has she done something wrong?"

"Nothing illegal. She's not in any trouble. It's more in the line of a personal situation."

"Oh, I see." She lowered her voice and became confidential. "You know, if those policemen last week had only told me that, I would have been, shall we say, a little more cooperative. But they were rude characters."

"They weren't real cops. Just studio security."

"Oh. Well, perhaps that explains it. One can't expect much from those kinds of people. Anyway, I just said nothing and sent them away with a flea in their ear. Mr. Miles was out on a sales call, and they didn't wait. It wouldn't have done any good anyway, because he doesn't know anything about where she went."

"But you do?"

She shrugged knowingly. "I have an idea."

"Care to share it?"

"I might." She paused and looked at me with a pretty good imitation of slyness. "But you know, times are hard, and a secretary doesn't make much money."

Life is full of surprises. It's not every day you get shaken down by a secretary in a polka-dot dress.

"Would five bucks help?"

"Yes, but ten bucks would help twice as much."

Well, it was Manny's money. I gave her two fives, which she folded primly and tucked away in a plastic change purse.

"Well?"

She lowered her voice even lower, even though there were just the two of us in the room.

"That whole story about getting married was a lie. She just wanted to get out from under . . ." Understanding the double entendre, she smirked and didn't blush. "Get out from under a relationship with some man who was rich but not especially . . . simpatico. I suppose that's who you're working for."

"Could be."

"Is your client simpatico?"

"Not particularly."

"I'm not surprised. Catherine was not very bright and she was not very efficient, but she was very good-looking in a trashy sort of way. She knew when she was being taken advantage of. She looked exactly like a former movie star. Minnie David."

"Really? Do you think she's still in town?"

"She told me she was going to quit this job and go out to one of the gambling ships and work as a cigarette girl. She said she could make twice as much money from tips alone, looking like she did. And I wouldn't put it past her if she found a little sideline, if you know what I mean."

"I know what you mean. But if she was that, shall we say, mercenary, I'm surprised she ducked out on her steady client."

"She said some things are not worth any amount of money. Besides, he may have been rich, but he was cheap, you know? She had those bracelets and that pin he gave her appraised, and you know what? They were fake. Not worth fifteen bucks. She said guys like him never married girls like her. They only wanted one thing. Well, that was all right as long as the diamonds were real. But when they gave you fake stuff, they were just taking advantage."

"What about the evening gowns?"

"Department store. Nothing special. Just copies of the real thing. She could make anything look good. Some women are like that."

Yes, some are.

"But those dresses were another signal that this arrangement was not only temporary, but not very profitable. You know?"

I knew.

"And there was something else. He never offered to get her a screen test. She kept waiting but he never did, until finally she asked him about it straight out and he said she wouldn't like the business. She was too classy. Can you believe that? If there's something she wasn't, it was classy. But he just wanted to keep her for his girlfriend. If he'd offered to make her a star or something, she would've listened and maybe stuck around even with the phony jewels."

Well, none of this seemed to say much for Manny's prospects, even assuming I could track her down, which seemed likely enough. It made me wonder, though, how sincere Manny's passion could be. A man who seemed so overthrown by love would not have tried to get by with fake diamonds and store-bought evening gowns, would he? Then again, maybe he would. Maybe in the back of his mind, he was saying "The schtupping is fantastic, and what's more, the price is right." But why hadn't he used the producer's standard hole card—a screen test? That could have bought him another year or so. Maybe he thought the girl was too dumb to catch on. If so, he was being naïve: no girl is *that* dumb. But the more I thought about it, the more it seemed like the answer was really very simple. He didn't want to turn her into an actress and expose her to all the temptations Hollywood could offer. He was in love with her and wanted to keep her all to himself.

"Do you happen to know which ship she went to?"

"No. She didn't know herself when she left. She asked me not to tell anyone about this, because she didn't want Mr. Unsimpatico to follow her. I didn't make any promises, though."

"Instead, you made ten bucks."

"Yes. We weren't really that close. We traveled in different circles."

That I could believe.

I went back to the elevator, pressed the button, and summoned the old guy in the old uniform.

I don't know why it happens, but it does. Something triggers it. Hard to believe it was an encounter with a homely secretary or a broken-down elevator operator. Maybe that didn't have anything to do with my mood, although the thought of what their lives must have been like was certainly a little depressing. Or maybe it was the thought of Manny Stairs aching for this woman who was willing to pass on a potential gravy train because Manny was not simpatico, which boiled down to the fact that the sight of him in his shorts, or worse, was not worth any number of diamond bracelets, even if they'd been real.

Anyway, when I got back to the Garden I felt a rush of sadness for Lily and for that lost opportunity, though I knew she wasn't really worth it. No, that's probably wrong. She was worth it. In fairness to her, she hadn't really had many options.

What's worse, I missed Myrtle. I'd hated the thought of turning her over to the studio hacks. It was turning her back on her authenticity. And most of all, I didn't like not being able to sleep with her. I missed her talking Croatian in her sleep. As well as everything else.

Well, whatever their reasons, Lily and Myrtle had made their choices, and I was without either of them. It was time to do some serious drinking. As usual, there was plenty of company around the pool to join in when I got back to the Garden, but I didn't need any company, because serious drinking is what you do alone. Otherwise you run the risk of making a fool of yourself. When you're alone, no one counts the number of drinks you've had, and there's no one to fight with. And there's no one to tell you that you're a pathetic loser. You can tell yourself that, but you won't believe it in the morning and you won't have made any enemies. And if you want to get maudlin, there's no one to laugh at you. No, the best way is to put some sentimental music on the victrola, pull the blinds, and settle into a comfy chair with plenty of ice in the ice bucket. In the morning, you may have a wicked hangover, but you won't have any apologies to make—or any scores to settle.

I missed Myrtle, though. The bungalow seemed especially empty now. Can you be in love with two women at the same time? Sure. Why not? After the second drink, it seemed that Myrtle was also a lost opportunity. At which point I told myself I really was a pathetic loser. Luckily, no one was there to confirm that judgment, and in the morning I decided I'd been wrong about that. Myrtle was only a few beach miles away, and I decided I'd drive out there that evening. She had called my office the day she moved out and left the Malibu address with Della. I did have a bad hangover, but time heals all hangovers. That and Goody's Powder.

I telephoned Manny Stairs from my apartment and told him I had a small lead and asked if he wanted me to stop by and give him a situation report.

"No, I'm busy. Just spill it over the phone." He sounded more peevish than I appreciated, and it changed my mind about how to break the news to him. I was going to try to let him down easy, but now I figured what the hell.

"Well, first of all, the information I have is second-hand, but I think it's accurate."

"And? I haven't got all day."

"Well, for starters she isn't married."

"Good!"

"That was just a story she made up. She quit her job as a secretary to go out on one of the gambling ships to work as a cigarette girl."

There was silence on the other end.

"Why would she do that?" he said after a long pause. His tone was decidedly less abrasive. It was as if he was asking himself that question. I let him answer it to himself. If he hadn't been so peevish, I would have covered him.

"Better money, I suppose," I said, finally, after a pause.

"Why would she need better money?" He sounded genuinely puzzled. "She must have understood that I was serious about her. I bought her things."

I hesitated for a moment, trying to decide what and how much to tell him.

"I don't know." I let him down easy after all. "But I can find out if you want me to. I don't know which ship she's on, but it shouldn't take too long to find her."

"Do it." He hung up.

I drove over to the office. It was another of those perfect California days. The sun was out, the sky was blue, the air was fresh—all in all, a set of lyrics for a bad song.

Della was typing and smoking when I walked in.

"Morning, chief," she said. She got a kick out of calling me "chief," since she was old enough to be my mother. The color of her lipstick matched the color of her hair. Magenta, I think they call it.

"Good morning, loyal employee. What's new?"

"Bugger all," she said. She had spent some time in England before the last war and had picked up a few Limey expressions. "Nobody's called, and no checks have come in."

"What are you working on?"

"A novel about a smart-aleck detective."

I almost believed her.

"What's Perry up to these days? Still in the water-taxi business?"

"That and other things best left unsaid."

"I'd like to talk to him. Where does he spend his days?"

"I've often wondered. But right around seven tonight you can find him in Santa Monica, in his boat at the pier.

He'll be the only one not wearing a tux or an evening gown."

❦

Promptly at seven I showed up at the pier. The gambling ships were open twenty-four hours a day, every day, but the evening trade was the more upwardly mobile. Anyone gambling during the morning or afternoon hours was likely to be a degenerate with little or no money to be spared for tips, so the evening hours were more desirable for the employees and contract workers, like Perry. The clientele was of a higher class; and when they won, they were happy to spread the wealth around.

I had met Perry before, so I didn't need to rely on Della's wisecracks about him. He was a former bosun's mate and looked the part—heavyset, with thick forearms tattooed with anchors, mermaids, and a woman not named Della. He had a close-shaved head and a no-nonsense expression. His boat was a sleek, fast inboard, about thirty feet long, and it could make the three-mile trip in no time flat. There was a canvas cover to protect the sports, while he stood at the wheel dressed in his navy pea coat. He made five bucks an hour plus tips, which meant his daily take was roughly twice mine. The fare was twenty-five cents. That went to the gambling ship and was earmarked for kickbacks to the various politicians and city officials who knew a good thing when they saw it.

Perry was getting his boat ready for the evening trade when I walked up.

"Hi, Perry. Got a minute?"

He smiled pleasantly, showing a broken incisor. "Well, if it ain't the private gumshoe. What's up? Need some more booze?"

"Not yet. I'm on a case."

"Good. That means you'll be able to pay my old lady again this week."

"Yes. Barely."

"Barely's better than rarely. What can I do for you?"

"You stop at all the gambling ships, don't you?"

"Yep. Some customers like one, some another, so I make all the stops."

"I'm looking for a girl who's working on one of them, but I don't know which. She's a new cigarette girl. What do you suppose is the best way to find out which one she's on?"

"Got a picture?"

I showed him the snapshot.

"Wow. A looker. Who's the midget?"

"He's the client."

"I get it. Well, it wouldn't be any trouble for me to show the picture to the greeters. They're always stationed right at the companionway to smile at the suckers. They generally know everything that's going on. And I know all of them."

That was what I figured, to begin with. Perry could get better and faster answers than I could.

"That'd be great. There's ten bucks in it for your trouble."

"It's no trouble, but I'll take the ten anyway. What's the broad's name?"

"Catherine Moore, but it's possible she's sailing under false colors."

"Yeah, it's possible. I once knew a cocktail waitress named Bubbles O'Toole. And do you know what her real name was?"

"Can't imagine."

"Bubbles O'Toole. Who but a Mick would name their kid Bubbles? But sometimes these broads do prefer an alias, especially if they have any ideas about selling more than just cigarettes. I'll show the picture around."

I took the snapshot and tore it in two and put the half with the grinning Manny in my pocket. I assumed he'd want to remain anonymous rather than risk the dreaded horselaugh. I gave the other half to Perry, along with the ten bucks.

"I'll check back with you in a couple of days. Okay?"

"Same time, same station. I should have your answer by then."

I went back to the car and took the coast road north, toward Malibu.

CHAPTER THREE

The next morning, I felt a lot better. First, I didn't have a hangover; and second, I'd spent the night with Myrtle at her new digs on the beach. It was a small house, but cozy, with lots of glass doors that faced the ocean and let in the sea air. The house was really only one room so that everything was open. There were sea-grass rugs and rattan chairs and couches with flower-patterned cushions and a stone fireplace with some sort of still life over the mantel and views of the coastline with lights shining off the water. The bedroom was separated by a half wall, and the only interior door in the house was the bathroom. Myrtle was delighted with the place and excited about her first day at the studio. She had spent most of the day with the publicity department, getting her life story explained to her.

"My real name is Yvonne Adorova but we shortened it to Adore to sound more American. I am a White Russian princess, and my family and I escaped from Russia during the Revolution. I was just a child then but old enough to remember and feel sad about it."

"Did you escape in a sleigh drawn by a troika while a pack of ravenous wolves was chasing you across the snow-covered steppes, gaining all the while as the horses grew tired until finally you barely made it to a peasant village and the wolves were afraid to come any closer?"

"I don't think so. They didn't say anything about that."

"Too bad. You might suggest it to them."

"Yes, that would be exciting."

"What happened to your family?"

"They're still working on that part. They're dead, of course, but they haven't decided how it happened. They say they are leaning toward assassination by a Communist hip squad."

"They probably said 'hit squad.'"

"Oh. Yes, I think you're right about that."

"My condolences anyway."

"Yes." She became suddenly thoughtful. "You know, my real parents are also dead. It was an influenza epidemic. It came through my village and killed almost everyone. I don't know how or why I survived. It was a very poor village in the mountains. Sanitation was a problem. And now, here I am in California where everything is beautiful and safe. All because of you."

"It may be beautiful, but I'm not sure it's all that safe. Of course, the sanitation is good. And remember, all I did was give you a ride and introduce you to Ethel. You did the rest."

"So you say. But I know better. Would you like some wine?"

"Shouldn't you be drinking vodka, princess?"

She made a face. "Vodka is nasty."

We had a wonderful evening. We grilled some fresh fish on the beach and drank a lot of wine and went for a naked moonlight swim and then to bed only slightly drunk, not drunk enough to take the edge off desire, and in the morning it was just like old times again, only better, and I began to think that half-in-love stuff might not be true after all, at least where I was concerned. Not that I was looking for it, but sometimes it finds you whether you're looking or not. Only twenty-four hours before, I'd been mixing bourbon with self-pity, in equal measures. Now, things looked decidedly rosier. For a minute, I wondered if this feeling of contentment meant that I was being disloyal to Lily. But how can you be disloyal to someone else's wife? No, that fresh morning in Malibu was a turning point, the end of something and maybe the beginning of something else. Whether that something else would involve Myrtle/Yvonne remained to be seen, but it was suddenly very clear that the time with Lily was well and truly over. And it was about time I found out about it.

The studio sent a car for Myrtle around nine o'clock. I went for a swim and then got dressed and drove to the office. It was Della's day off, so I left the door between the reception room and my office open. I wasn't expecting anyone, but strange things sometimes happened in this business.

My office was nothing to brag about—an oak desk and a matching oak office chair that swiveled and rocked, if you wanted it to. There was a black telephone on the desk and nothing else. I kept a spare thirty-eight in the top right-hand drawer, along with the pens and pencils and paper clips. On the wall was a copy of a Winslow Homer seascape that I'd bought at a garage sale for fifty cents, and a calendar advertising Barbasol that they'd sent me for nothing. There were two wooden chairs facing the desk for clients, although usually they came one at a time, that being the nature of the business. The only window looked out onto Hollywood Boulevard. I spent a few minutes staring out at the traffic, thinking about last night and feeling good about it. I didn't have any reason to be there, in the office I mean, but I didn't have any reason to be anywhere else just then. And you never know when someone is going to walk in. Like now.

My back was to the outer door and I did not hear it opening, so the first indication I had that there was a visitor was the smell of her perfume. It was an expensive smell. And she wore too much of it.

I swiveled around and saw her standing in my doorway.

"Mr. Feldspar?" she asked.

I hesitated a moment—I never could get used to that name. I got up then and held out my hand. She took it firmly. She was wearing gloves, expensive gloves.

"Yes. Please come in."

In Hollywood, there are three basic categories of women— the beautiful ones, the ones you don't notice, and the ones who were somewhere in between. This one fell somewhere in between. She was tall and slim and dressed in a gray tailored suit. She had long blond hair parted on the side and allowed to cascade carelessly to her shoulders in a manner that said she'd spent plenty at the hairdressers. Her face reminded me of Amelia Earhart—pleasant and attractive but not particularly beautiful, with just a suggestion of horsiness. She didn't wear a hat, which is something I approved of—not wearing them, that is. Women's hats just then must have been designed by men who hated women. She was somewhere around forty, I would guess. The sort of age when women hire private detectives.

"Won't you sit down?"

She sat down.

"My name is Watson. Mrs. Emily Watson. You were recommended to me by Ethel Welkin." Good old Ethel strikes again. "I gather you know her well."

"Fairly well, yes."

Emily Watson stared at me for a few moments, waiting, I think, to see if I'd make some sort of smirking gesture to reveal just how well I did know Ethel. If I did, that would indicate I was basically untrustworthy. I knew that game. So I put on my choirboy expression and simply waited for her to tell me why she was here. I noticed that she had very pretty gray eyes, though there were some dark circles that could have meant anything from tearfulness to sleepless nights to vitamin deficiency. Finally she seemed satisfied that I was discreet enough.

"I have a problem," she said.

I nodded reassuringly, not even tempted to make a wisecrack that the only people who came to this office were people with problems. I've always believed that one key to making yourself agreeable is not saying the obvious.

She opened her Vuitton purse and rummaged around in it. I noticed she was carrying a small-caliber automatic with a pearl handle. Probably a twenty-two. I would have thought she was too classy for a pearl handle, but then you never know where these wealthy ladies get their guns or whether they think they're fashion accessories and therefore need some sort of accent.

She found a snapshot and handed it across the desk. It was a picture of a young man, maybe twenty-five or so, dressed in a kind of yachting costume—white ducks, white bucks, dark blazer, silk scarf. He was strikingly good-looking with a slightly effeminate expression, obviously pleased with himself as though he were the reincarnation of Gatsby, with better taste in clothes. He was standing in front of an elaborate fireplace, above which hung an oil painting in a fancy gilded frame.

"This is the problem?"

"Yes. He has disappeared, and I want him found."

"Can you tell me why?"

She hesitated. There usually are these hesitations at this stage of a case.

"Ethel said you were trustworthy and could keep a confidence."

"I wouldn't be in business very long if I couldn't."

"You seem very young."

"Meaning that I haven't been in the business all that long?"

"Something like that."

"I'm older than I look. And if it's any comfort to you, I used to be with the FBI." This was not strictly true, but true enough.

"Why did you leave?"

"Too much bureaucracy."

That seemed to satisfy her. But she was still hesitant, not about me so much, but about her own story. You can always lie to yourself when you tell yourself your story, but it's harder when you tell it to a stranger.

She struggled with herself for another moment or two but then came out with it.

"His name is Wilbur Hanson, and he stole something from me and disappeared. I want him found and I want my property back."

"What did he steal?"

"A painting. A priceless Monet. In fact, that very Monet in the photograph."

I looked at the photograph again. I didn't know much about Monet, but I did know he brought in big numbers at the art auctions. That sort of thing was in the papers.

"Why not go to the police?" The answer was obvious, but I still had to make sure.

She looked at me, wondering if I was being dense or coy.

"Surely you will not be surprised to hear that there was something between us."

"Beyond an appreciation of Monet?"

"Yes."

"So, in plain words, you were lovers."

"Yes."

"Does your husband have any suspicions?"

She sniffed and tossed her expensive hair. "No. He's quite oblivious." The level of contempt was pretty high.

"Which means involving the police would complicate matters at home."

"Yes. My husband knows next to nothing . . . about art. When Wilbur stole the painting, he replaced it with a copy. I didn't notice it at first. It was a very good copy. My husband could stare at it until the moon is blue and never know it's a forgery. But if the police are called in. . . ."

"The jig will be up. I understand. But couldn't you just report it as a straight-out theft without mentioning any of the . . . context?"

"Wilbur has threatened to reveal everything if I report him to the police. Or if he's ever caught."

"Yes. Well, he would say that, wouldn't he."

"You don't believe him?"

"Oh, yes, I believe him. There's not much doubt he'd sing like the Rhythm Boys if the cops ever nabbed him. Was the painting insured for its full value?"

"Of course."

"Well, Mrs. Watson, the simplest way out of this problem would be to report the theft to the insurance company, collect your settlement, and forget the whole thing, while continuing to enjoy the copy. It would be perfectly honest, because the painting was in fact stolen. The only wrinkle in this story is that you happen to know who took it. But that is something you can keep to yourself. Your husband need never know anything other than you'd been robbed and restitution had been made. Apparently, he wouldn't care one way or the other about the painting. Of course, Wilbur would get away with the crime, which would be a shame, but your reputation and relationships would be protected. As well as your bank account."

"I've thought of that, of course."

"And?"

I could see the blood rushing to her face, and her expression changed so that she suddenly looked less like a pleasant Amelia Earhart and more like some evil stepmother in a scary children's book.

"I want the bastard found and caught."

So it wasn't the painting so much. It was "Hell hath no fury," with a side order of Medea.

I stared at her for a moment while she digested the fact that I understood her real motivation and the fact that she didn't give a damn whether I did or not.

"What happens if I do track him down?"

"That's my business. Finding him is yours, if you think you're up to the job."

"I think I can handle it. Of course, he could be anywhere in the world."

"I don't care where he is or how long it takes."

At twenty-five dollars a day plus expenses, this was the kind of client to have.

"May I keep this picture?"

"Yes. And when you're finished with it . . . burn it."

When she left after writing a check for two hundred fifty dollars, it occurred to me that this arrangement could end badly. I didn't like the combination of jealous rage and pearl-handled automatics, even a small caliber. I felt like a pointer sniffing out the quail. What if I found the guy, located him, and she said thank you very much just before she emptied the magazine into his midsection? If it happened, how was I supposed to feel about that? On the other hand, I did like her two-hundred-and-fifty-dollar retainer check. This is a business that requires conscious compromises.

My problem was solved for me the next morning when the headline in the papers said: SOCIETY MURDER/SUICIDE. EMILY WATSON SHOOTS INTRUDER, THEN TURNS GUN ON HERSELF. BEL AIR IS BUZZING. The rest of the copy contained the standard amount of lurid details. The victim, identified as "Wilbur Hanson, artist," had needed three shots to the abdomen. Emily had only needed one to the side of the head.

Things happen, don't they? I had deposited her check, but the job was over before it started. I'd been hired to find the immediate whereabouts of the boyfriend. That was easy. He was lying on a stainless-steel gurney in the county morgue, draining. I imagine she was there too, in a similar situation. I wondered whether I should call her husband and offer to return the money. I wouldn't have minded, but that would needlessly add to his shock and grief. Why did he have to know that she had hired a private dick to track this gigolo down? This way, he could maybe tell himself that she had defended her home and honor against a well-dressed intruder. A Raffles sort of gentleman burglar.

Of course, he might wonder why she had felt compelled to shoot herself, but maybe he could put it down to shock or even accident. As long as he didn't know the truth, he could tell himself anything that would be a barricade against obvious suspicions. On the other hand, I figured I owed her or someone something for the money, so I decided to call the boys at homicide and tell them what I knew. As far as the murder/suicide was concerned, I didn't know much, except the motive. But I did know there was a "priceless Monet"—her words—floating around somewhere. That now belonged to her husband, and the fact that he couldn't tell a real Monet from a Li'l Abner cartoon didn't change the fact that he had been robbed by some on-the-make sleazeball with the unwitting assistance of a wife with a bad case of the hots. Her husband deserved to get his property back.

I did wonder, though—what did "priceless" mean? A hundred thousand? Maybe even more. I wondered if the boyfriend had already disposed of the picture on the black market; I assumed there was a black market for art some-where. Or maybe he had been holding on to it for some reason known only to himself.

But why had he come back to her house? He must have known she'd be in a bad mood, and he also must have known she carried that pistol. Bad moods and pistols are a combina-tion anyone with an ounce of sense wants to avoid. Maybe he had had second thoughts about the theft; maybe he was returning the picture, smiling a sheepish smile and hoping to patch things up with the lady; maybe that picture now hanging above the mantel was genuine. Maybe he'd gone there thinking no one was home and replaced the fake with the real thing, at which point she'd arrived, emitting fumes of jealousy, and let him have it three times and then, distraught, ruined her coiffure with a .22 slug. But if that was what had happened, there was an extra painting to be accounted for, whether fake or original. It's possible he hadn't had time to replace the fake before she arrived in a murderous mood.

I called a guy I knew at homicide. He was one of the newer breed of L.A. cops—a college grad who preferred scientific interrogation methods and would only resort to a blackjack if the scientific methods didn't work.

"Kowalski," he said when he picked up.

"Hi, Ed," I said. "It's . . . Bruno Feldspar." Again I had trouble getting the name out.

"Hello . . . Bruno. How's life?"

"Okay."

"By the way, I know that can't be your real name. What kind of parents would name a kid Bruno?"

"Mr. and Mrs. Feldspar."

"Right."

"Would I lie?"

"Doesn't everyone? What's on your mind . . . Bruno?"

"Are you involved in the Emily Watson case?"

"I might be. Are you?"

"I was. Briefly."

"Really? And?"

"She came to my office yesterday and asked me to track down the guy who ended up with the leaky organs."

"Let me guess why."

"You'd be right."

"So you're telling me this was no intruder, but a regular visitor. The classic crime of passion."

"Yep."

"The papers are going to love this."

"You might consider keeping it under your hat for a while, Ed. There's an unsuspecting husband to consider."

"There usually is."

"Well, don't you have any feeling for the guy? He's grieving. Why add to his troubles?"

"What makes you think he's grieving? And besides, if he's so clueless as to think something other than the obvious, maybe it's time he wised up. But it's out of my hands, ultimately. The news boys will have this story sooner rather than later. What's your angle?"

"I don't have an angle. At least I don't know for sure. Just answer me one question."

"In exchange for?"

"What I know about the relationship between the dead guy and the dead woman."

"All right. Shoot."

"Was there an extra painting somewhere at the scene of the crime—a copy of the painting over the mantel, lying around, near the body, maybe? Or leaning against the wall? Even something rolled up somewhere?"

"No. Not that I saw. And there was squat in the after-action report."

Swell.

"So what's your story?" he asked.

"Here's the deal as far as I know it. The late Mrs. Watson was keeping company with this guy Wilbur Hanson. I have a photo of him that she gave me."

"I already know what he looks like, although I'm guessing he looks better in the picture than when I saw him. And just a word of advice—if you're going to be a private dick out here, you'd better find a more colorful way of saying 'keeping company.' Otherwise, people'll think you're some sort of fairy."

"Fine. I'll try to clean it up. How's this—she was banging the guy, and it was the classic story of the older woman and the younger man who was only putting up with her sagging charms and tinted hair because he figured there was something in it down the road. She had a bad case of the hots, and he had a bad case of wanting to get rich."

"That's more like it."

"The prize in this case was a painting. A Monet. Ever hear of the guy?"

"There's a black dude named Maurice Monay doing three-card monte on Figueroa, but I doubt it's the same one."

"No, this one's a French artist whose paintings go for six figures."

"Six figures. Hard to believe anyone would pay that for a picture of anything. Unless it was a nude. Was it?"

"No. A bunch of flowers."

"I swear the human race gets dumber by the hour. Anyway. . . ."

"So anyway, this guy Hanson steals the Monet from the aforementioned Emily Watson and replaces it with a copy. And, as is usual in such cases, she goes over the edge when she realizes she's been played for a sucker. When Hanson shows up again, she lets him have it and, then, after a moment of emotional turmoil and romantic despair, turns the gun on herself. Full stop."

"Romantic despair?"

"Maybe there's a better way to express it. Hysteria, maybe. Shock. Maybe even accident. What do you know about Hanson?"

"Not much. He doesn't seem to have any next of kin that we can find. He's just another one of these pretty boys who come to this town. How's the painting figure into this?"

"Who knows? I thought he might be trying to return it, maybe mend some broken fences. Or maybe he got cold feet and realized he wasn't cut out for the art underworld."

"What about the husband?"

"Clueless, according to his wife."

"About the boyfriend or the stolen painting?"

"Both. Out of curiosity, does he have an alibi?"

"Seems to. He was gambling out on the *Lucky Lady* pretty much all through the day and most of the night. Plenty of witnesses saw him. He called the cops when he got home. The boys said he was pretty shook up."

"I'll bet. But I keep wondering why Hanson came to the house that night. I keep thinking he was trying to return the original and get back on the side of the angels."

"No one in this town is on the side of the angels. Our name is a cosmic joke. But I see your point. If he was trying to make good, the other painting, whether real or copy, would be soaking up some gigolo blood when we got there."

"That was the idea."

"Good idea, but no cigar. There was plenty of blood, but it was being soaked up by a Persian carpet. The only painting was hanging above the mantel—not that I paid much attention to it. I'm looking at the crime-scene photos now, and there's definitely a picture above the mantel. But there's no second painting anywhere. Sorry."

"Hmmm. Maybe Wilbur stashed the painting somewhere safe and went to Emily's house to beg for forgiveness."

"Promising to return the painting later?"

"Right."

"It's possible, I suppose. Most likely we'll never know. But what do you want out of this?"

"The lady in question gave me a ten-day retainer. I'd like to earn some of it, anyway. Would you have any objections if I looked into the art-forgery business? It's a side story to the murder/suicide, which as you've said is pretty straight-forward—thanks to my information. I'd like to be able to set the husband right as far as his property is concerned."

"How do you plan to do that?"

"I thought I'd take a look at Hanson's place. Maybe he has the thing hidden there."

"Real or the forgery?"

"Who knows? Could be either one. If I can't find anything there, I guess I'll get ahold of the husband and tell him his wife thought there was something wrong about the painting and that she suspected it had been stolen and replaced with a forgery. She came to me to make a discreet inquiry, which will cover her if her husband looks over her cancelled checks. And it will cover her till the adultery story breaks—if it breaks."

"Oh, it'll break sooner or later."

"I imagine. But once I broach the idea of a forgery, he can hire an expert and take it from there. If the one he's got now is genuine, he can sit back and enjoy. Or sell it. If it's a fake, he can call the insurance company and get his money back. All neat and unconnected to the murder. Even when the adultery story comes out, the art angle doesn't really matter."

"It matters a little, but I take your point. It complicates something that otherwise appears pretty straightforward. Simple crime of passion. And it's better for us if it seems straightforward. Complications make paperwork. Better to have a good, clean story than one that's messed up with truth. So go ahead. Keep me informed."

"I assume you've checked Wilbur's apartment."

"Yes. It's got the standard crime-scene yellow tape across the door."

"I won't disturb anything."

"Okay. I'm guessing you can figure out a way of getting in."

"Yes. It's Lesson Two in the Private Detective Correspondence School."

"Anyone asks you what you're doing, have them call me. But just remember when you're poking around—it's no trouble putting a private dick out of business, if we don't like what he's doing and how he's doing it. If you find something, anything, I want to know about it. And if by chance you should happen to find the original, don't forget who it belongs to."

"I'll remember." I thought about correcting his use of "who," but decided against it. Almost nobody uses "whom" anymore.

"Stay in touch," he said and hung up.

I'm not sure I liked that part about putting somebody out of business. But maybe he was just practicing his tough-guy act. As a college graduate, he had to be especially hard-assed. The other cops were suspicious of anyone who wore glasses and was good at anything beyond shaking down a suspect, accepting cash in an envelope, and lighting a match with a thumbnail.

This guy Hanson lived in one of the countless semi-Spanish two-story apartment buildings. This one was U-shaped with a pool in the middle. It was on a side street in Santa Monica. That was convenient for me, because I was planning to meet Perry later that evening, hoping he would have some interesting news about Catherine Moore for me.

I parked on the street and walked a block or so to the building, known as the Hanging Gardens Apartments. It wasn't hard to locate Hanson's place, because of the yellow crime-scene tape across the door. There were a few aspiring starlets sitting around the pool, and they watched me as I went up the stairs to the second floor. I was wearing my fedora and so looked official, and I paid no attention to them, but I could hear them whispering something. I got out the piece of plastic that all junior G-men learn to carry and slipped it through the doorjamb and opened the lock. I ducked under the yellow tape, went in, and flipped on the light.

There was a funny smell in the room. I couldn't identify it exactly, but patchouli came to mind. Maybe that was it. The apartment obviously came furnished, because all the stuffed chairs and the sofa had that sagging, depressed appearance of things that had been forced to stay in service beyond their expiration date. It was only one room, with a kitchenette along the back wall, one closet, and a bathroom large enough to turn around in if you had to.

The distinctive feature of the place, though, was the amount of artwork on the walls. Even I could see that these weren't the usual cheap copies of senoritas or bullfighters. They were elegant-looking nudes—a half dozen of them arranged tastefully above the sagging sofa. I bow to no man in my appreciation of nudes, but I have to say I prefer it when the nudes are women. These weren't, and there was no attempt to disguise the fact, for all of the winsome lads in these pictures were facing the painter in various states of exuberance. The six paintings were all of different people, although they all shared a common well-endowedness. All but one were of young men with an effeminate look to them. The other one was of an older man, somewhere between forty and fifty and in good condition. I looked closer at each of them, checking for the signature of the painter, and was only mildly surprised to see the name "Wilbur Hanson" in the lower right-hand corner.

I wondered why Kowalski hadn't mentioned this aspect of the case, although it was possible he hadn't personally examined the apartment.

Even to my untrained eye it was clear that the recent Wilbur Hanson was a talented painter. Unfortunately, I didn't see any Monets anywhere on the walls. I looked in the only closet, but there was nothing in there except a few silk suits, a silk kimono, a half dozen pairs of shoes, and a rack full of ascots. I rummaged around in the dresser drawer but found nothing beyond what you'd expect to find.

The rest of the apartment seemed bereft of hiding places—no dropdown overhead, no hollow-legged tables or chairs. I turned over all the cushions, thinking he'd maybe sewn the painting amidst the springs, but there was no sign that the ancient material had been disturbed. The cushions themselves had no zippers. I gave the rest of the room a thorough going-over, but the only paintings in the apartment were the ones hanging on the wall.

So it would seem that if Hanson had the painting, he had it stashed somewhere, and the odds of finding out where were long, to say the least—which meant my next move would be to meet with the husband, tell him the semi-truthful tale about the possible forgery, and then let him take it from there.

I also wondered where Hanson had done the nudes. Obviously, this rather dingy apartment would not do as a studio, and besides there were no paints or easels or anything to indicate that he'd done these portraits here. It occurred to me that might be an avenue to investigate.

❧

I had a cup of coffee at a sidewalk café that had a view of the beach, if you stood up. There were the usual ragged hobos in the park across the way: drunks, drug addicts, the simple-minded, and the philosophers. They came here according to the season and got rousted by the cops and put on buses to Phoenix. But there were always others to replace them. They were like water coming in through the bottom of a leaky boat. Bail away, but there's no end of it. Well, it's hard to beat this weather if you have to sleep outside.

It was getting close to seven, the time I was going to meet Perry. I was just about to leave when a woman came up to my table. She was firmly in the first category of California women—a soul-selling opportunity.

"Do you mind?" she asked, as she sat down opposite me and crossed her legs—an exercise worth watching. If she'd been wearing silk stockings, they would have made an alluring swish. But she wasn't, and she didn't need them.

"Never minded anything less in my life, unless you have a commercial proposition in mind."

"Do I look like that kind of girl?"

"No." She did, of course, because those kinds of girls come in all shapes and styles. So I'm told. But one must be gallant.

And she was a stunner. Auburn hair that looked natural, blue eyes, full lips that, surprisingly, did not have too much lipstick despite the current fashion. She was wearing a tight-fitting low-cut jersey top with alternating blue and white horizontal stripes, like a French sailor, and cream-colored shorts. Everything was tastefully snug and left very little to the imagination. Her clothes were like the sheer curtain that gets drawn after the main curtain has gone up. A formality.

"Are you a cop?" She had a velvety sort of voice and precise enunciation, a phony-sounding combination that you can learn at any one of the acting schools in this town. These schools were generally on second-floor studios run by faded bit players with a theory and a nose for business. Somehow those places never made sense to me, because their basic message was "I can't make a living as an actor, but I can teach you how to become a star." They were the acting equivalent of a matchbook correspondence school in diesel mechanics or hairdressing. But as I said before, hopefulness was a widespread local affliction. Very contagious.

"So, what's the deal?" she asked. "Who are you?"

"I'm still working that out." I said this with a disarming smile, which she took for what it was worth.

"I saw you at the apartment a little while ago. You were in Wilbur's place."

"Oh. Yes, that was me." I know it should be "that was I," but it sounds so prissified.

"Well, are you? A cop?"

"No. Private. But I am working on the investigation."

"Private dick?"

"Right. Name's . . . Bruno Feldspar." Again, the difficulty. I gave her a card.

She smiled, showing just a trace of kindly ridicule. "What kind of name is that?"

"Just a name. You know the line—'What's in a name? A rose by any other name would smell as sweet.'"

"I heard that in a movie, I think."

"It's possible."

She studied me for a moment, trying to decipher something or other.

"You don't look like a Yid. Feldspar sounds like a Yid
name." That was true. It was one of the reasons Ethel suggested it. In this town, it helps.

"No, strictly Presbyterian. What's your name, honey?"

"Rita Lovelace. And don't call me honey."

"All right. And what kind of name is Rita Lovelace?"

"It's a name I figured the studios would like."

"I agree. It's nice. What's the real one?"

"Isabelle Fern. Not that it matters. I'm not in trouble anywhere."

Now it was my turn to smile. We understood each other,
at least on a superficial level.

"So what's on your mind, Rita?"

I could see her composing herself into an attempt to suggest sadness, if not exactly grief.

"It was terrible about Wilbur."

"I'm sure he'd agree, if he could."

"He was a friend of mine—nothing romantic. Just a friend.
I figured you must be a cop, so I thought I'd see if you'd
learned anything beyond what's in the papers."

"No, there's nothing much beyond what's been reported
so far. For some reason, he went to the woman's house, broke
in, and got shot for his pains. That kind of thing is an occu-
pational hazard for a burglar. We still can't figure out why
she shot herself."

Rita snorted.

"Some cops. It shouldn't take more than two seconds to
figure that one."

"What are you suggesting?" I asked, all innocence. "Lovers'
quarrel?"

"What else? Wilbur was no thief. Not a burglar, anyway. Besides, he told me he was seeing someone who was in the chips. Must've been her."

"She shot him and then, feeling guilty, shot herself? Is that your take?"

"No other explanation. I knew him. He wasn't a cat burglar. He told me he was on the way to a big score."

"Did he say what it was?"

"No."

"What's your angle, Rita?"

She looked me over as if trying to make a decision.

"You say you're not a cop, and yet you're working on this case."

"Just one aspect of it."

"Who're you working for?"

"That's confidential. But let's say it's a private client, not the cops."

"I get it." She took a deep breath and then made her pitch. "You know, I've been to a few auditions lately. I'm an actress."

"I never would have guessed."

"Smart guy, eh? Well, I am. But this is a tough town. Jobs are hard to come by. You go to bed with three assistant producers for a one-day gig as a stand-in."

"All three at the same time?"

"I wish. At least it would be over faster that way."

"What do you do to keep body and soul together— between gigs, that is?"

"What do you think? I'm a waitress. In a diner on Sepulveda."

"Maybe I'll come by some day for meat loaf and mashed potatoes."

"I wouldn't, if I were you. I've seen the kitchen. Anyway, here's the deal. I could use a few bucks to tide me over for a while. I've hocked the few things I have of any value, and my car tires are so shiny I can see my face in them. Tips have been poor lately, especially if they order the special."

"I understand. What do I get in return?"

She looked at me again, still trying to decide. "Are you sure you're not a cop?"

"Ever hear of a cop paying for information? Cops don't pay, they *get* paid. How much are we talking about here, anyway, and what do I get for it?"

She took a deep breath. "Do you have a hundred bucks to spare?"

"Yeah, I do. But that doesn't mean I'm going to spare it. Where I come from, that kind of money buys a lot."

"Wilbur left something with me. A package. He said to hide it and not tell anyone about it. He said it was the key to making his big score. Well, he's past caring now, so I figured I might as well make something for myself."

I felt a sudden surge of interest that went well beyond the interest I had in Rita, *qua* Rita. Could it be that lovely Rita, full-time waitress and part-time actress, had a painting worth six figures resting in a closet behind her shoes? Could be.

"What's the package look like?"

"It's a cardboard tube. About sixteen inches long."

"Did you look inside it?"

"No. Wilbur told me not to. It was sealed. But he said there'd be, ah . . . a hundred bucks in it for me, if I kept it for him for a few days. It was only for a couple of days."

That little pause told me he probably really only offered her twenty bucks and a hamburger dinner at some greasy spoon, but I didn't care.

"Where is it? The package."

"After I get the money."

"Deal," I said, trying not to sound too eager. I took out my checkbook and wrote her one for a hundred dollars, tore it off, and handed it to her.

She looked at it skeptically.

"You know, cash is better than a promise. And a check is only a promise. I've been stiffed before."

"Join the club. But obviously I don't have that kind of cash on me."

"What if we wait until tomorrow?" she asked. "The banks open at nine."

"All right." If she had what I thought she had, I didn't like the idea of waiting until morning. On the other hand, I didn't want to frighten her or give her the impression that the package might be worth more than a hundred. Tomorrow would come soon enough. After all, she had made the deal, and besides, where else could she go to find a better one? Between now and the morning, that is.

"It's not that I don't trust you. . . ." She smiled and looked at me from beneath some spectacular eyelashes. They almost looked real. The smile seemed a bonus, unrelated to the transaction in progress. I have to admit I felt a little fluttering here and there. Twenty-four hours ago, I'd been feeling sorry for myself about Lily. Twelve hours ago, I'd been congratulating myself about Myrtle. And now I was thinking lewd thoughts about someone I'd met ten minutes ago. There must be something wrong somewhere. Well, whatever it was, I did want that cardboard tube.

"Don't worry about it," I said. "In financial matters, prudence is always the best course."

She laughed and almost doubled over, revealing her flawless and braless breasts.

"What's so funny?"

"There was a girl in high school called Prudence, and all the boys used to say the same sort of thing. She wasn't much to look at, but she was very popular with the boys."

"Oh. Well, maybe some other time I can explore the rest of your biography. But let's do business first. How about if I pick you up at your apartment tomorrow at nine sharp? Meet me by the pool and we'll go straight to the bank, after which you can give me the package. I assume it's in your apartment?"

"No. It's in a safe place. I'll take you there when we finish at the bank."

"Fair enough." It was probably a bus-station locker. That was as good a place as any to stash something, for the time being, or, in fact, forever, as long as you didn't lose the key.

"Okay. See you tomorrow." She smiled again and then walked away, giving me the distinct impression that she knew I was watching the way those cream-colored shorts were moving. And, as a matter of fact, I was.

But I was also excited for another reason. It was hard not to believe that I was this close to getting my hands on the second Monet, whether it was the fake one or the real one. Either way, it was well worth a hundred bucks of Mr. Watson's money. What's more, I'd get the chance to know Rita a little better. You never know when you're going to get a hankering for diner food, although in this case I'd be sure to steer clear of the meat loaf. It also occurred to me suddenly that I had met Myrtle in a diner in Youngstown. Could it be that I was becoming a specialist in this kind of rare fauna?

I had fourteen hours to wait, so I figured I might as well check in with Perry to see what, if anything, he'd turned up.

He was getting his boat ready for the evening trade when I got there.

He saw me coming down the pier and waved.

"Hey, Perry."

"Hello, Bruno. Say . . . is that your real name?"

"Everybody asks me that. What do you think?"

"Beats me. But if it was me, I'd consider changing to something a little more believable for a private dick."

"I'll think about it. But to the matter at hand—were you able to find out anything?"

"Yep. I found the dame. She's working on the *Lucky Lady*, which is one of the better buckets out there."

Interesting. That was where Emily Watson's husband had been at the time of the murder/suicide.

"Working as a cigarette girl?"

"Started out that way, but didn't last. Right now she's not really working at all, unless you count staring at the ceiling a couple of hours a day. She got hooked up with Tony Scungilli. Ever hear of him?"

"Not that I remember."

"He's a wise guy, of course, and a gambler. His nickname is Tony the Snail. He runs the operation on the *Lucky Lady*. Nice enough fella for a goombah, long's you don't cross him."

"Why do they call him the snail?"

"I can see you ain't up to speed on your shellfish. A scungilli is a big salt-water snail. Like a conch. Very popular in Italian food. I like it in my pasta with tomato sauce."

"Is a snail a shellfish?"

"Comes in a shell, don't it?"

"I'll take your word for it. But you know, it seems kind of funny that Catherine Moore made such a quick conquest."

"Well, despite his nickname, Tony doesn't let any grass grow under his alligators."

"Alligators?"

"You know, his loafers, custom-made. But there's a funny angle to this story—one of the bouncers filled me in."

"I'm ready for a laugh."

"Turns out, this dame is a dead ringer for one of Tony's old girlfriends. She was a movie star a few years ago and ended up dead in some crummy motor court out in Joshua Tree. Drugs, of course."

"Not Minnie David?"

"That's the broad."

"I'll be damned."

"You know the story?"

"I've heard it."

"Anyway, Tony was with her when she bought it, because in those days he was peddling a full sample bag of booze and drugs. This was before he got promoted to running the gambling on the *Lucky Lady*. You got to work your way up in that business, same as everywhere else."

"He was with her when she died?"

"Yep, and the word is it hit him pretty hard. Word is, he loved the dame. Actually took the time to call the cops before getting the hell out of there. Anonymously, of course."

"And they say chivalry is dead."

"Whatever. But just because a guy's a gangster don't mean he don't have a heart when it comes to certain dames. They can be pushovers, too. So when he catches a glimpse of Catherine Moore. . . ."

"I get it."

"You understand that this little bit of information about Joshua Tree shouldn't get around."

"Sure. I'm surprised your friend was willing to tell you."

"We do some business together now and then, you know?"

"No, and I don't want to know."

"Usually the best policy. He was Tony's driver that day, which is how he knows. Told me the guy had real tears in his eyes as they got the hell out of there."

"Touching."

"Ain't it."

I wondered what Hobey, my writer friend at the Garden of Allah, would make of this coincidence. And it certainly was a fine coincidence. Two heartbroken swains suddenly jerked back into their lost romantic dreams by the same platinum blond lookalike, who only wanted to be left alone to pursue her dream of being a cigarette girl, and yet for reasons beyond her control got pulled out of her dream into theirs. I wondered what the Italian word for "schtupping" was.

"Is this Tony a dangerous character?"

"Do you have to ask? What's more, he's got a few guys around him that are worse. He's kind of—what do you call it?—flamboyant. Most of these hoods don't like publicity, but Tony's not shy. The suckers all like him."

"Any idea how she likes the arrangement?"

"Hard to say. My bouncer friend says she sort of drifts around the main salon when she's not on duty. Looks kind of vacant. Could be drunk or high, or could be just stupid.

Usually has a drink in one hand and a cigarette in the other. No way to read her. But she is a looker. Prime. Now and then, I hear, she works as a shill."

"What's that?"

"It's a good-looking dame who sits at an empty gambling table to attract customers. Tony don't like to see empty tables, so he scatters these girls around, knowing they'll draw a crowd."

"What's Tony look like?"

"Short and fat with slicked-back hair. Has a diamond pinkie ring and wears ties the same color as his shirt. These wise guys all read the same fashion magazine. He's nice and friendly to the suckers, but when he's off duty he goes around with a 'what're you lookin at' expression. You know that look."

"Yeah, I've seen it. Do these guys all live aboard the *Lucky Lady*?"

"Yeah. He's got plenty of muscle at his fingertips, if he needs them. You need that in a twenty-four-hour gambling joint. The rooms are pretty nice. Especially Tony's suite."

"You've seen it?"

"No. Just heard about it. 'Course, they all come into town every couple of days or so. You'd go stir-crazy living out there all the time."

"So Catherine Moore has moved in."

"Or *been* moved in, more like it."

Which meant that anyone wanting to have an immediate and private word with Catherine Moore would have to do it on board the *Lucky Lady*. Good luck. It wasn't my problem, though. My job had been to find her. Well, I'd found her. If Manny Stairs wanted to throw himself at her feet and risk the wrath of Tony the Snail, that was his business. He could take Perry's water taxi out beyond the three-mile limit and use whatever charm he possessed to talk her back to shore. Tony the Snail might not like it, but I was reasonably sure Manny could organize enough muscle to even up the odds. He didn't need my help. Which suited me just fine.

Besides, I had other fish to fry.

I went back to the Garden of Allah and called Manny Stairs's office. I didn't expect to find him there at nearly eight o'clock, but he picked up.

"This is Bruno Feldspar," I said. "I found Catherine Moore. She's working on the *Lucky Lady*. Do you know it?"

There was a pause.

"Yeah, I know it. Everyone in town knows it."

He sounded disappointed, as if he had been hoping that the initial story had been wrong. It's not an easy thing to know you've come in second place to a tray of cigars and cigarettes.

"Okay," he said, finally. "Let me think about next steps. Send me a bill."

And he hung up, not giving me time to tell him about Tony Scungilli. Well, he would find out soon enough.

CHAPTER FOUR

Promptly at nine the next morning, I presented myself at the Hanging Gardens Apartments. I was a little worried that Rita might have had second thoughts, maybe figuring there was more money to be made, since I had agreed to the hundred bucks pretty readily. That might have been a mistake. But she was waiting poolside when I pulled up, and she waved happily and came out and jumped in the Packard. She was wearing the same cream-colored shorts, but had changed her top to a skimpy T-shirt that said "Hooray for Hollywood," written in silver sequins. I took this as an ironic comment. It was also obvious that she didn't consider bras to be standard equipment.

"Nice car," she said. "The private-dick business must be pretty good."

"I guess there're worse ways to make a buck."

"You're telling me."

We drove to the local branch of Wells Fargo. Rita stayed in the car while I went in and cashed a check. I gave her the five crisp twenties, which she inspected carefully for a moment as though they were some exotic plant.

Then she gave me a radiant smile.

"I appreciate this," she said. "I hope you think the package is worth it."

There was a double entendre there, maybe, but I left it alone. "So do I. Where to now?"

"The Greyhound bus station."

That figured.

Rita shuddered when we pulled up to the parking lot.

"What's the matter?" I asked, more or less knowing.

"This place gives me the creeps. I see myself coming here some day with one suitcase wrapped with clothesline and getting on a bus for Sioux City."

"You could still hit it big. You have the look."

She smiled what seemed to be a genuine smile. "That's nice of you to say. Experience so far says something different. Maybe I'm no good in the sack. Not good enough, anyway."

"Hard to believe."

"Well, acting's not easy. In the sack you have to feel it, you know? A lot of women can fake it, but I can't. Not very well, anyway."

There was the hint of a challenge there somewhere.

"Is that your home? Sioux City?"

"No. But it might as well be. It's somewhere up north. In the middle of nowhere. It's like going back to nowhere from nothing, after having achieved exactly nothing except a few sessions with guys named Myron who promised nothing and delivered exactly that."

"Where's your real home?"

"Do you really care?"

"Just making conversation, but, yes, I kind of do."

"Akron. That's in Ohio."

"I knew that. I paid attention in geography class. Besides, I was born in Ohio too."

"Really? Whereabouts?"

"A little farm town called Poland."

"Never heard of it."

"You're not alone. It's outside of Youngstown."

"I've heard of that. Steel mills, foreigners, and mobsters."

"Pretty much."

I glanced over at her. She had a wonderful profile, top to bottom, and I could see why the various Myrons had made plays for her. And, let's be honest, used her. And suddenly the urge to do a good deed came over me. It happens now and then.

"I don't want you to misunderstand me, but I know some people in the movie business. They might be willing to arrange a screen test for you."

She looked at me skeptically. "I'm surprised you'd use that moldy line. You look like you could get over just on merit. Fact is, up till now I was kind of interested."

"I appreciate that. But I already have a lady friend, and, as a matter of interest to you, I arranged a screen test for her that resulted in a three-year contract at five hundred a week."

She stared at me for a moment. "Are you serious?"

"Yes. One of my clients is married to Isadore Welkin, the producer. We're on good terms, and she arranged for my friend to have a test."

"Really?"

"Really."

"And you'd make a call for me too?"

"Sure. No guarantees, but no strings attached."

"Why?"

"As a favor. After all, getting a test is a small thing if you know the right people. If you're good, it'll show up on the screen. If not, it'll be the bus to Sioux Falls or wherever. Or the diner on Sepulveda. That's all up to you. All I'm offering to do is make a phone call."

"Your real name's not Myron, is it?"

"No. And it's not Bruno Feldspar, either, just between us."

"Who cares? How soon can you make the call?"

"Just as soon as we pick up the package."

"Well, what are we waiting for?"

I parked the Packard in a litter-strewn lot next to the bus station. The litter included two drunks, whose attempts to panhandle us were so pathetically feeble that I gave each of them a quarter. For a moment, I wondered whether the hubcaps would still be there when we got back.

The station was pretty empty except for a couple of sleeping soldiers, a guy in a cheap suit who looked like a Fuller Brush salesman complete with clip-on leather bow tie and sample case, and some Mexicans of doubtful citizenship. It was three generations of poverty sitting there, big-eyed, on their way to what they must have thought was a better deal, and one that most likely would not be. Is there a more depressing place than a Greyhound waiting room? What sort of life stories gather or drift through there? Aside from the occasional soldier or sailor getting home on the cheap for a few weeks' leave, or maybe a high-school girl thrilled to be going anywhere away from home, everyone else is more or less broke, in all senses of the word, and the future not only doesn't look bright, it looks unlikely. The journey itself involved unpleasant smells and discomfort and long spells between bathrooms, and at the end of it you were in Yuma or Oakland or any other crummy town that's a stand-in for purgatory.

Rita hustled over to the banks of gray metal lockers and quickly retrieved the cardboard tube.

"Here you go," she said, a little breathlessly. "Wanna open it here?"

"I don't think so." I was burning with curiosity, but I didn't want to open it just yet. I needed to be careful with the thing, assuming it was a painting worth six figures, maybe more. Not the sort of thing you want to do in a bus station. "Let's get back to the car. I'll take you home."

"Okay. I have a telephone in the apartment, just in case you want to make a call, or something. And I have some gin. And tonic."

"Kind of early, isn't it?"

"You know what they say—it's five o'clock somewhere."

The "gin and tonic" seemed to be a pretty clear offer.

"Why not?"

Either way, I was still intending to call Ethel about her. A promise is a promise.

When we got to her apartment, Rita went into the kitchen to mix a couple of drinks. On the way there, she looked back over her shoulder and gave me what's known as a meaningful look. She couldn't smolder like Myrtle, but she certainly smoldered above the average. Plus, she had a good sashay. Not for the first time, I wondered what those cream-colored shorts more or less concealed. Her backward glance seemed to indicate that I'd find out.

But there was business to attend to first. I got out my pen-knife and very carefully removed the seal on the tube. I stuck two fingers into the tube and gently removed what certainly felt like a canvas. And so it proved.

It was a painting of a vase full of flowers. To me, it looked like something a bored housewife could produce in an afternoon at the country-club art class. The flowers looked kind of blurred. But in the lower right hand corner was the word "Monet." Put "Joe Schwartz" there instead, and you had something any canary would be proud to have on the bottom of his cage. Why that should be was an idea worth pondering at some point, but not now. For the present, I had either a hundred thousand bucks in my hand, or a worthless forgery. The question before the house was—which was it?

There was another question before the house, too. A bigger question. But I didn't want to think about that, just yet. I needed some time to think.

I stayed for lunch, which consisted of three gin-and-tonics, along with several generous portions of Rita, who by the way was much better than advertised and more than expected. She easily delivered on the promise of those cream-colored shorts, and I hoped that her story about not being able to fake it was true. This was after I had called Ethel, who responded to my request with a sly sort of tone in her voice that suggested she knew I was sending her a new protégé. Well, that didn't bother me. Ethel actually liked that sort of tomcat behavior. I guess it made her believe that she was still in the game, because deep down she must have known she wasn't.

Anyway, Ethel agreed to do me a favor and set up the test for Rita, which occasioned some ecstatic appreciation from my new friend, who wriggled out of her shorts and T-shirt and said thank you in a way that made me think those various Myrons must have had something wrong with them.

After lunch, I drove back to the office with the precious, or worthless, painting rolled up in the tube and sitting on the passenger seat.

When I got there, I took the painting out of the tube and very carefully pinned it up next to the Barbasol calendar. What better place to hide a priceless work of art than in plain sight? What better place to hang a forgery than next to a 1934 calendar showing a guy shaving and enjoying it? I guess he was a wealthy guy who didn't try to use his razor blades more than once.

Della had been there that morning and left me a note saying I should call Manny Stairs as soon as possible. "He sounded a little desperate," the note said.

Well, it was nothing to how he was going to feel when I gave him the news about Catherine and Tony the Snail. I have to admit that the thought made me smile a little.

I dialed Manny's private number. He picked up after the second ring.

"This is Bruno Feldspar," I said.

"Ah. It's about time. I left you a message three hours ago."

"I was having lunch."

"A three-hour lunch?" He didn't sound pleased. "How was she?"

"Michelin three stars."

"Is that all?"

"That's all they give."

"You spend three hours in the sack during lunch, maybe you should be a producer. You got the knack."

"I'll think about it. What can I do for you?"

"What I hired you for."

"I thought I'd done that. You wanted me to find her and I did. She's on the *Lucky Lady*."

"All right. But I also told you there might be a second phase to the job."

Swell.

"I want you to go out there and tell her I want her to come back. I'd do it myself, but there's a problem."

"Which is?"

"Everybody in this town goes out to those ships now and then. I can't risk being seen there sweet-talking a cigarette girl. I'd get the horselaugh for sure."

This didn't seem very plausible. I can't imagine that anyone in the business would sneer at a big-time producer chatting up a beautiful dame, even if she was carrying a tray of cigarettes and cigars and wearing a smile that said, for all the world to see, "I may be a dimwit, but ain't I gorgeous?"

"Well, I'd like to help, but there's a complication."

"Which is? I'll double your fee."

"I appreciate that, but it isn't a money complication. It seems that she's taken up with a character called Tony Scungilli. Ever hear of him?"

There was a pause on the other end of the line.

"Yeah, I've heard of him. A minor hoodlum." His contempt sounded genuine. Big-time Hollywood producers don't get where they get by being timid. Manny might be diminutive, but he knew what power was and how to use it. Tony the Snail didn't seem to scare him.

"So, what's the word? Just go out there and give her the message. Like I said, I'll double the fee."

"What if she refuses?"

"I'll jump off that bridge when I come to it. But Ethel says you're charming and persuasive, which in plain talk means you got a talent for bullshit, so I figure you make a good ambassador."

That was worth a smile. If there was anyone who needed persuading between me and Ethel, it was me. But as I've suggested, things have worked out well enough for all concerned, so I'm not complaining.

Well, I thought, I guess it couldn't hurt. At the very least I could go out there and see the shape of things, and if I saw an opportunity to talk to her in private, I'd do it. Most likely she'd give me a quick horselaugh, and that would be that. If I didn't catch her alone, I'd try again another day. Manny would want discretion, and so would I, given the array of goombahs wandering the passageways and gambling rooms.

"Would you consider offering her a screen test?"

"I don't want her in the business. I want her in the bedroom."

"I only ask because when I interviewed her friend at the insurance office, she told me Catherine was a little miffed that you never brought it up."

"Really?"

"That's what she said."

"That's interesting. Maybe I made a mistake there. Well, you can mention it, but only as a last resort." He paused as though coming to terms with something. "I'd much prefer she came back because she wanted to."

I don't care how many mirrors you have in your house, none of them reflects what you see or even expect to see, most of the time. And there are different kinds of mirrors, different from the ones that steam up in the bathroom during showers. It made you think about a fundamental question—which was better, to be a five-foot-two producer from the Bronx pining for a goddess, or a marginally secure fella posing as a private detective? I liked my situation.

"All right," I said. "I'll give it the old college try."

"Good. There's a bonus in it for you if it works. By the way, I thought you said you ain't a college boy."

"I'm not, but I've read about it."

"I'm counting on you."

Maybe he didn't know it, but he was leaning on a very thin reed. I'd give it my best, but I wasn't going to stick my neck out. What's more, I was armed with the discouraging knowledge that Catherine had decided Manny wasn't simpatico. I didn't think Manny needed to know about that. Not yet, anyway. And I supposed it was just possible that after a few days with Tony the Snail, her understanding of the real meaning of simpatico might have changed, maybe even in Manny's favor. After all, if she found Tony to be similarly unappealing, that wouldn't necessarily send her back into Manny's size-28 arms.

So, as usual, nothing was perfectly imperfect. At least I had the screen-test offer as a hole card. What Manny should do was obvious—he should lead with the offer, give her the test, and then string her along for a few months saying something might come up in the way of a movie role, and then sweeten the deal with some flashy jewelry that wasn't made with zircons. Then maybe marry her. That plan had a chance of working. But Manny wanted her to come back because she realized she really loved him after all. Even a Hollywood producer's ego has an Achilles heel. At least Manny's did.

My next call was long distance to Youngstown, Ohio. That was where my FBI contact worked. He and I had put together a money-laundering sting against the local mafia, with me masquerading as a shady New York banker. As I've mentioned, I'd had a hidden agenda involving scooting off with a large chunk of the money myself, but it hadn't worked out as planned, which turned out to be a good thing in the end. The FBI guy was named Marion Mott, and against all odds he actually went by that name. He was also a poster boy for the FBI—clean-cut, crew haircut, black suit, white shirt, black tie, black oxfords, and a perpetual expression that was a combination of eagerness, Christianity, and a Boy Scout's seriousness of purpose. All told, he might as well wear a sign that said "Kiss me, I'm a Fed." We had arranged a reasonably clever way for me to drop out of the sting before it went down—a matter of self-preservation, and Mott had agreed to hold off making the pinch for a month or two, so that there would be no connection between me and the arrests. That was the hope, at least.

I hadn't talked to him since then, and it had been three months.

"Mott speaking, sir." I guess he never knew when J. Edgar might want to call him.

"Marion, it's Riley Fitzhugh. How's it going?"

"Riley! Good to hear from you. I thought you changed your name."

"Only professionally."

"How's California?"

"Sunny."

"So I've heard. Some day, maybe. . . . So, what's up?"

"I've been wondering—how's the scheme working out?"

"Oh. That. Yes, well, we're still building the case. Could take a bit more time than we anticipated. We want it to be airtight."

Well, that suited me just fine. The more time, the greater the distance between me and the sting. But I thought I detected a slight hesitation or nervousness in his voice. Could it be that the local hoods had somehow put Marion Mott on the payroll? That thought had occurred to me before, and although it seemed unlikely, it's been known to happen. Well, that was none of my business. As I said, I had come to like some of those wise guys, and I felt a little sorry about setting them up.

"I understand," I said. "I really didn't call about that. I was wondering if you could give me some information."

"If I can, sure."

"Do you guys know much about the market for stolen art?"

"Not me personally, but I know we have a team working on that. I hear it's a big business internationally."

"How about art forgeries?"

"Same team. Apparently a lot of the underground buyers for this stuff are wealthy people—mainly Americans and Europeans—who think they're buying the real thing. They think they're getting stolen masterpieces at a deep discount when in fact they're paying through the nose for a forgery. They're the perfect suckers because they're afraid to display the painting and just put it in a vault or a locked studio or something. And they don't tell anyone about it, so the scam almost never gets exposed. One of our agents told me there were so many Whistler's *Mothers* out there, they could start a maternity ward. Everyone thinks he's got the real thing and that the one hanging in the museum is a fake. That's the standard sales pitch in the con. That's about all I know about it, though. Why do you ask?"

"I'm working on a case."

"Of course. What's your new name, again?"

I told him.

"Funny name."

"I agree. Are any of your guys working in L.A.—the art team, I mean?"

"I don't know, but I could make a few calls."

"That'd be great. And maybe you could find out if there's an art expert out here—some professor at USC or UCLA or someplace—that could examine a painting to see if it's real or a forgery. I assume the FBI would have some sort of contact in that line of work."

"I can ask."

"Thanks. How's your mother these days?"

"Oh, she's fine. She often asks about you." Marion still lived at home. "She'll be pleased to hear that you called."

I gave him my phone number, and he said he'd get back to me as soon as he could.

I glanced at my watch. It was only three in the afternoon. It didn't seem to make sense to go out to the Lucky Lady at this hour. Better to wait until evening, when the crowds would be bigger. That might improve my chances of talking to Catherine without being observed.

So, what to do until then? I could toss playing cards into my hat, read an improving book, or maybe take a pleasant drive up the coast to Malibu.

CHAPTER FIVE

Myrtle wasn't at home when I got there. I used the spare key she had given me and went inside to wait for her. There was a note on the table that said she was at the studio but would be back around six. There was cold beer in the fridge and some chicken salad. I was to make myself at home. There was lots to tell me. Three exclamation points followed by the standard hieroglyphics indicating kisses and hugs. She was obviously in a very good mood. Well, she deserved it.

Myrtle's note sounded so happy that I have to admit to feeling a little guilty about my morning with Rita. I resolved that Rita would be a one-morning stand and would remain only a fond memory, although I didn't throw away the scrap of paper she'd given me with her phone number and the inevitable words "call me." Well, I'd have to stay in touch with her just to see how her screen test turned out. Besides, Myrtle and I had been straightforward with each other and had not made any binding agreements. Even so, I felt a little funny about the morning.

Right at six, a car pulled up in front of the beach house. It was an open red-and-silver two-seater Duesenberg driven by a guy with shiny black hair parted in the middle and a Mediterranean complexion, meaning a combination of well-tanned and natural olive. He was wearing a white tennis sweater, white flannels, and an expression of self-satisfaction, like a man who had straight teeth and money in the bank. Well, who could blame him, driving a fancy car with Myrtle at his side. He was also, I have to admit, an extremely handsome young man, which meant he was on the acting side of the business, not the business side of the business.

I also have to admit to a sudden pang of jealousy. It was unfair, of course, but who cares about fairness when it comes to, well, whatever it was between Myrtle and me? Maybe this was the kind of character who might be the one Myrtle could fall completely in love with. You couldn't throw a brick in this town and not hit someone beautiful, male or female. And Myrtle would have to be a little susceptible, given her truly stunning change of fortunes. Anyone would be. Morally, of course, I didn't have a leg to stand on, given my morning romp with Rita. But that didn't matter just then. I've been morally legless before, and it didn't change the way I felt then, and it didn't change the way I felt now.

I opened the front door and went out to the car. It was an obvious, too-obvious, declaration of possession, and I knew it was kind of a low trick, but I did it anyway. Myrtle did not seem the least bit flustered when she introduced me.

"This is Rex Lockwood," she said, after introducing me. Lockwood smiled and displayed his, yes, perfect smile. "Glad to meet you, old sport."

Very lame, I thought—another guy modeling himself on Gatsby. He didn't look like what I thought of as Gatsby, but he did look familiar, somehow. That wasn't surprising, though; every young would-be actor these days was fashioning himself after someone who had already made it. Ramon Navarro was a popular model just then, and this Lockwood was doing his best to imitate him. No doubt somewhere Navarro was sincerely flattered.

"Rex Lockwood, eh?" I said. "What was it back in Topeka?"

"Chicago, you mean. But I'll never tell," he said, laughing. "What about you?"

"A dark secret."

Myrtle jumped out of the car, kissed me on the cheek, and danced into the house, pausing only briefly to wave good-bye to Rex as he reversed his astonishing car and headed back to wherever he'd come from. Central casting, most likely.

"Who was that?" I asked Myrtle, once she had finished kissing me, which took a while.

She smiled slyly and tilted her head coquettishly, something she had apparently picked up very recently. "Jealous?"

"Of course. I've always wanted a Duesenberg."

"Don't be jealous—that's not his car; it's his father's. We're in acting class together."

"You and Rex's father?"

"No, silly. It's every day between one and five."

"That sounds like fun." And it did, in a way. "How long will that go on?"

"Until I know what I'm doing, I suppose."

"That won't take long."

"Thank you, darling. Do you like me to call you darling? Everyone at the studio says it all the time."

"Well, then, it's not so special, is it?"

She thought about it for a moment.

"No, I suppose it isn't. I know. I will call you 'miljenik.' That's Croatian for 'darling.' How do you like that?"

"Better." But to be honest, most Croatian sounded like a hysterical fundamentalist speaking in tongues. I did like listening to her talking it in her sleep, but that was because I liked listening to her talking in her sleep. Esperanto would have been equally appealing.

"Would you like a drink?"

"Afterwards."

I missed Perry's seven o'clock run, but I caught up with him at nine. I gave him a wink as I stepped aboard and joined a couple dozen eager gamblers. Perry acted as though he'd never laid eyes on me, and we shoved off for the *Lucky Lady*.

It took about fifteen minutes to cover the three miles to where the ship was anchored, fore and aft, as Perry would no doubt say. We could have gone faster, but there was a choppy sea that would have sprayed the gamblers despite the canvas coverings. The *Lucky Lady* was lighted up like the proverbial Christmas tree. The ship had started life as a four-masted merchantman, but the gambling investors had torn away all the masts and superstructure and replaced them with a three-hundred-foot deckhouse—not that they did the work themselves. It took several months in the shipyard. They also widened the main deck by building platforms all around the ship, so that sports could walk around the outside of the deckhouse, bemoaning their luck or getting some fresh air or thinking about putting an end to it all. With its rounded roof, the deckhouse itself looked like an airplane hangar. The name LUCKY LADY was on the side facing the beach, in neon red. There was a row of lifeboats hanging from davits, and it occurred to me that there weren't nearly enough of them to accommodate a capacity crowd. And three miles is a long swim, especially when the tide's going out.

The upper deckhouse had eleven roulette wheels, eight craps tables, and a dozen or so blackjack, faro, and chuck-a-luck tables. Chuck-a-luck was a dice game in which three dice were rotated in an hourglass-shaped wire cage. It was almost impossible to win, but it was easy to understand and bet—a real sucker play. You had to pick the correct sequence of three dice. You figure the odds.

There was a long bar at one end of the room and slot machines, a hundred and fifty of them, along the other. Off to one side was a dining room complete with dance floor and seven-piece band. The dining room was packed. The twenty-five-cent taxi fare also bought you a free meal, as long as you ordered turkey. If you wanted something else, it cost extra, and there were more than a few down-and-almost-outers who came there solely for the free food, although inevitably many of them were drawn to the slots or the card tables even though they couldn't afford it.

For those who could afford it, there was a private card room for high rollers. A lot of Hollywood big shots were in that room each night, and no doubt those were the people Manny Stairs was worried about: he did not want them to know about his obsession for Catherine Moore.

When the investors remodeled the ship, they had also cleared out the lower deck and put in a bingo parlor that could seat five hundred. You wouldn't think there'd be five hundred people in the entire city who were so starved for entertainment that they'd turn to bingo, but you'd be wrong.

All told, the *Lucky Lady* was quite an operation and could accommodate up to two thousand losers at a time. And there must have been almost that many there that night. There were three hundred and fifty employees, including waiters, musicians, dealers, bartenders, bouncers, and, yes, cigarette girls. Since the *Lucky Lady* was open for business twenty-four hours a day, they needed that many employees to work the various shifts. Almost all of these except the crewmen who operated the ship's power plant commuted to shore after their shift, although Tony Scungilli and a platoon of goombahs stayed aboard most of the time. There was too much money on board at any one time to take any chances. They made daily runs to the bank, of course, but when you're running a twenty-four-hour operation, the money keeps flowing in like water through a leak. The ship had no engines—they'd been removed—but it had gasoline-powered generators that provided light and electricity.

Presiding over this floating empire was Tony the Snail Scungilli. Behind him were the investors. It was no surprise that they were also experienced bootleggers. That was convenient, because they had well-established sources of supply. They ran supply ships down from Vancouver, where they bought liquor from a consortium of distilleries. Booze and gambling made a combination that would attract any enterprising mobster. All that seemed to be lacking to make a perfect trifecta was prostitution, but, as Perry told me, there were lots of cabins on the lower decks of that ship. No doubt things could be arranged. Loans could also be arranged for the unlucky, and the word was that the ship's cash room had a safe filled with expensive watches and jewelry that had been turned in by people who were positive the next card would win them a fortune, and were wrong. There was also plenty of cheap stuff that any hock shop would be pleased to put in their dusty display cases. Whether this sort of business fell into the loan-sharking category, I didn't know, but I had a pretty good guess. So there in the shape of one former merchantman, you had the essence of gangster enterprise— gambling, loan-sharking, booze, and prostitution, the latter being informally organized.

All of this sinful fun was highly exasperating to the local keepers of city morality—Methodist preachers and some of their congregations, ladies' temperance groups, and assorted politicians and officials—the ones who weren't taking bribes, which probably put them in the minority. Every once in a while they tried to interrupt the action. The cops had no jurisdiction on the high seas, so they hassled the water taxis, but since those taxis had long been a staple of the various communities, taking people from town to town or to places like Catalina Island, they provided a legal and useful service. As a result, the hassles didn't last long enough to interrupt the mostly one-way flow of money from the gamblers to the gambling ship operators. Most of the cops didn't have their hearts in it anyway. A lot of them were on Tony's payroll.

There were a few decent-looking women on the ride out there. One or two fluttered their eyes at me—I don't mean to be egotistical, just honest. But the guys they were with pulled on their elbows and looked peeved. They shot a few glances at me, but I ignored them.

Perry pulled alongside the *Lucky Lady*'s landing platform, and two greeters helped the sports off the taxi and made sure they were able to climb the stairway to the main deck without falling overboard.

I was the last one off.

"See you later, Perry."

"Good luck," he said.

When I walked into the main salon, the air was heavy with cigarette smoke and the noise. It was a cacophony of screams of joy and groans and laughter—roulette dealers saying "place your bets," and craps players shouting orders to the dice, and other people yelling drink orders to the wandering waitresses, and the orchestra playing and a girl singer warbling into the stand-up microphone, while a hundred or so diners scraped plates and clinked glasses, and at the far end the sound of a hundred and fifty slot-machine arms being cranked and occasionally paying off with a cascade of coins, mostly nickels. It was an unholy din. Only the blackjack players were quiet, being satisfied with a tap on the cards to substitute for "hit me."

Contrary to what Della had implied, the gamblers there were not particularly stylish. There were very few tuxedos in evidence, and ninety-five percent of the women were not in evening gowns. It was more like an Elks convention than a night at the Trocadero. Most of the men were wearing hats, straws, fedoras, flat cloth caps. There were quite a few sailors scattered around—up from the base at Long Beach. Apparently Tony Scungilli was smart enough to realize that a more relaxed atmosphere would attract a wider audience, and if the swells resented mixing with the hoi polloi, they had very little in the way of alternative places to gamble and drink. There were several other ships out there, but they too followed Tony's lead in encouraging a come-one, come-all style. Besides, most of the swells in that town were in the movie business and had started life in very different circumstances, whether in the garment district of New York or the farms in Kansas and such places. Even the smattering of actors with British accents sprang from vaudeville or the circus. There wasn't enough blue blood in Hollywood to fill a milk jug, so there was surprisingly little snobbery, even among the newly rich—which covered just about everyone with money in that town. Oh, some of the women, wives or actresses, would swank around and call each other "dahling," but deep down they didn't have the self-confidence to be real snobs. They were all "nouveau," and those who weren't yet "riche" were trying like hell to get there.

At first I thought it might be hard to find Catherine Moore in such a place, but the main salon was really just one gigantic room, as long as a football field. I didn't think she'd be hanging around the bingo parlor, so I stayed in the main room, walking around and keeping my eyes open. There were cigarette girls here, there, and everywhere. They wore short, satiny dresses with plunging necklines, and fishnet stockings, and they walked through the crowds with smiles pasted on their faces, carrying their trays before them and singing their mantra—"Cigars, cigarettes, cigarillos." Needless to say, they were all good-looking women, although they wore too much makeup, and most of them had a shade of hair color unknown in nature. I thought about asking one of them if she knew Catherine but decided against it. I felt sure that Tony had the whole crew on a pretty short leash, and any one of them would be pleased to tell the boss that someone—"that guy over there"—was asking about his new girlfriend. Anonymity was the better part of valor.

It wasn't hard to spot the security guys who were stationed strategically by the doors that led out to the main deck. Others mingled with the crowd. They were conspicuous by design. They were all bulky guys with serious, self-important expressions, and they were constantly surveilling the room. There was obviously a lot of money on board, most of it being transferred from the gamblers to the *Lucky Lady*, and Tony was taking no chances. You'd have to be an idiot to try to pull a heist on board, but the world was full of idiots and what with the Depression in full swing, the economy was bad everywhere except on board the gambling ships, especially the *Lucky Lady*. A lot of people were desperate. It only took one to try it.

I bought some chips at the cashier's cage and then circled around the outside of the action, trying to look like a rube in search of a likely-looking table, one that looked ready to pay off. I was three quarters around the room when I saw her. She was sitting alone at a blackjack table—alone except for the dealer. Apparently, she was doing double duty as a shill—as well as Tony's girlfriend.

She must have just sat down, because otherwise she would have been surrounded by men eager to impress her with the size of their bankrolls. She was of a quality to attract men the way a bitch in heat starts a fight between otherwise well-mannered dogs. Not that she gave off the impression of being in heat. Quite the contrary: she looked like an ice princess in a sequined gown whose idea of a good time was being left alone. The platinum hair added to the image. It would take a confident man to approach her with any hope of success.

Even so, she wouldn't be alone long. Already I noticed men at other tables glancing in her direction. I'd have to make my case, or Manny's, quickly. What's the line? "If t'were done, t'were well t'were done quickly." But there was the problem of the dealer. He'd no doubt be standing there with his ears flapping, eager to gain points with the boss afterward by telling him about the encounter. The situation didn't look promising for doing a John Alden routine. On the other hand, she was beautiful, and I didn't see any harm in sitting down next to her. It was only a five-dollar table, so I figured I could risk a little of Manny's money just to make contact with her for a few minutes, if nothing else.

"Anyone sitting here?" I asked with as charming a smile as I could muster.

She looked at me with a bored expression. Her look didn't dent my ego too badly. I'd already been in bed that day with two startling-looking women, so I could ride out a mild wave of indifference.

"You see anyone?" she asked.

I didn't, so I sat down next to her. She smelled of expensive perfume and champagne. At least I think it was champagne. She also had a Camel going, and that didn't add to the quality of the air. Almost everyone smoked, but I didn't care for the scent of it on a woman. It was hard to escape, though, in a casino.

"What'll it be, sport?" This from the dealer.

"This is called blackjack, right?"

"That's right."

"Remind me of the rules. I don't gamble often." That was true enough, but not because I didn't know how things worked, but because I did.

"Twenty-one is the highest score. Closest one to that wins. Dealer has to hold at seventeen. A player can take as many cards as he wants, but if you go over twenty-one you lose."

"Seems simple enough."

"It is." He smiled insincerely.

"How have you been doing?" I asked Catherine.

"I just got here." She smoked languidly and gazed off into the middle distance, as though to give new meaning to ennui.

"Aren't you playing?" I asked.

"I guess." She tossed a chip and so did I, and the dealer slid two cards to each of us. I had two threes, called for another and got a ten, called for another and busted out with a seven. Catherine won with two kings. I assumed this was part of the shill, showing gamblers that it was actually possible to win now and then. She didn't seem surprised.

This was going nowhere. Luckily, we were very close to the long bar.

"Would you care for a drink?"

"No, thanks." If she had, she wouldn't have needed ice, although I guess I'm pushing the frosty theme too far.

I got up and went to the bar and ordered a gin and tonic. While the bartender was fixing it, I got out one of my business cards and wrote on the back: "I represent a well-known producer. He has seen you here and would like to discuss a possible screen test. Call me for further details."

I got my drink and went back to the table. A few other men had arrived by now, so I merely tapped the beauteous Catherine on the bare shoulder and handed her the card. She glanced at it briefly, read what it said, and thought for a minute. Then she looked at me with narrowed eyes, obviously trying to decide whether this was legitimate or just another cheap trick. I looked her straight in the eye with no hint of flirtation and then nodded.

"For real," I said. I stood there emitting sincerity and seriousness of purpose. I can pull that off sometimes.

She studied me for a few moments more, made her decision, and then suddenly smiled. It was that smile that made me understand a little better why Manny Stairs was infatuated with her. She was nothing more than another pretty woman when she was playing a sullen shill; but when she smiled, she was radiant. All her perfect body seemed to come into sharper focus—at least from where I was standing, which was behind and above her. Always a good vantage point. I began to have impure thoughts.

She nodded discreetly, turned and winked at me, and I took my cue to leave and take my impure thoughts with me. I had done the best I could under the circumstances. It was pretty clear that it would be a lot easier to make Manny's case in the privacy of a phone conversation than in this madhouse of hopeless hope, with bouncers and dealers all on the *qui vive* for smart guys trying to make the boss's girl. I didn't see whether the dealer noticed anything. With luck, he had been paying attention to the new arrivals. But even if he had, the simple business proposition was perfectly innocent, wasn't it? Catherine might even tell Tony about it, and it was just possible that he wouldn't object. He had a taste for actresses, after all. What's more, he was well acquainted with the big shots in the business. Most of them at one time or another had enjoyed his hospitality at the high rollers' table. None of them would have seemed a threat to Tony, most likely. Gangsters generally have good-sized egos.

Maybe when Catherine thought about it, she'd figure out who that interested producer might be. But that didn't necessarily queer the deal, because the screen test was what she had wanted all along—that and some real jewelry. The combination might push Manny's simpatico quotient just over the bar.

I took the water taxi back to Santa Monica. From there, it was only a short drive to Malibu.

CHAPTER SIX

The next morning, Della was pounding away at the typewriter when I got to the office.

"Mornin', chief," she said without breaking stride. She had the eternal Pall Mall dangling from the corner of her mouth. Her daily quota was about three packs, which no doubt accounted for her baritone voice.

"Good morning, loyal employee. What's happening?"

"Bugger all."

"Still working on the detective novel?"

"Yes."

"How's it going?"

"Okay. I'm doing a chapter on the smart aleck detective's visit to a gambling ship."

"What's he doing out there?"

"Looking for a dame. What else?"

Apparently she and Perry had been having a pillow talk.

"Sounds good. Let me know if you need any local color."

"Perry's as much local color as I can stand. By the way, Manny Stairs called. Wants you to call him back. Also, some guy named Marion Mott called. Said he had some info for you."

"Good. I thought you said nothing was going on."

"I was just pulling your chain."

"Consider it pulled. If a woman named Catherine Moore calls and asks about a screen test, don't tell her she's got the wrong number."

"Don't tell me you're using that old line." Her smirk radiated disdain mixed with the kind of disappointment a mother feels for a wayward child.

"Not for myself personally, although I can tell you—it works."

"It's been working in this town since Sunset Boulevard was Sun*rise* Boulevard."

"Good line. One of yours?"

"Sure. I got a million of them."

I called Manny's private number, and he picked up after one ring.

"This is Bruno Feldspar."

"Ah. Good. How did you make out?"

"Well, I made contact with her, but there were too many of Scungilli's people around. I couldn't make the case in that environment. But I did give her a note asking her to call me."

"Why would she wanna do that?" He sounded wary, as though he sniffed another possible rival.

"I used the last resort. A screen test."

"Sounds like it was the first resort."

"I didn't see any other way to get to her privately. She's surrounded out there by Scungilli's goombahs."

He thought about it for a minute. No doubt he had been on the *Lucky Lady* many times before and understood the problem.

"Yeah, I see what you mean. I guess that was the only way to lure her out of there, although I'm not keen on the idea."

"Well, it's only bait. You really don't have to go through with the test, if you can get her to come back to you strictly on the merits of. . . ." Of what, I wondered—imitation jewelry and a distinct lack of simpatico? If he wised up, he'd realize that the screen test was the best card he could play. And I figured it wouldn't take him very long to come to that conclusion. It might bruise his ego a little, but what, after all, was the object of the exercise? To schtup or not to schtup—that was the question.

"Yeah, yeah. I get your point. Did you tell her the offer was from me?"

"Not yet. I figured I needed to talk to you first."

"Good. Let me think about how best to do this. I'll get back to you."

"There's one more thing—she had that jewelry you gave her appraised."

"Oh." He sounded more than a little subdued at the news. "I guess I should have expected that. Did she tell you that?"

"No. It came from what the news boys call a reliable source. One of her friends."

"I see."

"You might want to shop somewhere other than Woolworths, next time."

"I also get that point."

He hung up. Ten seconds later, he called back.

"You have an office, right?"

"Sure."

"Have her come to your office."

"What do you want me to tell her when she gets here?"

"I'm still thinking about that." He hung up again.

It seemed to me I'd gone about as far as I could. The rest was up to Manny. I suppose he'd come up with some scheme to waylay Catherine in my office, maybe hide behind the coat rack and jump out at her just as she was sitting down and waiting to hear about how she was soon to become a star. As the French would say, *quelle surprise.*

Next, I called Marion Mott.

"Marion. It's Riley."

"Hello, Riley. I have some information for you. Seems that we don't have anyone in the L.A. office who's working on art theft and forgery. Most of the guys are looking into the union problems in the movie business. They're rotten with Reds."

"So I've heard."

"But there is a guy we sometimes use to examine works of art. Name is Dennis Finch-Hayden. He's a professor at UCLA and writes art columns for some national magazines. Gets interviewed on radio a lot, too. Apparently he's quite the boy."

"Meaning what, exactly?"

"Kind of a celebrity in that business. Flamboyant."

"Pansy?"

"Just the opposite. A real ladies' man and bon vivant. His friends call him 'Bunny.'"

"Swell."

"Now if you want to contact him, don't be shy about mentioning your connection to the Bureau. He makes a tidy sum from us on a regular basis. He should be happy to cooperate with you. If he wants any verification, have him call me."

"Thanks, Marion. I appreciate it."

"You're welcome. Let me know how you make out."

As I hung up the phone, Della opened the inner door that separated my office from the reception room.

"Someone to see you, chief." She winked a watery eye.

"A lady?"

"Maybe, maybe not. But she's definitely a female. The one doesn't necessarily go with the other, you know."

"Yeah, I've heard."

"Just like gentleman doesn't necessarily go with smart-aleck detective."

"Point taken. In the back. Well, show her in."

It was Catherine Moore.

She was wearing a tight-fitting green sweater that matched the color of her eyes. It was one of those sweaters that buttoned up the front, but she hadn't bothered with the top buttons. Or some of the middle ones. She apparently shared Rita Lovelace's aversion to bras. And like Rita, she didn't need one. Catherine was also wearing a short white skirt designed to display her legs to best advantage, and it worked. On her head was a green beret that gave her a rakish look. It was perched on the side of her platinum blond hair. She wore too much red lipstick, but that was the style. I didn't like it, but I was in the minority.

Aside from that, she was, of course, a knockout, but there was also a no-nonsense look about her, too, a kind of attitude and posture that said she'd been to the ballpark and back a time or two. The word "demure" would not enter anyone's head on first seeing her, and everything about her clothes and her manner said she didn't care. "Alluring," on the other hand, would spring to mind without any effort at all. Also springing to mind—to my mind, at least—were the same impure thoughts that she had aroused the first time I saw her on the *Lucky Lady*. They must have shown in my expression, because she noticed, and it made her smile. It was nothing more than what she expected; she'd have been disappointed otherwise.

She sat down, crossed her legs making that swishy, silky sound with her stockings, took out a silver cigarette case, selected a Camel, and lit it with an onyx-and-silver Ronson.

"Mind if I smoke?" she asked, after blowing a smoke ring.

"Not at all."

She looked around at the spartan décor of my office.

"Looks like you didn't waste any money on decorators."

"I did it all myself. Oak modern. It's the latest thing."

"Latest thing, eh? Let's hope it passes quickly. Last time I saw stuff like this was in a police station in Enid, Oklahoma."

"Interesting that they're up on the latest fashions in Enid. What were you doing there?"

"Just passing through." She noticed the Monet tacked to the wall. "You should get that picture of flowers framed, otherwise people'll think it's a wallpaper sample."

"What if it *is* a wallpaper sample?"

"Yeah, well, if I was a private dick that liked flowered wallpaper, I'd get into another line of work."

"I'll think about it."

She smiled at me and then blew another smoke ring.

"I'm just razzing you," she said. "I don't suppose you've got a pint of rye in that drawer."

"No. But I do have a pint of bourbon."

"That'll do."

"Paper cup suit you?"

"Just like whistling Dixie. No pun intended."

I poured out two shots of my best bourbon, which was everyone else's middle of the road. I gave her one, and she tossed it back with professional ease, crumpled up the paper cup, and tossed it into the wastepaper basket. Then she smiled at me and asked "So, what kind of name is Bruno Feldspar, anyway, huh?"

"Lithuanian."

"Yeah? How 'bout that. Where the hell is Lithuanian?"

"Not far from Mexico."

"No kiddin'? You learn something every day. So tell me, what's a Lithuanian private dick doing scouting for the movies?"

"Jobs come in all shapes and sizes. I'm not picky. Besides, I'm not scouting, I was just delivering a message for my client."

"Who is, exactly?"

"That's confidential for the time being. But it's someone you've probably heard of. A legitimate player. Assuming, of course, that you're interested."

"Damn right I am." She brightened at the prospect and sweetened up a little, too. She even favored me with one of her higher-voltage smiles. "You know, I have some experience. I was the star of our high-school play my senior year. It was a play called *No, No, Nanette*. Ever heard of it?"

"Vaguely."

"Yeah. I played Nanette. Want to hear my big number?"

"Sure."

She obviously was not troubled by inhibitions, because she stood up and started singing "Tea For Two," which apparently was one of the hit songs of the play. She moved with surprising gracefulness, doing subtle dance steps that came under the "less is more" category and at the same time displayed her body in a way that would make your average housewife blush with envy. She was a natural; and what's more, she had a remarkably sweet voice that was an interesting contrast to her Mae West attitude.

"You sing beautifully," I said when she'd finished a couple of bars.

"Thanks. It's one of my two talents."

"I'll bite. What's the other one?"

"Acting, of course." She batted her eyes at me, half mockingly. Or maybe totally mockingly.

"Somehow I think there's a third talent."

"Could be." She laughed, and it sounded as though she was sincerely amused. I was glad she had dropped last night's ice-princess routine. And it wasn't hard to see how two rather rough characters could have fallen for her. She was brassy, all right, but some men go for that. I didn't mind it myself.

"Well, stage experience is always valuable," I said, "but the real question is how you will look and act on film. It's a different business."

"I know. I used to date a producer. I kept asking him to give me a try, but he was only interested in one thing and it wasn't my acting career." She grimaced at the memory. Not a hopeful sign for Manny. "All I wanted was a chance, but he was a real heel. Even gave me phony diamonds. Can you believe a guy would do that?"

"It's been heard of."

"I hope it isn't him you're working for."

"As I said, that's all confidential until we get to the next step."

"Which is what?"

"The client wants to meet with you and have a chat before setting up the test. Just to see if you're . . . simpatico." I couldn't help it. The word just popped into my head.

"Oh, sure. That's fine with me. He'll see I'm simpatico as hell. I practically ooze the stuff."

"There is one question, though," I said.

She smiled flirtatiously. "Well, seeing as how we only just met, the answer's most likely no, but maybe if you play your cards right. . . ."

"That's not the question," I said. "At least not now."

"Well?"

"What about your relationship with Tony Scungilli?"

"How'd you hear about that?"

"Word gets around."

"Well, that's no problem. Tony's just nuts about the movies. He likes actresses. He said I looked just like one of his old girlfriends who was an actress, too. She died trying to rescue her poodle from a burning building. It was tragic."

"Funny, I didn't see that story in the papers."

"They hushed it up. Don't ask me why. Tony was real upset for a long time until he met me." She grinned, as if to say "and who could blame him?" "I showed him your card and he was all for it. Told me to get right on it, so that's how come I came here today."

"Do you . . . see Tony as a long-term proposition?"

"I thought a proposition was always short-term. Like one night and maybe breakfast."

"All right. How about 'a long-term relationship'?"

"I get it. As for Tony, I don't know. He's okay, but no Douglas Fairbanks, if you know what I mean. You know what his nickname is? The Snail. Well, there's one thing he's not slow about, if you get my drift. A girl's just getting started and he's already finished and halfway through his cigarette. He thinks 'foreplay' and 'afterglow' are only separated by a dash."

"A hundred-yard dash?"

"No, the kind that comes between words."

I was beginning to like her. There's nothing like a good-looking woman with a sense of humor. She wasn't someone you'd want to take home to mother, but that wouldn't bother her any; she could take your mother or leave her. Most likely her own mother, too.

"So you wouldn't object to moving out and coming back to Hollywood . . . if the test works out?"

"Not for a minute. Tony might get upset. He says he loves me. But if he really loved me, he'd go a little slower, you know? What's more, the presents have been scarce as hen's teeth. Just a couple of pearl earrings. I mean, what kind of love is that? Pretty cheap, if you ask me. For all I know, they're fake too, like those diamonds that other rat gave me. I haven't had time to get them appraised yet, but you can bet I'm going to. Plus, a lot of the time that boat's rocking and I get queasy. I like it better on dry land. Besides, all those goons he has around all the time give me the creeps. They know better than to make a play, but they're always eyeing me, you know? Like they're wondering what I look like without any clothes."

"Shocking."

"Ain't it?" And she laughed again.

Well, all of that added up to a glimmer of hope for Manny, despite being labeled a "rat." Catherine was obviously not any more attached to Tony than she had been to Manny. But Manny could offer one thing that Tony couldn't. With either guy, she'd be holding her nose in the bedroom, but at least with Manny she'd have a shot at the movies. It began to look a little brighter for my client, the more I thought about it. She had said she hoped I wasn't working for Manny, and that was a dampener. But she would soon figure out that if the test went well and she got a contract, she'd have a lot more leverage with Manny, as well as some jewelry that didn't come from the five-and-dime.

"So, when do I meet this bird?"

"I'll make a call and set it up. Are you going back to the *Lucky Lady*?"

"I don't feel like it. I think I'll check into a hotel and charge it to Tony."

"You might try the Garden of Allah. Lots of movie people hang out there."

"Yeah? That sounds good. Where's it at?"

"Eighty-one fifty-two Sunset Boulevard, just across from Schwab's Drug Store. Any cabbie knows the place."

"Great. Thanks." She looked at me suspiciously. "I don't suppose you get a kickback from that place—for sending people there. I hope it's not a dump." She was obviously a girl with a nose for the angles.

"Nope. It's a nice place. And no kickback. As a matter of fact, I live there myself."

She turned her head slightly and looked at me slantwise and knowingly. I switched on my choirboy expression.

"I'm just trying to be helpful," I said.

"A real philosopher, eh?" I imagine she meant to say philanthropist, but I let it go. Either way, I wasn't one anyway. "Okay. Well, maybe I'll see you there later."

"Good. I'll introduce you to some people in the business. I have a feeling they'll like you, assuming you like gin."

"Gin? It's practically mother's milk to me, and if you knew my mother you'd know I wasn't kidding. Well, see you later . . . Bruno."

After Catherine left, I called Manny.

"The lady in question just left my office."

"I thought you were supposed to wait to hear from me." Again, the unwelcome peevishness. "I'm still working on my pitch."

"It wasn't my idea. She just dropped in."

"Oh. Well, what'd you tell her?"

"Not much. I said the client, meaning you, would remain confidential until you actually met with her."

"Good. She still set on a screen test?"

"It's the only reason she came in. But she's very excited about it."

"I guess there's no way around it."

"I don't think so. And if you want a little friendly advice, I'd play it straight with her. She doesn't seem to me to be the kind of girl who'd give you three strikes. And you've already swung and missed once."

There was a pause while he swallowed this medicine.

"Did you ask her about Scungilli?"

"Yes, and I don't think that'll be a problem. She's not romantically involved with him."

"Meaning she's not banging him?"

"I didn't say that. I said she's not romantically involved. It appears to be strictly a business arrangement for her, although she says he's in love with her. That could be a complication."

"I suppose he's showering her with jewelry." He sounded a little glum at that thought.

"Only pearl earrings, so far. She's not impressed. Thinks he's kind of cheap."

"In that case, I wonder what she thinks of me."

"Do you really have to wonder?"

"No, I suppose not. Well, all of that can be taken care of. Did you set up a time for us to meet?"

"No. I wanted to talk to you first. Figured you'd have some thoughts on where and when."

"Better not bring her to the studio. If there's a bad scene for some reason, I wouldn't want it to play out in front of so many witnesses."

"The horselaugh."

"Right. Bring her to my beach house in Malibu. We had some good times there, and it's private." He gave me the address.

"When?"

"Tomorrow at lunchtime. I'll have a caterer put something nice together. For two. You can scram after you drop her off."

As if I'd want to hang around and watch Manny maneuver.

It occurred to me that I might have trouble setting up the meeting tomorrow, if Catherine decided she'd skip the Garden of Allah and go back to the *Lucky Lady* after all. If so, I'd have to go out there and deliver the message firsthand. Well, after what she'd said about Tony's enthusiastic reaction to her potential acting career, there should be no trouble about that. She might even introduce me to the man. After my experience with the mob in Youngstown, I was kind of curious how Tony would compare to my erstwhile gangster friends back east, if you consider Ohio the east. On balance, though, it would be better to meet her around the pool at the Garden, later. It would save me a trip and also give her the chance to get to know some aspiring actresses and some expiring writers, to say nothing of a stray private dick with impure thoughts. Like Scungilli's goons, I too wondered what she looked like without her clothes. Finding out might constitute a professional conflict of interest, but as someone once said, perfection is the enemy of the good. Voltaire? Maybe.

"One more suggestion," I said. "I'd stop by the fanciest jewelry store you know and pick up something big, shiny, and expensive. I don't think 'discreet' or 'subtle' will do the job."

"I already thought of that. And this time I'll show her the receipt."

It's a shame all the romantic poets are dead. True love and sensitive souls like Manny and Catherine deserved an ode. *What men or gods are these? What maidens loth? What mad pursuit? What struggle to escape? What pipes and timbrels? What wild ecstasy?*

Obviously, Catherine didn't quite qualify as a "maiden loth," or a maiden of any kind, for that matter. Still, you have to take your romantic inspiration where you find it. And although I wasn't sure what a timbrel was, I was pretty sure my old English teacher, Granny Graves, would have been pleased that I remembered those lines.

CHAPTER SEVEN

My next call was to Dennis Finch-Hayden at the Art Department of UCLA.

The secretary who answered the phone told me Doctor Finch-Hayden was not in, and she didn't know when he was expected. She was a little frosty, until I told her I'd been referred to the good doctor by my friends and colleagues at the FBI and, further, that I'd like to meet with him about evaluating a potential forgery of a Monet. She thawed out at the mention of the FBI—and the prospect of a fee, I suppose. Or maybe it was the magic word "Monet." She said she would make sure Doctor Finch-Hayden got the message and called me back.

The next afternoon, I went to see Professor Dennis Finch-Hayden in Westwood, on the impossibly beautiful campus of UCLA, where impossibly beautiful coeds walked gaily by, wearing saddle shoes and plaid kilts and white blouses, their hair, blond as a rule, tied back casually, faces tanned. Here and there a few boys lounged in the shade wearing letter sweaters, white bucks, khakis, and expressions of confidence. No one was discussing Kant or Keats, but whatever they were discussing made them happy, for they were all smiling and laughing. I envied them their insouciance. In years, they weren't all that much younger than I was, but in other ways we were from different generations. And certainly from different worlds. And I have to admit to breathing a mild sigh of jealousy. I wondered if they had the slightest conception of their good fortune. Some must have, surely.

Dennis Finch-Hayden's office was in the university museum, so I had to walk through the main gallery that was festooned with paintings in gilded frames and the floor crowded with statues in marble and bronze, most showing the human form in unlikely perfection. Well, why not. Who wants to look at ugliness in a museum? The rest of the world is filled with it. You want to see ugliness, walk down any city street—even in Hollywood.

These days, mostly because of the Depression, there was a school of thought that wanted to emphasize depressing reality in any sort of art, even including the movies, which were or should have been nothing more than sugar on the corn flakes and uniquely valuable for that reason. But according to the gloom merchants, life was nothing more than a Russian novel in which everything is dreary, right up to and including the point when the main character jumps in front of an express train, while the peasants resignedly starve to death in the background.

I didn't care about any of that. I had long ago rejected the importance of being earnest. I had worked in a steel mill, so I knew more about the working class than the guys writing about them oh so solemnly. Hell, if I was anything, I *was* working-class. At least, I'd started out that way. The days in the mill were long and hot, but after work, the pitchers of beer and the shared packets of Lucky Strikes restored tired muscles and even made the work seem worth doing. There really is such a thing as feeling good after a good day's work.

Of course, I hadn't worked in the mills for very long; greener pastures beckoned. So I could afford to be philosophical on the subject. But the men I worked with were not beaten down by a sense of hopelessness, even though they all knew they weren't going anywhere else. Nor did they think of themselves as cogs in some ever-turning gear. Most of them were happy to have a job and to spend time after work with their friends in a beer joint. I've forgotten nine tenths of the jokes I heard. But I can tell you there was more laughter than complaining. And if you've never tasted cold beer and a Lucky after a full day of hard, sweaty work, you've missed something. Add a pickled egg from the jar on the bar and some good-natured vulgarity from a buxom barmaid, and you have a recipe for happiness, albeit temporary.

I found the professor's office midway down a long hallway off the main gallery. His name was on the door, and although I was expected, I knocked politely.

"Come in!" If this was Finch-Hayden, he sounded energetic and cheerful. "Feldspar?" he said. "Glad to meet you. My name's Finch-Hayden. My friends call me Bunny."

"Yes, I've heard."

"Silly sort of name, I know." He said this with a self-assured grin, as if he enjoyed the joke as much as everyone else.

"Well, you're certainly the first man I've ever known who was called that." The only other "Bunny" I'd known was a girl back in high school; she had the nickname for reasons not difficult to figure out.

"It's absurd, of course. Been called that since before I can remember. Came from Nanny. She was a ruthless old trout, just the kind to saddle an innocent child with a ridiculous nickname. I'm surprised I don't have nightmares about her still. Anyway, the name stuck, and I've become used to it. Has an element of agreeable irony. Care for some coffee?"

"I'd like that, yes."

"Splendid." He pushed a button somewhere and a secretary magically appeared with a silver tray bearing a silver pot, two expensive-looking cups and saucers, the kind that light almost passes through, milk jug, sugar bowl, and a dish of macaroons. All the crockery matched and was decorated elaborately with pink flowers and green leaves. The secretary laid the tray on the coffee table, smiled pleasantly, and then dematerialized.

"I hope you like macaroons. My secretary adores them and therefore assumes everyone else must like them, too. Personally, I don't care for them. I don't tell her that; she is a sensitive soul. I take them home and give them to my Labrador retriever. He shares her enthusiasm. Every suit coat I own has crumbs in the pockets."

"I'm an Oreo man, usually."

"Yes. Now that makes sense, artistically. A simple but elegant circular arrangement in black and white. Very modern.

Take a pew," he said, indicating two chairs separated by the coffee table. "You know, for just a moment I thought you said you were an Oriel man. That's an Oxford college. Perhaps you've heard of it." He said this without any discernible condescension.

"I've heard of it, yes."

"I was at Magdalene." He pronounced it "maudlin."

"And yet you seem so cheerful."

"Yes. Well, who can explain these things?" He smiled amiably. "It may not surprise you to learn that that witticism has been used before."

"No, I'm not surprised."

Finch-Hayden was tall and lean, with hair the color of straw, clear blue eyes, and a hawk nose, which as he told me later was a legacy from a distant ancestor, the Duke of Wellington. ("It's the only legacy our side of the family got, I'm afraid," he said.) He was dressed in a blue pinstriped suit, white shirt, and blue-and-white striped tie which I assumed meant something, either a regiment or an old school. (Eton, as it turned out.) I noticed that the buttons on the sleeve of his jacket actually buttoned, a sign of Savile Row tailoring. No doubt Manny Stairs would approve.

Finch-Hayden was not especially handsome, but he was elegant-looking. A Leslie Howard type, you might say. About forty, he exuded good humor and total self-confidence—as witnessed by the gold signet ring on the little finger of his left hand. When he wasn't teaching, he was busy cutting a wide swath through the eligible and ineligible women of L.A., New York, and London. At least that was the rumor, and it was not difficult to believe. He had the look, and he had the manner. And of course he was an expert in the arts—a sure winner with wealthy women who liked to give or attend fundraisers. He offered them the chance to combine a little civilized adultery with pre- and post-seduction conversation about Picasso's blue period. Or Braque's billiard tables.

I didn't know anything about Picasso's blue period or any other period, for that matter, but Bunny was not shy about explaining how art talk paved the way for some high class "shagging"—the British version of "schtupping." "The secret to the business is very simple, really—it's what you say to them afterwards. You have no idea how a few words about Matisse's brushwork can convince them that you really are interested in them as individuals. Especially if you ask their opinions. The same talk beforehand would rightly be viewed as a mere means to an end and accepted as such. But afterwards, my boy, afterwards. That's the key. Unless of course you are not interested in any afterwards."

This was after I got to know him a little better, of course. He said he avoided coeds, though. "Tempting, but apt to become clinging. Or demanding. Or now and then given to blackmail. And certain old women in the administration frown on such things."

"I didn't realize there were many old women in the administration."

"There aren't any, literally. Just a figure of speech. Reminds me of something someone said about the poet Housman—that he was descended from a long line of maiden aunts. Yes, all things considered, it's much better to stick to married women. They only want a little excitement, sprinkled with culture."

"I'll make it a point to read up on Picasso's blue period."

"Yes, do. And don't neglect the rose period. It has its own merits."

His office was like the library of a men's club—leather furniture, well-used but not worn, floor-to-ceiling shelves crammed with books, and one window looking out over a quadrangle. The window faced west so that the afternoon sun was slanting through in yellow shafts created by the wooden blinds. Where there were no bookshelves, there were photographs of young men on sports teams, all smiling and wearing college scarves and white outfits. Above one of the shelves was a rowing scull, and hanging from a hook on the side of one shelf was a cricket bat, much scarred.

There was a desk in front of the window, facing inward, and on the desk an Underwood typewriter with paper inserted, a notebook, a Mont Blanc fountain pen, a telephone, a pipe rack, and an index-card file. The desktop was inlayed with red leather. Like the rest of the office, the desk looked well used, well kept, well aged, and expensive. The Persian carpet was not new and in fact gave off the impression of having been trod upon in earlier times by slippered Paynims. But it was in elegant condition nonetheless. The room smelled of pipe smoke, of course. It was a good smell. I could have cheerfully lived in that room.

When we were seated in opposing leather wing chairs, sipping coffee, he looked at me with friendly curiosity.

"What sort of name is Feldspar?" he asked.

"Made up."

"Ah. I'm not surprised. I would have pegged you as Scotch-Irish."

"You would have pegged correctly."

"Good. I like being right. I won't ask why you travel under false colors. No doubt you have your reasons. Many people out here do."

"Travel under false colors, or have reasons?"

"Both, I would say. One leads to the other. What's your relationship with the FBI? I gather it's not official."

"Well, I collaborated with them on a case involving organized crime. In Youngstown, Ohio."

"Very dreary, those places."

"In some ways, yes." But, as I've said, in other ways, not so bad, if you didn't mind the slag heaps. But there was no reason to get into that with "Bunny."

"I've traveled through some of our own factory towns in England," he said. "It's the sort of thing everyone should do, if only to understand D. H. Lawrence—or, should I say, if only to forgive him his literary sins. Those awful row houses, smeared with grime. Pathetic gardens in the back. Dirty streets in front. Dirty children sitting on the curbside. One wonders how people stand it. That anyone fights his way out of such places is a minor miracle. Have you read Lawrence?"

"*Lady Chatterley*, yes."

"Of course. It's not bad, really, if you can get by the smutty parts. Not that I'm a prude. Far from it. But it's a jar to see some words on the page. You know, I once met a couple in Scotland, at a pheasant shoot near Loch Lomond. I was the guest of the local squire. Nice chap. Something out of Trollope or Fielding. Anyway, his gamekeeper was a typical dour Scot, complete with black beard and a scowl. And yet he was living with a very posh Englishwoman, not his wife. She cooked and cleaned their little cottage and didn't seem to mind the constant odor of blood, manure, and wet dogs—a gamekeeper's stock in trade. They seemed poorly matched and quite happy. Queer, isn't it?"

"Life imitating art."

"Yes, quite right, although I think that expression has become a little shopworn, wouldn't you say?"

"Sorry."

"Oh, I didn't mean to be rude or critical. Just a lecture point. Always doing it. Bad habit outside the lecture hall."

"I don't mind. You never know where you'll pick up something of interest."

"Spoken like a true detective. Have you been at it long?"

"A year. Maybe less."

"That's not very long. You must have a talent for it."

"Now and then I'm afraid that I do."

"I think I understand what you mean. Did you go to university?"

"No. But I like to read."

"An autodidact. I'm impressed. Most of the great artists were, too. Not many graduated from art school. Gauguin started out as a stockbroker, if you can believe it. Well, let's not waste any more of your time. Tell me, what is this all about?"

"It involves a lost, or possibly stolen, Monet."

"Ah. Big money. How nice. Was it in a private collection or a gallery? Or museum, God forbid."

"It was private."

"And you say the painting has been stolen?"

"That's the way it looks, although other scenarios are possible."

"Yes, that's usually the way of it."

"And to cover the theft, or the loss, a copy was made."

"So there are at least two possible paintings. I say 'at least' because in these cases there are sometimes several made."

"Yes. There may well be another floating around some-where. But I have gotten ahold of one, and I need to know whether it's the original or a copy."

"How did you come by it?"

"Luck."

"Ah. Life's most important and elusive commodity. You know what Napoleon said about it."

"As a matter of fact, I do."

"Bravo! Well, I see you have the tube. Let's have a look."

I passed the tube to him, and he carefully extracted the painting and spread it on his side table.

"A forgery," said Finch-Hayden after no more than a few seconds of gazing at the painting through a monocle. "Couldn't fool a child."

"I see." This was disappointing, of course, but there was more to the question. "As far as I know, there aren't any chil-dren who need to be fooled. Only a middle-aged husband with little or no knowledge of art. Could something like this fool him?"

"Well, since I don't know the husband in question, I can't say definitively. But I assume he's wealthy, owning a Monet and all that."

"Yes. But it was his wife's idea to acquire it."

"That's usually the way. Most of the husbands I have met are not interested in art but are happy to stand by, checkbook in hand, looking the other way while the good lady acts the role of patron of the arts. Of all creatures great and small, middle-aged, wealthy husbands are Nature's most perfect fools. Touching in many ways. Of course, there is the other kind—the ones who are jealous and wary and hover over their wives like Othello with a pillow. But they are in the minority. Most are a byword for gullibility. I suspect it is often a willful gullibility. 'What the eyes do not see, the heart does not feel,' as the Spanish say."

He smiled, as if to indicate that, having never been married, he was the beneficiary, rather than the victim, of this widespread gullibility, real or self-induced. "Is the wife in this case young and beautiful? They generally are."

"No, she's forty-ish and dead. Emily Watson. I'm surprised you haven't heard about it. It was in all the papers."

"I don't read the papers. And I don't listen to the radio news. I find them depressing. I prefer to edit reality, letting in as little bad news as possible. I find my own mind is a more than sufficient source of distress. I don't need more. Of course, it's too bad about the lady."

It didn't sound like he was feeling very sorry for the victim. But, then, he hadn't known her. And I sympathized with his technique of editing reality. I tried to do the same thing myself.

"Too bad in what sense?"

"Well, it's an aesthetic problem, a departure from the usual scenario. You know, wealthy older man, beautiful young wife. There's usually a younger lover in the picture somewhere. Although he needn't always be *that* young." He smiled self-referentially. "Was her death a crime of passion? Or did she die of natural causes, like La Dame aux Camellias? Forgive me if I seem flippant. One does this to keep emotions at bay."

"More editing reality?"

"Yes. But it's an annoying English trait, I realize."

That seemed odd to me. He hadn't known the woman, so why should there be any emotion to be kept at bay? Of course, he was an Englishman. Perhaps that explained it. Still. . . .

"I don't know about passion," I said. "But it certainly was a crime. She died from a twenty-two-caliber bullet through the temple."

"I see. Hardly natural causes." He became serious now. "Murdered?"

"Possibly. Suicide hasn't been ruled out. There was also another shooting. The victim was a younger man. . . ."

"Ah. The plot thickens—according to form."

"Yes, this part of the story does seem to run true to form. The younger man was not only Mrs. Watson's lover but also a painter. That is confidential, for the time being at least—that he was her lover, I mean."

"Yes, I supposed as much. I assume this forgery has something to do with the case."

"Something. We're not sure what, exactly. Not yet, anyway."

"Naturally you've considered the possibility that the young lover in this case was the forger."

"Yes, of course."

"And what's your role in the case, if I may ask? You're not officially with the police or the FBI."

"No. I'm a private investigator. I was hired by the victim the day before she died, and I'm working with the police to look into the way this painting might have a bearing on the case. They're hoping it has no relationship at all and that the two shootings were a simple matter of a lover's tiff resulting in one murder and one suicide."

"That the theft of the painting is a separate matter entirely. Yes. Very clean. Very simple."

"As for the FBI, I worked with them on that other case, so they're willing to vouch for me."

"I know. I checked before agreeing to see you. I hope you don't mind."

"I would have done the same thing."

"Yes. A mere precaution."

"Somewhere there's a genuine Monet floating around. I was hoping this was it, of course. But I figured that would be too good to be true."

"Yes, unfortunately. Whoever did this has talent; I won't deny that. But there is a vast difference between talent and genius. One is a Model T, the other a Bugatti. Both run on petrol, but the similarities end there. I should know. I have talent, but nothing beyond, I'm afraid. I'm talking about my own painting, you understand."

"Better than nothing. To be talented, I mean."

"Yes, of course. Still, when one spends one's life teaching people about the elements of genius, one becomes all that much more aware of one's own shortcomings. Now and then it can be depressing. You'll notice I don't have any of my paintings here in the office. I can't stand to look at them for very long."

"You seem to have done all right, otherwise," I said, gesturing to the fine fixtures of his office.

"Well, yes. No doubt. As an artist I have discipline, ability, and energy, and I have that single prerequisite to a happy career in the arts—a reliable private income. Still, I know I'll never produce anything so good as the original of this painting."

"I assume copying a masterpiece is significantly easier than creating one."

"Of course. You have the detailed blueprint in front of you."

"I don't suppose you recognize anything about this forgery that might suggest who did it."

"Nothing at all, I'm afraid. It could be any of a thousand artists, assuming the deceased Lothario did not do it. There are some well-known master forgers loose in the world, mostly in Europe. But I doubt it was one of those. They would have done a better job."

"If I showed you examples of other paintings by some artists, original paintings, could you detect any similarities of technique. . . ?"

"That might enable me to deduce that the same man painted both? I doubt it. After all, the forger was trying to copy Monet's technique, not adapt his own."

"I see."

"But I'd be willing to have a go at it, if you like."

"Can't hurt."

"No, I suppose not."

"Well, I won't take up any more of your time, Professor."

"Call me Bunny, if you like. I know it takes a little getting used to."

"All right . . . Bunny."

"And what shall I call you? Surely not Bruno."

"Well, my real name is Thomas Parke D'Invilliers, so I guess you could call me Tom."

He looked at me and smiled knowingly.

"Thomas Parke D'Invilliers, eh? Interesting name. I have the feeling that I've run across it before, somewhere. Is that possible, do you think?"

"I don't know. It's possible, I suppose." From the amused look in his eye, I knew I had put my foot in it.

"Yes. I'm sure I've seen it," he said. "I know! It's quoted as an epigraph to a novel. *The Great Gatsby*. Do you know it?"

"Vaguely. I read it when it came out a few years ago."

"No one reads it these days, of course. But I rather like it. A little overwrought in places, but not disastrously so. Now, how does that epigraph go?" He got up and started looking through his bookshelves, and in a few moments found the volume he was looking for. "Here it is. *The Great Gatsby*. And the epigraph reads: *Then wear the gold hat if that will move her; If you can bounce high, bounce for her too, Till she cry 'Lover, gold-hatted, high-bouncing lover, I must have you!'* Words to live by, eh?"

"I suppose so, in one sense."

"The author is identified as Thomas Parke D'Invilliers. That's you! Did you give that line to the author, what's his name—Fitzgerald?"

"No. Of course not. It's obviously a coincidence. I remember wondering about it when I first saw it."

"Yes. Anyone would wonder about that. Of course, D'Invilliers is a common name, to say nothing of Thomas and Parke. It's easy to see how the coincidence could occur."

I have to admit I could feel my face getting red.

"No need for blushes, Tom," he said, with a friendly smile. "We all have our little secrets. *The human heart has hidden treasures, in secret kept, in silence sealed.* That's Charlotte Brontë. Know her?"

"No, we've never met," I said, trying to regain a straight face. "Does she live around here?"

He laughed at the joke, politely.

"Well, we will peel the onion of your various identities until some day we may perhaps arrive at your real name. Not that it matters. After all, 'what's in a name?'"

"Four roses would smell as sweet."

"Good God. Surely you don't drink that vile stuff."

"Only when there's nothing else."

"Well, you must come to my place for dinner some evening. I can give you something better."

"Thanks. I'd like that." That was true. Bunny had charm to spare, and it was so natural that it worked even on someone like me. Besides, he was interesting and knew things that I didn't know. Getting to know him better would be fun.

"Bring someone along if you like. I intend to have company too, and a foursome is always more pleasant."

"Thank you. I will." Myrtle would like him too, and there was something about him that said he would never poach on a friend's territory. It was not "the done thing."

"Good. That's settled then. I'll call your office with date and time. Now, be so kind as to take some of these damned macaroons with you, will you? My dog will never know, and besides he's getting much too fat."

It was getting close to cocktail hour by the time I got to my car and wound my way back to the Ocean Highway. I turned north into the traffic and headed for Malibu. A cold Stella Artois, a swim, and a shower, followed by fresh fish grilled on the beach, some chilled wine, and an evening with Myrtle all added up to a hard-to-beat program.

When I pulled close to her driveway, I saw the red-and-gray Duesenberg parked outside her door. It had the look of having been there for a while. I don't mind admitting to a sudden pang of jealousy. Or maybe it was sadness. Certainly

I felt a little deflated. I waited a few minutes to see if that guy, I'd forgotten his name, was just leaving. Maybe he was dropping her off after acting class. Then I waited a few more minutes, and still nothing seemed to be stirring. After a while, I noticed that the wait had stretched to almost half an hour.

Life seems to come in half-hour chunks, I thought—both the good and the bad. This was one of the bad chunks. I had no claims on her, of course. I had even told her that some day she would meet the man of her dreams. Yes, I had told her all that, but that doesn't mean I *meant* it.

When the sun started to dip into the ocean, I started the engine and headed south, back to the Garden of Allah, wondering if Myrtle's young Lochinvar had finally "come out of the west" driving a Duesenberg. It kind of looked that way.

I had forgotten that I needed to get ahold of Catherine Moore and arrange for the next day's meeting with Manny Stairs. I remembered all this as I drove back to Sunset Boulevard, hoping that Catherine had followed my advice about the hotel. It would save me a trip out to the *Lucky Lady*, and I wasn't in the mood for a boat ride just then: I was in the mood for a gin and tonic.

The usual crowd of inebriants was gathered around the pool, and the usual bevy of starlets was splashing joyfully in the water, doing what they could to attract attention and succeeding. I checked to see if Catherine was in there with them, but she wasn't. As soon as I'd had my drink, I'd check with the front desk to see if she was registered.

My friend Hobey, the writer, was sitting by himself at a table; he was cradling a drink and peering into it as though it were a crystal ball. I guess in some ways gin had answers for him, although you couldn't be sure they were the right answers. He looked up and saw me and waved at me to join him.

"You look a little down in the dumps," he said. "Have a drink."

"Thanks. I will. And I am, I suppose."

"Women, eh?"

"Does it show?"

"Kind of."

"It'll pass." It always had, although some took longer than others. Hobey didn't look so chipper himself, and I mentioned it to him.

"Oh, it's just the usual thing with this writing game."

"Producers driving you crazy?"

"No, not this time. I'm working on a novel. Just about finished with it, but now and then I get stuck."

"Does drinking help?"

"Not really. But neither does not drinking."

"What's the book about?"

"About a man with a difficult wife."

"Should appeal to a wide audience."

"I hope so. But how would you know? Are you married?"

"No. But I read a lot."

"A wise policy. Vicarious misery is much better than the real thing. Well, I hope you will read this one, if I ever get it finished."

"I look forward to it. What's it called?"

"I don't know yet. I always save that bit for last. I'll dig up something. Maybe a quote. Bartlett's is always good for finding titles."

We sat drinking in silence for a few minutes. I was still a little confused by what I had seen at Myrtle's place. I was trying to sort through what I really felt about it, but I wasn't having much luck.

But after a few moments I said to my companion in mild misery: "Do you remember that story I told you about the producer who fell in love with the woman who was a dead ringer for his former wife?"

"Sure. It's a good story. I've been toying with it a little. Maybe that's why I'm having trouble finishing up the other thing."

"Well, look over yonder and you will see the woman herself, coming this way."

He looked across the way, squinted, and drew in his breath.

"Why, it's Minnie David," he said, astonished. "I mean, her exact double. I knew her, you see. Lovely woman. Physically, that is. Otherwise, not so much." He thought for a moment and then made the logical connection. "So Manny Stairs is the lovelorn producer of the story."

"Good guess. This one's named Catherine Moore."

"Remarkable."

Catherine hadn't seen me. She was wearing a skimpy bathing suit the color of a California sunset, and she sat down in one of the chaises longues beside the pool. I assumed she'd bought the suit that afternoon, although she could have brought it from the *Lucky Lady*; it might have easily fit in a change purse.

"Remarkable," he said, again.

"Would you excuse me for a while? I've got some business I need to do with her."

"I can well imagine," he said. "While you're at it, ask her if she'd like to meet a down-at-the-heels, formerly famous writer."

"I think she's got her eye on a currently famous producer."

"Can't say I blame her."

I walked over to her, and she brightened up when she saw me. I took that as a hopeful sign. I don't know of what exactly. Maybe just that she was in a good mood and ready to hear that her secret admirer was in fact the well-known cheapskate Manny Stairs.

"Hiya, Sparky," she said, grinning playfully. "You were right. This is an interesting place."

"Glad you like it."

"I saw Francis X. Bushman in the lobby."

"That must've been a treat."

"He looked old."

"That happens. And in Hollywood it happens faster than anywhere else."

"So, what's up? When do I get to meet the mystery man?"

"Tomorrow. For lunch. In Malibu. I'll drive you there."

Her eyes narrowed into a "Wait a minute, buddy" look, and then she smiled slyly. "That wouldn't be at an unfinished house on the beach, would it?"

"How'd you guess?"

She laughed. I had to admit she was even more beautiful when she laughed than when she thought someone was watching her and she was posing.

"I figured it was him. He had a bad case."

"Bad case?"

"Bad case of yours truly. What else?"

"Does it matter? That he's the one, I mean?"

"Not if he comes through with the screen test. I've been thinking about it, and I realized I could put up with a little schtupping in the short run. Hell, name me a dame in this town who's made it who didn't have to put up with putting out."

"You said—for the short run."

"Right. If I make it big, I'll give him the push again. What's he going to do about it, anyway, huh?"

"What if you don't make it big?"

"If I don't, I'll turn off the honey supply until he promises to marry me. Then once I'm safely married, I'll live my own life and he can either lump it or pay the alimony. Won't matter to me which."

"What if he gets tired of you?"

"Think it's likely?" She ran her hands down the sides of her breasts and down along her thighs. Impure thoughts returned to me, as she intended.

"No, but just for the sake of discussion."

"If that happens, I can still say 'cigars, cigarettes, cigarillos' with the best of them."

"Which brings up another question: What about Tony?"

"Tony'll keep. Besides, he wants me to become a big-time star, and he knows how the game is played."

"What about the phony jewelry? Still mad about that?"

"No. He won't try that trick again. If anything, he'll go overboard the other way."

"Seems like you've thought it all through pretty carefully. I'm impressed."

"I didn't do it to impress you, Sparky. I'm out for number one, and I'm just like Tony: I know how the game is played. I was mad as a wet hen at first—when I had those fake diamonds appraised. And I figured I wasn't ever going to talk him into making me an actress, so I said what the hell and buggered out. But after I talked to you and more or less figured out who your client was, I saw things clearer. Things had changed, and good old opportunity was staring me in the kisser. I'd be a fool to turn it down, now that I had the upper hand. Which I do."

I had to smile. She was beautiful and sassy, but that's not why I was smiling. It was the thought of what Manny's future would be like. During office hours, he might terrorize nervous directors, but at home he'd be singing a different tune, or I was missing my guess by more than a little bit.

"What are you doing for dinner?" I asked.

"Why, I'm surprised at you, Sparky. Didn't you know? I'm having it with you."

By midnight, I no longer had to wonder what Catherine Moore looked like without her clothes. Neither did a half dozen or so shattered writers and a handful of extras who were flush from five days of work and blowing their earnings at the Garden. She treated us all to a stripping exhibition from the high-diving board, after which she attempted a swan dive that turned out to be something more like a duck committing suicide. A quart of gin or thereabouts will ruin even the most professional diver's timing, and Catherine, for all her naked physical perfection, was strictly an amateur off the board. The splash she made, both literal and figurative, was stupendous; that sort of thing happens when you land flat out on the water, like a gigantic beaver slapping its tail. And it was only because I was still moderately sober that she didn't sink to the bottom of the pool and stay there, for the rest of the audience wasn't capable of realizing that she'd knocked herself out in the fall, much less of jumping in and rescuing her.

You would think that someone so well endowed would be more buoyant, but not so. Once she hit the water, she headed straight down. I dove in after her and reached her just as she was settling onto the bottom. When she felt my arms going around her, she actually opened her superb green eyes and smiled, as if to ask "What took you so long to make a pass?"

It was something of a struggle getting her to the surface, because when she smiled at me, she had also swallowed a pint or so of water and began flailing her arms and kicking her legs. But I made it after all; and when we broke the surface, me holding her under her breasts in the approved Dick Champion lifeguard technique, the various writers and extras all broke into applause and someone started singing "For He's a Jolly Good Fellow." I managed to get her into a sitting position on the edge of the pool, and she continued coughing up the water she'd inhaled, after which she passed out again. It was at this point that the various onlookers decided to offer their help; but I firmly resisted and, lifting her by the arms, threw her over my shoulder in what they call the fireman's carry and staggered the few yards to my bungalow.

I dropped her on the imitation Spanish sofa and went to get a towel. When I came back, she was awake again. Apparently her swim had sobered her up, a little.

"Hey, Sparky. Did I have a good time?"

"Exquisite."

"That'll be a first. How about you? Was it good for you?"

"So-so."

"Yeah. Pull the other one. Why am I so wet?"

"Diving into the pool bareassed will do that."

"Oh." Apparently a dim memory was beginning to flutter around her. "So, are you saying . . . we didn't get around to it?"

"Not yet."

"I figured that when you said 'so-so.' If there's one thing I'm not, it's so-so. In that category, I mean."

"I believe you. Do you want any help drying off?"

"No, thanks, Sparky. What I really want is a place to go to sleep." She yawned and stretched elaborately. It was one of the best stretches I'd ever seen. "Mind if I bunk with you? I'm too tired to make it back to my room."

"Do you snore?"

"Nobody's complained so far."

"In that case, let me show you to the bedroom."

"Smooth talker." She paused as if processing a new thought. "I wonder where my bathing suit went."

About three in the morning, I found out that she wasn't lying when she said she wasn't so-so. For an hour or so, all thoughts about Myrtle disappeared. I know that's not very noble, but as I've said before, I'm just a blue-collar guy trying to make his way in the world. Nobility and I are more or less strangers.

I woke up to the smell of fresh coffee. It was about seven.

"Mornin', Sparky," she said as she delivered a cup of coffee laced with cream and sugar. I normally drank it black, but

I have to say this one tasted pretty good. She was wearing what's been called a roguish smile. The fact that she was also wearing only a bath towel added a certain something. Despite the amount of gin she'd taken on board the night before, she looked fresh and bright. "How'd you like last night?"

"The three A.M. version, or the swimming party?"

"You know," she said, with an ironic imitation of coy girlishness.

"It was so-so," I said with my own version of the roguish smile.

"Oh, sure."

"How about you?"

"What was the word you used before?"

"Exquisite?"

"That's it. Pretty much. I may have to put you in my card file."

"I'd be honored."

"Don't go falling in love with me, though. I'm going to be pretty busy for the next few months." She winked elaborately.

"Thanks for the warning."

"What time are we going to meet Shorty?"

"Manny? Around noon. He's putting together a lavish lunch out at his place."

"Lobster and champagne, I'll bet. Jews aren't supposed to eat shellfish, but he doesn't pay any attention to that kosher stuff. And afterwards a little schtupping, I suppose. Well, you gotta take the rough with the smooth in this life."

"You're a philosopher."

"That's one word for it. I'm going to go out and see if I can find my bathing suit. Do you think anyone'll mind if I'm only wearing a towel?" She laughed again and left me to finish my coffee, musing about the fact that a woman with a sense of humor was one of life's great treasures, especially if she had a body like Catherine Moore's—and an equally voluptuous willingness to share it. True, she was a little coarse, but that didn't bother me any. Moonshine whiskey was a little coarse, too, and I didn't mind that either.

CHAPTER EIGHT

A few hours later, I drove Catherine to Malibu. Manny's Rolls, immaculate and shining, was parked in front of his house. There was no chauffeur to be seen, so I assumed Manny had driven there himself. I smiled as I pictured him peering just over the steering wheel.

As soon as the Packard's tires crunched on the gravel driveway, Manny came out the front door. He was dressed for yachting, I guess. Blue blazer, white ducks, and a yachting cap covering his dome. When he saw Catherine, his face lit up in a hopeful and nervous grin. It would have almost been funny had it not been so sincerely pathetic. He waved to her weakly, and she turned to me and raised her eyebrows as if to say "well, here goes nothin'," and then she whispered "don't lose my number," and jumped from the car and said to Manny, "Hiya, Sparky," apparently her favorite all-purpose term for men. And when he saw her smiling at him, all his well-founded doubts disappeared, and he beamed with profound relief and opened his arms to her.

She accepted the invitation and more or less swallowed him up in an earth-motherly embrace. While they clung together, his head buried up to his ears between her breasts, his yachting cap knocked askew, he waved his hand dismissively toward me, and I took the not-so-subtle hint that I was no longer needed in the tender scene. So I drove away. That job was done, apparently. And "'twere well done." The thought didn't carry with it the level of satisfaction like a cold beer and a Lucky after a day in the steel mill, but this work did pay better and you got to wear a tie and drive a Packard.

Since I was in the neighborhood, I decided to drive by Myrtle's bungalow. I'd always known I was going to do that, but you know how you play these little games with yourself. I assumed she'd be at the studio for her acting class, but I thought I'd have a look around and see if there were some telltale clues about what, if anything, was going on between her and that guy with the Duesenberg. Telltale clues like a man's slippers under the bed. There might be other clues, too. These weren't worthy thoughts, I know, but I did think them. I guess I was trying to figure out where I stood with her, and the less secure I felt about it, the more I wanted to get on firmer ground. And if our futures involved a parting of the ways, the sooner I found out, the better.

Her bungalow was hidden down a fairly long driveway that was bordered on each side by tall oleander bushes. I eased the Packard down the drive. To my surprise and disgust the Duesenberg was still there, in what seemed like the same spot as last night. I guess they both must've called in sick.

I was about to put it in reverse and drive away, when something seemed not quite right. Maybe it was one of those instincts, or maybe it was the drawn drapes—Myrtle loved the morning sunlight. She always made a big deal out of opening the drapes wide in the morning. So I pulled up behind the Duesenberg, walked quietly to the front door, and listened. No sound. The door was locked, but I had my key and I carefully unlocked the door and pushed it open, gently. The first thing that hit me was an unusual smell, one that didn't belong there. It was the smell of blood. And maybe some other stuff, too.

Now a little panicked, I pushed through the door and switched on the lights.

Myrtle was lying on the floor in the middle of the room. She was naked and moaning. Next to her lay Rex, the Gatsby wannabe. He was wearing a button-down polo shirt and his pants were down around his ankles, just above a pair of black-and-white saddle shoes. He was apparently the source of the blood smell, for he had a terrible-looking gash across the front of his head, and his head was lying in the middle of a dark stain. Though his complexion still looked a nice balance between olive and suntan, that would soon begin to fade after all the blood he'd lost. Reluctantly, I put my finger on his throat to check for a pulse, but there wasn't any. Lying next to him was the poker from the fireplace. It had blood on it, and some strands of hair. Someone, most likely Myrtle, had whacked him with it and put an end to his promising career. There were parts of his brain exposed that were never intended to see the light of day, though as I thought about it I realized that no part of the brain was intended to see any part of the day.

"Myrtle," I asked quietly, "are you all right? What happened?"

She moaned again and then opened her exquisite blue eyes and tried to focus. There was a small bruise on her left cheek. I noticed that her clothes were scattered around the room. They were torn to shreds. It didn't take too much imagination to figure out what had happened.

"Oh, Riley," she whispered. "Thank God." She sat up slowly and touched the bruise with her fingers. Then she saw Rex lying there in the pool of blood. "Is he dead?" she asked.

"I think so. What happened?"

"Get me my robe, please. It's hanging behind the bathroom door."

I did and draped it over her shoulders as she sat up and stared at the body. She was trembling.

"Can you tell me what happened?"

"He raped me and I killed him," she said in a low monotone. "I'm glad."

Well, after all those years of living near Youngstown, I knew you didn't mess with the Slavs. They were good at manual labor, and they were good at religion, and they were good at violent hatred, not necessarily in that order.

"How did it happen?"

"He came to pick me up for class, the same as always."

"He wasn't here overnight?"

She looked at me, disbelieving and a little hurt. I felt justifiable guilt.

"What? No. Of course not. He brought me home last night, and I asked him in for a drink to be friendly. I thought you would be coming soon. I saw no harm in it. But he took it the wrong way and tried to make a pass, but I sent him away. He was very angry when he left. Then when he came this morning, he had a terrible look in his eye; and when he came into the house he started closing all the drapes, and then he punched me in the face and knocked me almost out and then tore off my clothes and stuffed my panties in my mouth so I couldn't cry for help. And then he raped me."

"How badly are you hurt?"

"I am very sore. Could you get me a wet towel, please?"

"We should get you to a doctor."

"No," she said. "I will be all right. A doctor would ask questions."

"Are you sure?"

"Yes."

I got her a towel and helped her clean herself. Then she told me the rest.

"So when he had done that, he rolled away and lay on his back and smiled and said something like 'that'll teach a cockteaser.' Is that the right word?"

"Most likely."

"That smile was a bad thing. Then he started laughing and I could see he was getting ready to do it again, so I rolled over and grabbed the fire poker and swung as hard as I could and hit him in the head. That was a surprise to him, I could see. Then I hit him again and again, and you see how it is with him now."

"Yes. You were very thorough."

"He had it coming."

"Yes, again. How long ago did all this happen?"

"I don't know exactly. Maybe only a few minutes before you came. Maybe longer. What am I to do now?"

"Well, the police generally like to hear about things like this. We should call them. It's obviously a case of self-defense."

"The police! Oh, no, Riley."

The word clearly terrified her. In the "old country," the police were never interested in protecting the rights of their citizens; they were more often the hired thugs of the ruling party. And when she emigrated to Youngstown, the cops there were hardly models of civic virtue either; everyone knew they were corrupt, and regular people like Myrtle went out of their way to stay out of their clutches.

Then, too, there was her acting career. She was just getting started in a new life, and this sort of publicity would ruin her before she even got established. The studios might, and I emphasize *might*, go all-out to protect one of their big stars, but they'd think nothing of throwing Yvonne Adore to the wolves. There were plenty more where she came from. The studios were getting a lot of heat from the state and federal governments about the racy nature of their product. Censorship was nipping at their heels. The bosses would run from salacious and negative publicity faster than their ancestors ran from the Cossacks.

"Let us wait until dark and then throw him in the ocean," she said. "Let the fish take care of him."

I made a mental note not to get on her bad side.

"That won't work. There's the little matter of the Duesenberg."

"Oh. Yes. That will be a problem."

"Yes, I'm afraid so."

Fortunately, the driveway and the cars were hidden from the main road by the winding driveway and the overgrown oleanders. Anyone wanting to see the house would have to come at least halfway down the drive, the way I had last night. Most likely, then, there wouldn't be any problem with random witnesses to whatever we decided to do—or, rather, try.

"What can we do?" she asked, still trembling.

"Well, the best thing is to call the cops."

"Oh, no, Riley. Please. There must be a better way."

I knew there was another way. I was pretty sure it wasn't better, and I didn't like it. But considering the state she was in, I couldn't very well refuse her.

"Maybe there is."

"Yes. Please."

"All right. Let me think."

"Yes, think for both of us."

Well, this was one of those turning points. I had made a pact with myself to protect her, regardless of what happened. And now something very bad had happened. That didn't change the pact. But it made it harder to live up to.

"For one thing, you must go to your acting class," I said finally. As soon as I said that, I realized that all future decisions would come under the "how" rather than the "whether" category, as in how to get away with this situation rather than whether to call the cops. I remembered my old teacher's Latin class and the big deal she had made out of "Alea jacta est." "The die is cast." That's what Caesar said when he crossed the Rubicon with his army on the way back to Rome to take over. Still, at that moment I didn't feel much like Caesar, but I did recognize we were at a turning point.

"Are you up to going to class, or are you too badly hurt?"

"No, I can do it. If someone asks why I am walking strangely, I'll tell them it's monthly cramps."

"Don't overdo it. Don't give any information you don't have to. Be careful."

"Yes. I will. Don't worry."

And so we had moved on to the next stage. What was it Frost said? We had taken the fork in the yellow wood, and it was decidedly not the road we should have taken. Frost and Caesar had some of the same things in common, it seemed. As for Myrtle and me, any further rationalizing was beside the point.

"All right. Take my car. If anyone asks you where Rex is, just tell them he was supposed to pick you up but he never showed, so you borrowed your boyfriend's car to come to class. You don't know anything else about it."

"Are you my boyfriend?" she asked, quietly, sweetly.

"You bet." I put my arms around her and kissed her very gently.

"I'm glad," she said. "You make me feel safe."

"I'm glad too." I wasn't sure I was, but I was in it now, and half of me was in fact content, if not exactly happy, about it. Who knows where love starts and stops?

"Don't make a big deal of your friendship with Rex," I said, trying to think fast. "The less connection between you and him, the better. Especially romantic connection. It's better if people think you're involved with someone else and that Rex was just an occasional ride to work."

"But that is the truth."

"Well, sometimes the truth is useful."

"I will tell them that he made a pass at me the night before and I sent him away"

"No. Don't do that. The last thing we need is the whiff of a motive. Nothing turns on the cops like a lover's spat after which one of the lovers ends up missing or dead. Better that he was just a professional acquaintance who gave you a lift to acting class now and then. Not every day. Nothing more."

"Yes. I see. You're right."

Then it occurred to me that Rex might have mentioned something to a friend or maybe a roommate, something about wanting to teach a cockteaser a lesson.

"Do you know if Rex lived alone?"

"Yes. He told me last night that he had an apartment in Bel Air. He was proud of that."

"What about friends in the class? Is there anyone he might have . . . confided in, maybe mentioned that he was interested in you?"

"I don't think so. We only started this week. And he was the only man. And the two other girls were just fourteen and fifteen. I don't think anyone will know he came here. He'd have no reason to tell those little girls."

"How about your instructor?"

"No one likes him. He prances around and wears cologne. Rex thinks he's a homosexual."

So, it looked as though no one would know that Rex had had designs on Myrtle.

"Can you cover up that bruise with makeup?"

"Yes, I think so. If not, I will tell them I ran into a door."

"No one ever believes that story. Say you had an automobile accident on the way to class. Bumped your face on the dashboard when some yahoo from Oklahoma ran into you from behind."

"Oklahoma?"

"Yeah. Details add believability." As long as you can remember them afterwards, I thought.

"What will you do if I take your car?"

"I'm working on that."

A little while later, she left for her class, driving away in my Packard. And when she left, I felt extremely alone, because my only company was a dead film actor with his pants down around his ankles. He was not a pretty sight. Things happen to a body after it dies.

Looking down on the recent Rex, I began to wonder whether Myrtle was worth the coming difficulties. As in previous, similar musings, I decided she was. It was not an easy decision. But to understand, you would have to see her eyes and her mouth and to listen to her speaking Croatian in her sleep. And it was more than that.

The Duesenberg was the problem. It was too damned distinctive. Myrtle had said it was Rex's father's car, so it seemed reasonable to assume that people in town would recognize it if they saw the chiseled features of yours truly driving it away. And I couldn't just leave it parked somewhere, because inevitably that would raise questions about what had happened to the driver. They both had to go.

Then I remembered that Rex had mentioned he was from Chicago. Maybe the car had come from there, too. Maybe Daddy was not a local. Maybe no one would know who the car belonged to. Maybe I could just drive it away and leave it somewhere and let the cops wonder what had happened to the driver. Better yet, maybe I could take it up to Mulholland Drive and send it over one of the many cliffs, complete with a dead Gatsby lookalike behind the wheel. If we were lucky, it would blow up.

I went out and checked the rear end of the Duesenberg. Illinois plates! Here was a piece of luck in an otherwise sticky scenario. It was not a Hollywood car after all. Apparently, Junior had driven it out here from Chicago.

I went back into the house and called Della's home number.

"Della!"

"Hello, chief. What's the rumpus?"

"Is Perry around? I need to ask him a question."

"That's what the cops always say. Last time I saw him, he was on the couch looking at smutty magazines and drinking beer. It's Friday."

"Let me talk to him, please."

"Is everything all right with you?" This time she sounded sincere.

"Not exactly."

"Hold on."

A minute later, Perry picked up.

"What's up, chief?" Perry's use of the word was more generic and had nothing to do with the employer/employee relationship.

"I have a hypothetical question for you," I said.

"Good. That's usually the opening line in a deal."

"Okay. Here's the question—what's the going rate for getting rid of a dead body and a car?"

There was a slight pause on the other end of the line.

"What kind of car?" he asked, finally.

Leave it to Perry to home in on the heart of the matter.

"A two-seater Duesenberg, maroon and gray. Illinois plates. I was thinking of maybe running both items up to Mulholland Drive and pushing them off the cliff. Two birds with one stone, but I need a helper to meet me there and drive me back."

"How did the departed meet his maker?"

"Several blows from a fire poker."

"Hmmm. I assume he had it coming."

"Take my word for it."

"Your handiwork?"

"No. A friend."

"Gotcha. Well, the staged accident might work in that case. You'd expect the head to be a little damaged from a tumble down those cliffs. And with luck—or a little planning—the car just might explode."

"That's what I was thinking."

"It might work, but I wouldn't do it that way."

"Why not?"

"First of all, it's risky. Mulholland Drive is a regular lover's lane. All those remote cliff roads are. You can't be sure you won't be seen either arriving or leaving the scene. Or, worse, pushing the car over the side.

"Second, when a car goes over a cliff, there are usually skid marks on the highway and ruts in the edge of the cliff. But in this case there's no way to duplicate the signs that the driver was going too fast and lost control. Cops get suspicious when the usual signs aren't there. This sort of thing has been tried before, you know. It ain't easy to stage it right, especially when some horny kids might come around the corner just when you're shoving the car over."

"I see your point."

"There's something else. Something practical."

"Which is?"

"I don't think you have to waste the value of an expensive car just to dispose of a body. I'd think of this hypothetical as two unrelated problems—how to get rid of the body and how to get rid of the car. The body is no problem to someone who has a boat and knows the tides around here.

"But the car is an expensive item. There are all sorts of rich Mexican crooks outside Tijuana who'd jump at the chance to get ahold of one of those beauties at a discount, no questions asked. All it would take is for the same enterprising boat owner to feed the departed to the fishes and then drive the valuable car across the border and turn it over to people he knew who'd be happy to act as agents. Everyone benefits, and you're out no cash. Capisce? The car pays for the whole deal, and then some. I figure a car like that's gotta be worth close to fifteen grand. The going rate for getting rid of a body's no more than a grand, tops. So even if the car gets sold at a big discount, there's plenty to go around."

"That could work."

"It always has."

I let that one go.

"This way is much neater than a staged accident," said Perry. "Our cops couldn't do anything against the boys across the border, even if by some chance they heard about the car being down there. But if they did hear about the car, they'd naturally assume the departed got departed when his car was stolen by banditos. That would give our cops enough to close any missing-person case. Open cases give 'em heartburn, and they'd jump at any excuse to wrap this one up. This is all hypothetical, you understand."

"Hypothetically, do you know anyone with a boat and contacts across the border?"

"I'll be there in an hour or so. Where is there, by the way?"

I figured I had about five hours between now and darkness. That was five hours of sweating and wondering whether what I was about to do made sense. I didn't care about the financial aspect of Perry's plan. Perry and his intermediaries could keep all the money from selling the car. I didn't want any part of that.

I was concerned about Myrtle. Her ingrained fear of the police wasn't really a good excuse for not reporting the killing. There was plenty of physical evidence to prove self-defense. She had been torn up pretty badly and would take time to heal, and during that time a doctor's exam could prove rape and therefore self-defense.

But there was the thought of her career and her hopes that had just been kindled by this big break. Did it make sense to destroy those hopes? Who would benefit? The rapist was dead. Dragging Myrtle through the court system and most likely ruining her career wouldn't bring Rex back. And while it was no doubt too easy to say that Rex had gotten what was coming to him, there was an element of truth in that, wasn't there? I would have done the same thing in her place, but then no one had contacted me to write a book on morality. And there was the bare fact that all of this was academic; it had gotten academic when she left the scene of the crime and went off to acting class as though nothing had happened.

I did wonder, though, about Rex's family. Did he have a sister or sweetheart somewhere, someone who would forever wonder how and why he had disappeared? And what about his parents? They would never know what had happened to their handsome and promising son. Was it better to let them wonder, or for them to learn the brutal truth? And just how much of the truth was enough? Without question, there were details that wouldn't do them any good to know. There was a writer once who said mankind cannot stand too much reality. Was it T. S. Eliot? Whoever said it had it right.

I thought about finding out who Rex really was and thinking of some way to let his family know that he'd been killed, in some sort of accident or incident related to the disappearance of the car. Maybe we'd tell them that Rex had decided to take a weekend drive into Mexico and that was the last we ever heard from him. No one knew anything more than that; it was all a big mystery. I figured we owed them that much.

Then it occurred to me that if I was in the family's shoes, I'd want to know more than that: I'd want the details. They obviously had money or they couldn't have given junior such an expensive car. In all probability they'd hire private investigators to try to fill in the blanks. They'd do that anyway, after some time had elapsed and they hadn't heard from him. But did it make any sense to give them a lead by making up some story about a Mexican lost weekend that apparently had led to car theft and murder? Any detective worth his salt would then start in Mexico and try to retrace the steps. It wouldn't be hard to find a Duesenberg two-seater in Tijuana.

There seemed to be no percentage in giving the family a starting point that could possibly lead them to Myrtle's front door. They might find out that Rex and Myrtle were in the same acting class, and that he occasionally gave her a ride to and from. No, the best plan would be to say nothing, and if and when the family's investigators questioned Myrtle, to say that Rex had skipped Friday's acting class and no one knew why. Thursday's class was the last anyone had seen of him. The greater the mystery, the safer it would be for Myrtle. And for her accessories after the fact.

I have to say I didn't like it, though. We'd turned down our chance to come clean, and now we'd have to live with the crime of silence.

About an hour and a half later, I heard the sound of an engine and of tires crunching on the driveway. I looked out the front window. It was a large flatbed truck covered completely by a canvas awning on which was painted the words SICILY'S FINEST OLIVE OIL. A rough-looking character got down from the driver's seat, and Perry came around from the other side. It was a relief to see Perry, I can tell you.

"Hey, chief. Meet Vinnie." It would be a Vinnie, of course.

"How ya doin'," said Vinnie, in the approved fashion.

They came into the house, and both glanced at Rex but showed nothing more than casual interest. He might have been a piece of furniture.

"What's up with the truck?" I asked, although I had a pretty good idea.

"I got to thinking about our problem," said Perry, "and I decided that it wasn't all that bright to take the chance of being seen driving that heap to Mexico. So I called my friend Vinnie who I knew had a truck and what's more was a regular visitor to Tijuana to pick up various items that the pissants on this side of the border think are immoral and a hazard to the health of the nation. What's more, now and then he takes a fancy automobile down for sale to his friends."

"It's called free trade," said Vinnie with a grin and an emphasis on "free," which I supposed was a reference to the cost of acquiring the cars he transported.

"Vinnie knows some places to cross where the eyes are not so watchful."

"Or where there ain't any eyes at all," said Vinnie.

"I get it," I said. "I assume you have a winch in the back of the truck."

"Naturally."

"Good. Let's get the thing loaded up and out of here," I said.

"In a minute," said Vinnie. "First we gotta be clear about how to split the money from the sale. I made a few phone calls and got a guy lined up, but I wanna know my share before I do anything."

"That's between you and Perry. I don't want any of it."

Vinnie made a gesture of approval that was mixed with a slight element of contempt for someone who would pass on such easy money.

"You sure about that, chief?" said Perry.

"I'm sure. You're doing me a hell of a favor and so you should get well paid. How you split it up is up to you."

"Deal," said Vinnie. "What about the stiff?"

"We'll worry about him," said Perry. "You just handle the car sale and forget everything else—except how much you owe me."

"Fair enough. Let's load the merchandise."

It didn't take long. Vinnie had obviously done this sort of thing before. He and Perry lowered a ramp from the back of the truck, hitched a steel cable to the front of the Duesenberg's undercarriage, and then turned on an electric winch that slowly and surely pulled the car up and into the truck, where Vinnie and Perry tied down the car on all four corners, lowered the canvas covering in the back, and finished the transaction by checking the vehicle identification number and the name of the owner listed on the registration and filling out a bill of sale.

"I don't suppose you'd like to take the . . . departed," I said to Vinnie.

"No, thanks."

In a matter of a few moments more, Vinnie was off down the road to Mexico.

"What happens if he gets stopped?"

"No problem. That's one reason why he didn't take the body. That's also why he made out the phony bill of sale. It's details like that that separate the professional from the amateur. Only amateurs get caught."

That made me wonder whether I was an amateur or a professional.

"Well, that was efficient," I said. "I wouldn't mind all that much if I never saw him again."

"Don't worry. You won't, unless you start hanging out at the Sons of Sicily Social Club. Vinnie's nickname is 'the fog.' One minute he's there, next minute he's gone, leaving no trace."

"Well, that seems to solve problem number one. Now, what are we going to do with the body?"

"We just have to wait a little bit till the boat gets here."

That was a little alarming. A boat meant yet another accomplice and therefore another possible leak in any investigation.

"Who's bringing the boat? I hope he's trustworthy."

Perry laughed. "It ain't a he, it's a she. And you see her three days a week, so you must know by now that she's trustworthy."

❧

By the time Myrtle got back that evening, all traces of the recent Rex had disappeared. Della had run Perry's motorized fishing skiff up on the beach just after dark, and we'd loaded Rex and the sea-grass rug into the boat.

"How'd this happen, chief?" asked Della as we man-handled the cargo into the skiff.

"The guy raped Myrtle, so she bashed him with a poker while he was basking in the afterglow."

"Serves him right," she said, lighting a Pall Mall with a Zippo. "Well, he learned his lesson."

We didn't waste any time with moralizing or with loading the cargo, and the last I saw of them, Perry and Della were headed out to sea, toward the horizon. Della had been thoughtful enough to bring two concrete blocks and a chain that would assure Rex a permanent spot on the ocean floor. It made you think. It was one hell of an end. But then, what wasn't?

And that, it seemed, was that. It occurred to me, of course, that Perry and Della now had something on me and Myrtle, but that didn't bother me much. After all, they were the ones taking a body out for burial at sea; we all had something on each other. Besides, I didn't think Perry and Della were the kind to betray a friend. They might be involved in a few nefarious things, but I trusted them.

When Myrtle came home that evening, she looked at the floor where the rug had been.

"Is everything all right?" she asked.

"Yes."

"What happened to . . . ?"

"I don't think you need to know. The less said, the better. But I think everything is taken care of."

"Are you sure?"

"As sure as I can be."

"All right."

"How do you feel?"

"Not too bad. A little sore."

"How was class? Did the instructor make a fuss about Rex not being there?"

"A little. But I did what you said. I told him I hadn't seen him. That I drove my boyfriend's car to class this morning."

"Good. Did he notice the bruise?"

"Yes, but I told him what you said. He seemed to accept it."

"How about a glass of wine?"

"Yes. And then I want to go to sleep and sleep until noon."

"Yes. You've earned it."

"Will you stay with me?"

"Of course."

I didn't know whether she meant for this evening or for the long term. But it didn't matter, anyway. Not right now.

CHAPTER NINE

I spent the weekend at Myrtle's house, cooking her food and delivering it to her in bed. She seemed to be recovering, physically and—especially—psychologically. On Sunday afternoon, I found out why.

"How do you feel—about what happened to Rex?" I asked. We had not talked directly about it.

She shrugged. "It is too bad, of course. But what else could I do?"

"Nothing, I suppose." Of course, we knew she could have refrained from bashing him, and equally of course we should have called the cops, but that pair of horses had left the barn long ago.

"Shall I tell you something?" she asked, maybe with a certain amount of indecision.

"Sure."

She didn't say anything.

"What is it, honey?"

She looked at me, and there were tears in her eyes. "This is not the first time this has happened to me."

"What do you mean?"

"In the old country, one day a gang of Serbs came to our village."

"Uh-oh."

"Yes. We were always fighting with them, you know. They are beasts, like the Russians. Worse than Russians, really."

"What happened?"

"They came to steal and they came to rape and to kill. They started shooting many of the men and dragging the women into the streets. Everyone was screaming. The noise of the screaming and shooting was terrifying. My father told me to run away. I ran into the woods, but one of the Serbs followed me, and . . . well, you can imagine the rest."

"Yes."

"And when he had finished I grabbed a rock and hit him, more than once. I don't remember how many times. But many. And when he was lying there unconscious, I took his knife from his belt and . . . well, I made sure it was the end of him. I hid in the woods until the Serbs had gone and then went back to the village. That was how my parents died. Not from disease. Not the way I told you. But from being shot. My mother, even worse. I didn't want to tell you this before. Maybe I didn't want to think about it. Or remember it."

"I can understand why."

"But now you can understand that I feel very little, almost nothing, about what happened to Rex. It was like being back in my village again, being attacked for no reason.

"It is too bad it happened with Rex," she continued. "But I know I can live with the memory. I have done it before, so I know."

"It's a bad story," I said.

"Yes. I am glad I told you."

"I am too." It explained a lot. Two rapes, two dead rapists, two cases of self-defense. That was more than enough for any woman to have to endure, and yet she had done it. With her history, it was a wonder she was so giving and passionate with me.

"You know, it's amazing to me that you and I can have such. . . ."

"Such fine times in bed?"

"Yes."

"It's not so amazing. Don't you remember that we are half in love? That is what makes the difference." She smiled, teasing.

I put my arms around her and felt something I had not felt before. A bond? A connection? Something stronger than friendship or the desire to look after her. Something more.

"How would it be if we were all the way in love?" I whispered to her, smelling her dark hair.

"Who knows?" she asked. "Maybe we will find out. But we must wait a little while longer. I want you, but we must wait."

I nodded. I wanted her more than anything just then, knowing that it was impossible.

❧

On Monday, Myrtle called the studio to pick her up for class, and I went to my office. Della was there, cigarette dangling, right eye watering. She was banging away at her Underwood.

"Mornin', chief," she said.

"Mornin', loyal employee. How's the novel coming?"

"Not bad. I'm doing a chapter about how the smart-aleck detective got his shorts in a wringer trying to cover up a killing."

"Did he have any accomplices?"

"A couple of shady characters and one glamorous middle-aged woman with henna-colored hair."

"Does she smoke Pall Malls?"

"Practically non-stop."

"I look forward to reading it." I often wondered what Della was really writing. I knew it wasn't a detective novel. Much later, I learned it had something to do with her escort business. I guess there was a fair amount of paperwork involved, though I can't imagine what it might have been. Maybe carefully worded blackmail notes. "Anybody call?"

"As a matter of fact, yes. Ethel Welkin."

"Did she say what she wanted?"

Della looked up and smirked. "Lube, oil, and filter?"

"Very droll. Any other calls?"

"Yeah. A guy named Charles Watson. Name mean anything?"

"Yes. Any message?"

"Just that he wants you to call him back. He sounded as if he thought he was important. You know the type."

"All too well."

I went into my office and dialed the number Della had given me.

A gruff voice answered: "Charles Watson."

"Mr. Watson, this is Bruno Feldspar."

"Ah. Good. I have a little mystery on my hands."

That was understating it by a fair amount, it seemed. But I let it go.

"Yes?"

"I have been going through my late wife's checkbook. I suppose you have read the papers and seen that she was killed by an intruder."

"I saw that report, yes." He did not seem broken up about it, or even a little dented. But it was interesting, if not particularly useful, to know how he was interpreting what happened to his wife and her boyfriend.

"Anyway, in looking through her checkbook, I see here a check for two hundred and fifty dollars written to you. I'd like to know what it was for."

"That's understandable."

"You are a private detective, I believe. I looked you up in the Yellow Pages."

"That's right. And I was working on a case for your wife."

"I'm not sure I like the sound of that."

"I think you'll feel better when you know the details. Suppose we get together."

"Yes. Come to my office this afternoon at two." He gave me the address. It was a fancy one. Then he hung up.

I never did like taking orders, and I felt pretty certain I wouldn't like this guy. As it turned out, I was right.

⚜

Around lunchtime, I met Ethel at the Beverly Hills Hotel. She felt nostalgic about the place, because it was at the Polo Lounge there that we'd first met. At the time, I'd been going by the name of Victor Raskolnikov, a Polish poet. There's no sense going into why; it seemed to be a good idea at the time. Anyway, Ethel quickly figured out that my only link to Poland was growing up in a tiny Ohio farm town by that name. And she had read *Crime and Punishment*, so she sniffed a fraud from day one. But instead of being annoyed at the pathetic deception, she thought it was funny, and that's how we started whatever it was we had. It was nothing more than friendship sprinkled by a little passion—pretty strong physical passion on her part and the mildest sort of passion on mine, hardly worth the name. A moralist might say that I was using her in exchange for favors in Hollywood—access to potential clients and that sort of thing. And I suppose there's some truth in that. But any moralist who could be a fly on the wall during our afternoon gallops would have second thoughts about who was using whom.

So we had a quick roll in the hay—Ethel's efficiency in these matters was one of her strongest attributes—and then an even quicker lunch in the Polo Lounge. Ethel as usual opted for something in which the primary ingredient was garlic, while I went for a mushroom omelet with pommes frites, lightly salted, because they reminded me of a French woman I had met the first time I was in California. Her name was Dany and the memory of her was still bright, even though she had given up trying to make it in the movies and had gone home to France to marry a doctor. Or maybe it was a dentist. That might have turned into something special if she had stayed around a little longer. But she hadn't. Too bad. She was beautiful and had the most charming accent.

"How's Myrtle these days?" Ethel asked between bites of pastrami and a dill pickle that had its own, almost visible, atmosphere.

"Okay. She's enjoying her acting class."

"Good. You know, I think she has the 'it,' as they call it. She reminds me of Garbo. Not so much in her looks—which are frankly better—but in her aura. She gives off a complicated message."

"I agree."

"She's going to be a star, you watch."

"I hope so. She's been through a lot. She deserves the chance."

"She's going to get it, believe me. Manny is almost never wrong when it comes to spotting 'it.' She just needs to keep her nose clean—which means that you and she had better be pretty damned discreet."

"I understand." And, boy, did I.

"They're going to turn her into a virgin, you know."

"I heard. It's remarkable, the things Hollywood can do."

"Tell me about it."

"What happened with that other one I sent you?" I asked. "Rita Lovelace."

"Isadore tested her, and she came across pretty well." Isadore was Ethel's husband, a big-time producer. "He's going to offer her a contract. Nothing elaborate, but worth having. She'll go into the studio stable. She has potential; but, unlike your Myrtle, she doesn't quite have 'it.' Not yet, anyway. It's the difference between a headliner and the girls in the chorus. But you never know, Rita may develop into something. I doubt she'll have to become a virgin, though."

"I'm glad. She's been working on the fringes for a while now and was just about ready to give up."

"Getting tired of banging assistant producers?"

"And their nephews."

"What's her real name, by the way?"

"I think it's Isabelle Fern."

"No wonder she changed it. How'd you run into her?"

"By accident. I've been working on a case involving stolen art, and she happened to have some information. I traded her a phone call to you for the information. Which reminds me, do you know a guy named Charles Watson?"

"The real estate developer?"

"Maybe. I don't know what he does, but I have the impression that he's wealthy."

"Yeah, he is, if it's the same guy. He likes to play cards with Isadore and a few of the other big players in town. Isadore loves it when he shows up for the game because he's such a lousy poker player. Watson, I mean. There's nothing like taking money from the goyim. At least that's what Izzy says."

"Did I ever mention I was a Presbyterian?"

"I don't mind. I don't have Izzy's prejudice. Besides, I'm not taking any money from you."

"Watson's a steady loser?"

"Big-time."

"Do Isadore and his crowd ever go out on the gambling ships, or are the card games all in the comfort of someone's mansion?"

"It varies. Sometimes they go out there in a party. The guy who runs the *Lucky Lady* hangs around Hollywood because of the glamour. It gives him a cheap thrill when the movers and shakers call him by his first name. He goes out of his way for them. It wouldn't surprise me if he didn't spice things up with a little female talent, just for variety."

"Everyone likes variety."

"You should know."

I don't think I ever met anyone so forgiving of human frailty as Ethel. Of course, she expected the same indulgence in return. On the other hand, maybe she just didn't give a damn. Where does one perspective start and the other end? Does it matter?

You know how sometimes you meet people for the first time and yet they seem so familiar that you feel as though you must have run into them before somewhere? That's how it was when I sat down with Charles Watson in his office on Sunset Boulevard, just down the street from the hotel.

Watson was a virile-looking man of about fifty. He did not look the part of a clueless husband of the kind my new friend Bunny described. He had a tough no-nonsense air about him which I gathered was the direct result of having come up the hard way in the construction business. He'd started working life carrying steel reinforcing rods, and he never let anyone forget it, one way or another. And yes, he was the same Charles Watson that Ethel said was in the real estate business these days. He had graduated from manual labor to land speculation, at a time when land speculation paid off in a big way. Things had changed a bit, though, recently. It was called the Depression.

"Have a seat," he said, when I was ushered into his office by an efficient-looking secretary. The fact that the secretary was a man seemed a little odd.

There was nothing notable about the office, aside from a stuffed owl hanging, wings extended, on the wall behind his desk. I didn't care for that. My Chippewa friend, Rocky, who was my partner in that heist from the Purple Gang, always said owls were bad luck or harbingers of doom. I never knew an Indian who liked owls, and I knew quite a few Indians. So I didn't like them either.

"Thanks," I said as I sat down, eyeing the stuffed owl. "I was sorry to hear about your wife, Mr. Watson. I had only met her the day before, but she seemed like a nice lady." This was just pro forma, of course. To me, she had really seemed more like a modern rendering of Medea.

"Yes. A terrible thing. This city is becoming a sewer of crime. It just goes to show you, when things like this can happen in Bel Air. No one is safe."

This was the kind of thing you didn't bother discussing, so I just nodded.

"Let's get right to the point," he said.

"Suits me."

"What was the assignment my wife gave you? What was worth two hundred and fifty dollars?" His tone was aggressive, but there was something in his expression that seemed wary. Observing him, someone might come to the conclusion that he was worried that his wife's private dick might have turned up something Watson would rather not have turned up. No doubt he had a girlfriend somewhere; no doubt he didn't want that known; and no doubt Mrs. Watson could not have cared less except for using the information as a bargaining chip in the divorce settlement. Well, I suppose Watson was no different from everyone else; we all have something to hide, saints and infants excepted.

"How much do you know about art, Mr. Watson?"

That threw him off stride a little.

"How much do I know about art? I know it's expensive—at least the kind my wife liked. That's about it."

"She hired me because she was afraid the Monet she'd bought had been stolen and that a copy had been put in its place. She suspected Wilbur Hanson, and she wanted me to check up on him."

"Hanson? The guy she shot?"

"The same."

"So you're saying she knew him?"

"That's what I'm saying."

"Implying what, exactly?"

"Implying nothing more than the fact that he traveled in the same sort of art circles as your wife. Fundraisers, auctions, exhibitions, that kind of thing."

"I see."

Did he, I wondered? It was hard to tell.

"If she thought there was a theft, why didn't she go to the cops?"

"I think she thought I might be able to get it back quietly. That's just a guess."

"You could apply some muscle?"

Did I detect a note of sarcasm?

"I don't think she thought that. But maybe. Or maybe she just didn't want to see her name in the papers. There are people like that."

"So, what did you find out?"

"I got permission from the cops to look into Wilbur's apartment. I thought he might have kept the real Monet there. He was a talented painter and probably was the source of the copy. And I thought I had found the original, but it turned out to be a copy."

"So the painting that's in the house is the original? I'm confused."

"It could be. Or it might be another copy."

"Why would anyone make two copies?"

"I don't know, but you should have it appraised. I can give you the name of a UCLA professor who could tell you whether it's real or a forgery in about five seconds. Then if it's real, you're in good shape. If not, you can apply for insurance and turn the cops loose on the theft. But if Hanson was the thief, I'd be surprised if you ever recover the painting. He probably sold it as soon as he took it. There's a lively market for stolen art."

"The thing I don't understand, though," he said, "is why this guy Hanson came to the house that day. I'm quite sure Emily shot him in self-defense. But I can't understand why she shot herself afterwards."

"It's a puzzle," I said, knowing that we both knew it really wasn't. "Shock, maybe. Maybe an accident. Guns have a way of going off when you don't expect it. Especially in the hands of someone unfamiliar with them. But I don't suppose we'll ever know."

"Probably not," he said. "Well, I think I'll take your advice and have the thing appraised. Then I'll be able to decide what to do next. Seems like you earned your fee, Feldspar, so I'll take it from here."

That was my cue to leave. We both stood up, and he didn't bother shaking my hand and I didn't waste any time in fond farewells. It was only as I was leaving the office that I realized why he had seemed so familiar. I had seen him before, in a way. He reminded me very strongly of the only middle-aged man in Wilbur Hanson's gallery of male nudes.

I couldn't be sure, though, so I figured it was worth the time to check it out. I drove out to Santa Monica and pulled up outside the fake Spanish apartment building, wondering whether Rita Lovelace would be there.

She was.

She was sitting by the pool, wearing a two-piece bathing suit that rivaled Catherine Moore's for skimpiness. When she saw me, she jumped to her feet and ran to me, displaying her three-dimensional virtues as she came toward me at a gallop. She threw herself into my arms and whispered "Thank you, thank you" in my ear in a way that suggested more than simple gratitude.

"I heard," I said. "The producer's wife is a friend of mine. Congratulations."

"I didn't think it would ever happen," she said breathlessly.

"No more nephews, eh?"

"Nope. Nothing but full-time producers and directors from now on. And no more meat loaf. I can't thank you enough."

"Happy to be of service."

"Speaking of that," she said coyly, "how would you like a gin and tonic?"

"I've had lunch," I said. "And besides, I'm here on business, and I need to pay attention."

She looked at me skeptically. "Really?"

"At least initially. I want to check Wilbur's apartment one more time."

"Can I come?"

"If you want." It occurred to me that she might be able to shed some light on what exactly was going on with those portraits. "It won't take long."

We went to the second floor. The yellow crime-scene tape was still there, but I didn't have any trouble getting the door open, and we ducked under the tape and went in. I turned on the lights.

"Gee, it's spooky being in here, knowing what happened to Wilbur," she whispered. "What are we looking for?"

"Something that used to be here."

In the space where the middle-aged male nude had been, there was nothing but a rectangular patch of darkened wallpaper and a picture hook.

CHAPTER TEN

Rita didn't know any of the guys in the remaining gallery. She did know that Wilbur was a free spirit, as she put it, by which I assumed she meant he didn't care whom he went to bed with.

"How did Wilbur make his living, do you know?"

"Same as a lot of us out here. He scrambled, I guess you could say."

"Hustled, you mean?"

"You could say that, too. I think that woman who shot him was helping him along, if you know what I mean."

"I don't suppose you remember the older guy whose portrait used to be there."

"Not really."

"If I showed you a photo of him, do you think you could recognize him?"

"I doubt it. I saw people coming and going, but I never really paid much attention to them."

"Did Wilbur ever sell any paintings?"

"I don't think so. What's the word when you trade something for something else?"

"Barter."

"I think that's about the extent of it." She said this with just a hint of disdain, the tone of someone with a new and unexpected contract. Money in the bank, or the prospect of it, changes things. But she said it with a flip of her auburn hair, which was designed, I think, to be seductive, and was.

"You said you'd already had lunch. But how about some dessert?"

It made me wonder. What was my responsibility now with Myrtle? An afternoon encounter with Ethel Welkin was one thing—nothing more than friendship. Even Myrtle wouldn't worry about that. But had I entered into new territory with Myrtle? Did I owe her something now? Something like loyalty? It felt that way. On the other hand, here was Rita, available and willing, even enthusiastic—not so much about me personally, but about her entry into a new and promising future—and eager to share her happiness with someone who had helped make it happen. What was another gin and tonic, more or less? In the grand scheme of things, did it matter?

There was some small voice in my head that said it did.

After a couple of drinks back in Rita's apartment, that voice grew harder to hear, but it was still there, whispering, and so I finally told Rita I had to get going. She made a face designed to indicate disappointment, but I could tell that my taking a pass didn't damage her new and robust self-esteem all that much.

"You sure?" she asked.

"Pretty sure. Tempted, but pretty sure."

"You have someone else?"

"Kind of."

"You didn't have her the last time, I suppose."

"Not really. She's a recent arrival."

"You work fast."

"Sometimes."

"Well, I understand," she said, smiling. "If things change, you know where to find me."

Glowing with a newfound sense of righteousness mixed with a dollop of regret, I drove back to the office, wondering about the disappearance of that painting. If it was in fact a portrait of Charles Watson, a whole new line of thought opened up. If it was Watson, then he obviously knew Wilbur and knew him in an intimate way. It must also have been Watson who'd gotten into Wilbur's apartment and stolen the painting. Obviously he didn't want the relationship to become public, for any number of reasons. Why he'd waited until after the cops searched the place was a mystery. But it's possible he woke up in the middle of the night, horrified to remember the picture and understand how it could link him to the murdered Wilbur. One thing seemed pretty clear—if it was his portrait and if he took the painting, and if he had any sense at all, which I assumed he did, he'd have already burned it.

When I got to the office, I called Ed Kowalski. He had specifically told me to report if I found anything that might have to do with the case, and I understood that it was in my long-term best interest to stay in the good graces of the cops.

"Ed, this is Bruno."

"Bruno! For crissakes, why don't you come up with a different name?"

"Can't. I'm building my brand."

"What's on your mind?"

"When you searched Hanson's apartment, did you notice his little picture gallery?"

"How could I miss it? A bunch of pansies with extra large wangs. I didn't spend much time gazing at them, though."

"Well, there's a strong possibility that one of the pictures was of Charles Watson."

There was a pause while Ed digested this.

"Hmmm. That's interesting."

"I met Watson this afternoon and thought he looked familiar, and then I remembered why. So I went back to Hanson's apartment to double-check."

"And?"

"That one painting was gone."

"Even more interesting."

"Does his alibi hold up?" I asked.

"Yep. He was out on the *Lucky Lady* the night of the shootings. Lots of witnesses."

"Still, the fact that he must've known this guy Hanson is quite a coincidence."

"Do you believe in coincidences?"

"Only in Charles Dickens."

"Good for you. Let me think about this bit of news. Meanwhile, lemme know if you run across any more coincidences."

He even sounded appreciative.

Next, I called Manny Stairs's private number. He actually sounded happy to hear from me. It seemed that today would be a good day for me to enter a popularity contest.

"How's life treating you?" he asked.

"Not bad. But I'd like to ask a favor."

"If I can." By which he meant, if he felt like it.

"I'd like to get ahold of Catherine and ask her a couple of questions about her time out on the *Lucky Lady*. She might be able to give me some insight into a case I'm working on."

Manny paused to think it over. "I guess there's no harm in that. She's at my house." He gave me the number.

"How's everything working out between you?" I asked, just to be polite.

"Smooth as silk," he said. "First-rate. Take my word for it."

Of course I didn't have to take his word for it, but there was no sense going into that.

⌖

"Hiya, Sparky. How's tricks?"

"Not bad." It was Catherine, making her entrance into the Polo Lounge, where I was waiting for her. It was the following day. Meeting there was her idea. She seemed to think it was appropriate, now that she was in the movie business, almost.

She was wearing a diaphanous white silk dress, a rope of perfect pearls, and a diamond-crusted Cartier watch— altogether an outfit that conveyed two points she wished to make: she was being well kept by a rich man, and the rich man was getting his money's worth. The men in the room and a few of the women watched her entrance with understanding and appreciation. As usual, she had decided that underwear was superfluous and even might get in the way of her message.

She sat down at my booth and gave me a hundred-watt smile.

"So? To what to I owe the pleasure of this meeting?" she asked in a mock grande dame accent. "Did you fall in love with me like I told you not to?"

"Not yet. This is more in the line of business."

She looked at me skeptically. "Monkey business, I'll bet. But I don't mind. Manny's going out of town today. There's a western being made out in some godforsaken hole in Utah, and the director's gone way over budget. Manny's going out there to knock a few heads together, if he can reach them. So I'll have a break for a few days."

"I imagine you can use it."

"Tell me about it. How do you like my new jewelry?"

"Beautiful. Like the one wearing it."

"Smooth talker. So, what's on your mind?"

"As I said, it's business."

"And to think I went to all this trouble getting dolled up. Well?"

"How long did you work on the *Lucky Lady*?"

"About a week. Seemed longer. Why?"

"Can you keep a secret?"

"No."

"It doesn't matter, I guess. I'm working on a case involving Charles Watson. Does the name mean anything to you?"

"Not offhand."

"His wife shot her boyfriend and then killed herself. It was in the papers."

"If it ain't in *Variety* or the funny papers, I don't read it. Or the rotogravure. That's where the celebrity pictures are."

"Well, the story is this guy Charles Watson is a local real estate developer and a high roller. Runs with the Hollywood crowd. And likes to gamble. Now and then, these guys would go out to the *Lucky Lady* and Tony would set up something special for them—a private room, drinks, other treats."

"Oh, I know what you're talking about. Some of the other girls got involved. So?"

"Charles Watson was out there on the *Lucky Lady* the night his wife shot herself after killing her boyfriend."

"Seems like a waste. I can see killing a rat, assuming he was a rat, but why kill yourself?"

"I see your point, but that's what happened."

"So what do you want from me?"

"I'd like to know anything you can tell me—or find out—about the relationship between Tony and Charles Watson. Or anything about Watson, alone. Anything at all."

"What's in it for me?"

"I promise not to fall in love with you."

"That's it?"

"Well, a fair-minded person would also understand that I have been the Cupid in your new and profitable arrangement."

"You're saying I owe you one?"

"Kind of. And don't forget who rescued you from the pool at the Garden of Allah."

"I thought I paid you back for that sometime around three A.M."

I had to admit she had a point. "All right. So let's just say I'd like you to do me a favor."

"Okay," she said with a grin. "I'm as fair-minded as all hell. And speaking of profitable, these are real." She fingered her pearls. "I checked."

"I'm not surprised."

"That I checked or that they're real?"

"Both."

"Well, I don't mind playing junior detective for you. The fact is, now that Manny's going to be gone for a few days, I was planning to go out and see Tony anyway."

"Wanting to keep your fallback position in place?"

"Something like that. A girl's gotta look out for number one. But how am I supposed to ask Tony about this bird? I assume you don't want him to know it's part of a case you're working on."

"If at all possible, no. But I haven't come up with much of a cover story. I thought maybe we could discuss it."

She thought for a moment or two.

"I got it. I don't talk to Tony about it at all. I talk to one of the dealers. There's a guy named Al Cohen who's Tony's top dealer. He'd be the one to handle those high-roller private games. He knows more Hollywood dirt than Louella Parsons. And he likes me."

"Who could blame him?"

She batted her eyes with no trace of demureness, if there is such a word.

"Smooth talker," she purred. "So. Whaddayah think of my idea, huh?"

"It sounds good," I said. "At least it's a discreet place to start."

"Well, you know me. I'm discreet as all hell. Now let's eat. I'm starved. All I ever get for breakfast is lox and bagels served on a tray. And fruit. After a while, a girl wants some bacon and eggs."

⁂

I went back to the office. Della was there reading the paper and smoking.

"Hiya, chief."

"Good afternoon, loyal employee. No writing today?"

"I got writer's block. Say, did you see this piece in the paper? BODY WASHES ASHORE IN MALIBU. VICTIM APPARENTLY BRAINED AND DUMPED AT SEA."

"What?!" A bolt of panic shot through me.

She lowered the paper and grinned maniacally. "Just pulling your chain, chief."

"Jesus, Della, I didn't need that."

"How's Myrtle doing?"

"Better than you might expect."

"I'm not surprised. She's got some deep currents, that girl."

"You have no idea how deep," I replied. "Any calls?"

"Some guy named Bunny, if you can believe it."

"I can."

"Sounded like one of those English pansies who are over-running our fair city."

"He's English, but that's the extent of it. Teaches art at UCLA. Did he say what he wanted?"

"No. Just that you should call him back."

Bunny answered after the first ring. "Finch-Hayden," he said.

"Bunny, it's Bruno Feldspar."

"A.K.A. Thomas Parke D'Invilliers?"

"The same. But you can call me Tom. What can I do for you?"

"I came across a bit of information that will be of interest to you. It's not the sort of thing I'd like to discuss over the phone, though. Could you manage to stop by my office? Whenever it's convenient, of course."

"I could come over there now."

"Splendid. I'll be here all afternoon, so just turn up whenever you like."

"I'm on my way."

I drove down Hollywood Boulevard to Santa Monica Boulevard and turned right on Wilshire past the Los Angeles Country Club. I could see a couple of foursomes in plus-fours and sweaters and neckties. Most were hacking futilely at balls in the deep rough or pushing putts five feet past the hole. A lot of them were short and pudgy. The rest were tall and pudgy. I envied them their membership, but not their golf swings. Well, maybe someday, although I knew being a private detective was not the avenue to membership. The committee would regard that as putting a fox in the henhouse. But I didn't intend to be doing this forever. And I fancied myself in plus-fours and a necktie. I wasn't the least bit pudgy.

It was another perfect day for having a convertible. In fact, so much of Los Angeles was beautiful—the palm trees, the sunshine, the clean smell of ocean air, the mountains to the east that looked closer than they were—and yet here I was; my reason for being in that paradise was to investigate multiple crimes and misdemeanors—murder, suicide, theft, forgery, gambling, clandestine sex of all descriptions.

Well, the common denominator in the seamy side of life was always people. The more beautiful California was, the uglier the human inhabitants seemed to be. I'm not talking literally here, you understand. Obviously there were more physically beautiful people in L.A. than in any other place on the globe, although it had its share of gargoyles too, mostly people who worked behind the cameras. But there was something missing here that was always missing wherever numbers of humans congregate. Mark Twain said that God invented man because he was disappointed with the monkey, and I never argue with Mark Twain. Of course, there's the dissenting view—"What a piece of work is man! How noble in reason! How infinite in faculty! In form, in moving, how express and admirable! In action how like an angel! In apprehension how like a god!"

Well, maybe somewhere. But not in L.A. (If you're wondering how I came up with that Shakespeare quote, it's easy to explain—I was helping Myrtle out with one of her homework assignments. *Hamlet*, if you can believe it. Based on our practice sessions, she wasn't ready for the Bard quite yet, but she was coming along.)

Having helped cover up a homicide, I, of course, had no grounds for moralizing, and I understood that I was not much different from everyone else. But I could live with it. And then there was the undeniable fact that all the various foibles and sins committed in this paradise were good business for me.

I parked near the UCLA art museum and walked through the crowds of depressingly beautiful coeds, bright and fresh. They were part of the good scenery of California. They hadn't been corrupted yet. At least they didn't look like it. But then you couldn't always tell by looking. One or two gave me a sly smile that indicated they might be in the starting gate.

I knocked on Bunny's office door and heard his cheerful "come in."

"Hello, Tom," he said. "Or have you changed your name since we last talked?"

"Not yet. I'm thinking of going with Felton Hardy, but I haven't quite decided."

"It would be a sad step down from D'Invilliers. I advise against it. Have some coffee?"

"Sure. But I thought this was always the time of day the Brits had high tea."

"It is. But I'm an iconoclast."

"I'm a Presbyterian, myself."

He smiled, indulgently, like a fond parent regarding an imbecilic child. And I admit, as witticisms go, mine was pretty lame.

Once again his prim secretary materialized with a tray and the inevitable macaroons. That aroused a sleeping black Labrador retriever, who waddled over to the tray and sniffed appreciatively.

"This is King Arthur," said Bunny. "Goes by Tom. Seems to prefer it. Not one to stand on ceremony, our King Arthur. 'Large, divine, and comfortable' about describes him. Do you know the line?"

"Can't say I do."

"It's from *Idylls of the King*. Tennyson."

"Hence 'King Arthur.'"

"Bravo, my good D'Invilliers."

I made a mental note to tell my friend Hobey that I was "going by" D'Invilliers. I figured he would get a kick out of that.

As soon as the secretary left, Bunny put the dish of macaroons on the floor. Tom dispatched them quickly and noisily and then went back to his place below the window and resumed his nap.

"Have you ever thought about the differences in our language?" asked Bunny. "For example, we call these things 'biscuits,' whereas you call them 'cookies.' Who said the

English and Americans were two people separated by a common language?"

"I don't know, but for me a biscuit is something you pour gravy on."

"I rest my case. It was either Shaw or Wilde. They both said something along those lines, I believe. Not surprising. They both were always straining after the bon mot. Shaw's still at it, as a matter of fact. The word is, he wants to come to Hollywood and write for the pictures. Imagine that."

Bunny lit his pipe, and the sweet smell of expensive tobacco drifted through the room. It made me think about taking up the pipe at some point. It looked very elegant. But I wasn't sure I could quite pull it off the way Bunny did. He was wearing a brown tweed jacket with a checked shirt and a blue-and-white ascot. Now, there was nothing unusual about ascots in this town, but Bunny was one of the few who actually didn't look or feel self-conscious wearing one. Passing a mirror or a plate-glass window, it wouldn't occur to him to look at his reflection. It was part of his quite genuine self-assurance. He was the kind all the others were trying to imitate.

"I apologize for dragging you here," he said. "But I thought it best not to tell you anything over the phone. It's a habit I've picked up since I started working with the FBI. Telephone operators have large ears. Besides, I think the story will raise a number of questions."

Was that really the reason? I wondered. It seemed a little overly cautious. Then I remembered Gertie, the telephone operator for my office building. Then Bunny's caution made more sense. Gertie was a friend of mine, but I knew she doubled as an escort for Della's service, a bit of information the building manager and the phone company would frown on. A little implied blackmail and chocolates now and then went a long way toward guaranteeing confidentiality.

"It's no trouble," I said. "What's up?"

"Something interesting to us both. An art dealer I know stopped by to tell me that an important French Impressionist painting will be coming on the market in the next week or so."

"The Watson Monet?"

"Very possibly, although the dealer wasn't specific. It was just a preliminary conversation. He was a little cagey, which sent up a small-ish red flag. The interesting aspect, though, is that the sale will be private. No auction house involved."

"Why would this guy come to you?"

"Well, we've done business before, you see, and he wanted to know if I was interested in getting involved. I told him I just might be."

"In what way?"

"Helping to place it."

"'Place' it?"

"Sell it, to be more precise. I know a great many people who are both wealthy and acquisitive, here and in New York and London. And a few other places where money lives. There is a large appetite internationally for Monet."

"And they say we're in a Depression."

"Soup kitchens and bread lines notwithstanding, people with money are quite happy to look for bargains in the arts. Of course, the dismal economic climate affects the selling price, but the demand is still there if you know where to look."

"And you do."

"Frankly, yes. As a sideline, I've often helped place artwork with private buyers. It's a nice arrangement for everyone, because there are no auction-house commissions to be paid. I also authenticate the work, so that the buyer is assured that he is getting a genuine article. Of course, there are other experts who do similar work. We tend to specialize in certain periods. I'm best known for my work on the French Impressionists." He smiled, ironically. "No doubt you've read my book."

"It's on my nightstand."

"I'm pleased to hear it," he said, indicating that he knew better than to believe me.

"But how does this market work—I mean, with no auction, how do you know what something is worth? How does anyone set the price?"

"I help with that, too. You rely on knowledge of what has sold in the past and set a provisional price. And then there is a bidding war of sorts, albeit private. You don't just contact one potential buyer. But the contacts are confidential, the opposite of a noisy auction room."

"Do you get paid for this?"

"Of course, but my fees are much lower than those of an auction house. No overhead, you see."

It occurred to me that this private-placement business was the perfect way to move stolen art, and I said so.

"It is the only way, my boy," said Bunny. "The only way."

"And I suppose with your contacts, you have an idea of who might be in the market for a piece of art—with no questions asked?"

"You mean stolen art?"

"Yes. Or forgeries."

"One gets around. And hears things too. The private-placement market is actually quite active, and sometimes just as cutthroat as an auction, but entirely sub rosa. And fragmented. Lots of one-on-one confidential contacts. An ideal environment to move stolen artwork. Or forgeries, for that matter."

I stared at him for a moment. He must have detected the shadow of suspicion in my expression.

"Have you. . . ."

"Ever placed a piece of stolen art?"

"Yes." It was an offensive question, but Bunny did not seem in the least offended.

"Not knowingly," he said. "But no one knows the where-abouts of every piece of an important artist's work. Things come on the market that you've never heard of. Didn't know existed. And therefore had no idea who might have owned it or where it came from. Happens more often than one would imagine."

"A hundred years ago, a starving artist traded a café owner a painting for a glass of beer? And then it stayed in the family attic for generations while the artist became more and more famous—after his death in the poorhouse?"

"Something like that, although in the case of the French Impressionists it was more often a glass of absinthe they traded for—which accelerated their passage to the poorhouse, or sometimes the madhouse. But the fact that such pieces bob up regularly has created and supported the private-placement market. And it works the other way round—the fact that there is an active private market opens the door to the sale of forged as well as stolen works. If everything were sold only in public auctions, the art thieves would be essentially out of business."

"Are the private buyers conscious co-conspirators in this business?"

"Not for the forgeries, for obvious reasons. No one is a conscious dupe. But in the case of thefts, the answer is 'quite often,' yes. It is a wicked world, I'm afraid. You have no idea of the passion of a true collector. Many of them would jump any number of legal and moral fences to acquire something they wanted. Many are not in the least burdened by legal scruples. Not when it comes to acquiring great art. And let's face facts, people who amass great fortunes are not always the kind of people you want to take home to mother. One does not usually become a multi-millionaire by taking soup to the poor. In fact, I firmly believe that many of them enjoy the intrigue. They think—in fact, they know—they are getting a valuable asset at a discount from its true open-market value. That is part of the thrill of acquisition. Of course, countries have been acquiring art this way for centuries. The Elgin Marbles, for example. Pure theft. Ask the Greeks."

"This all must take place pretty quickly. I mean when a painting is stolen, wouldn't the cops or the FBI be on the case almost immediately?"

"In theory, yes. But if you were a thief, you'd probably steal a painting in, say, Budapest, ship it quickly to New York or London, and put it into the market, privately. The better the piece, the faster it sells."

"And way ahead of the law."

"Way ahead, yes. And don't forget, the sale is completely private—a conversation between a dealer and his client, usually a regular client. Word of the sale does not get out, regardless of how efficient the international police might be. And you won't be shocked to hear that international cooperation between law-enforcement officials is highly *in*efficient. What's more, if the thieves were clever enough to replace the stolen object with a credible forgery, the owner might not know for a week, a month—or ever, for that matter."

"Would a good forgery, especially one masquerading as a previously unknown work, almost always find its way to a buyer through the private-placement route?"

"Usually. A particularly good forgery might be offered at public auction, but generally there are too many people examining the piece to make it quite comfortable for the forger. Better to take a little less and sell it privately."

"How do you authenticate these sudden mysterious arrivals, then?"

"From the style, most of all. And some technical tests. It's generally easier with a stolen piece, because, after all, it is genuine."

"Although you don't know it's stolen."

"No, because it's presented as one of those 'found in the attic' pieces. Authenticating forgeries is another story. If I have even the slightest doubt, I don't guarantee authenticity, just give an opinion. Say 'it's in the style of so and so.' That's usually good enough, though. At the right price, collectors are willing to take a chance now and then. It may knock down the price a bit, but the forger paid nothing for it to begin with—just a few tubes of paint, a canvas, and a little time—so anything is almost pure profit to him. And most of these people are extremely talented. They can turn out a credible forgery in a matter of days. So anything they get for their work is like the stuff you pour on biscuits."

"I get it. But it would have to be a master forger who could slip one by an expert. Like you."

"Yes, in all modesty. I don't say it couldn't happen, though. Or even that it hasn't happened. Besides, there are other authenticators who may not be as, shall we say, fastidious. Or as expert."

"An expert who might be in on the deal, possibly?"

"I wouldn't say that. But *you* might."

"Getting back to the dealer who contacted you—let's assume for a minute that the painting he's talking about is the Watson Monet. Can you find out from him who's behind the sale? Who's offering it?"

"There's the rub. As I've said, these private placements are usually done in complete secrecy. The owner is not always identified. A dealer who does not honor that privacy would be out of business very soon if word ever got out, which it would. That is why forgeries and stolen pieces can be moved—secrecy. Besides, there are often several middlemen in the transaction, so that a dealer sometimes has no idea of who the original owner might be."

"A daisy chain."

"If you like. I can ask my dealer friend, of course, but I would not be at all surprised if he doesn't know or isn't allowed to say."

I mulled these elements over, wishing I had some talent as a painter. It was only a fleeting thought.

"Has Charles Watson contacted you?" I asked.

"The owner of the Monet?"

"Yes."

"No, I haven't heard from him. Why?"

"I gave him your name as the best person to examine the painting in his house—to see if it's genuine or another copy like the one I showed you. Strange that he hasn't done it."

Bunny studied me for a moment, took a few puffs on his pipe, and then gazed out the window for a few more moments. He let the smoke out gradually, savoring it, and he did not blow smoke rings. It wasn't his style.

"You think there may be something overly ripe in Denmark?" he asked finally.

"It's possible."

"Ah. Very interesting. Let us therefore consider those possibilities. Suppose this new painting that's coming on the market is in fact the Watson Monet. And suppose, further, that it is genuine and currently hanging above the Watson mantel, protected no doubt by an elaborate alarm system. The Watsons would be foolish not to have very good security. But the point is, in that scenario, there is nothing at all nefarious, right?"

"Correct."

"Right. And Watson is selling it because he's not an art lover and simply wants to turn an asset into cash and get rid of a bad memory at the same time. The painting would have unhappy associations, even if he appreciated Monet."

"Which he doesn't."

"I'm not surprised. Anyway, that's scenario one. Everything on the up-and-up. But let's consider scenario two. In that case, let's suppose the painting above the mantel is a fake. Then what?" he asked.

"Then we can assume it's a second fake that was almost certainly painted by Wilbur Hanson so that he could cover his theft and sell the genuine article through these private-placement channels."

"But why bother with a second fake, I wonder?"

"I've wondered that too."

"Perhaps it was a better job," said Bunny. "Perhaps Wilbur thought he might improve on the first. He had talent, no question. The one you showed me couldn't pass muster with anyone who would be interested in buying Monet. But if he did a better job the second time around. . . ."

"But why bother?"

Bunny put a fresh match to his pipe and leaned back in contemplation.

"How about this for a scenario," he said through a cloud of aromatic smoke: "Wilbur somehow exchanged his first copy for a new and improved second copy. How or when he did that remains to be seen. But let's suppose he managed it. As Mrs. Watson's lover, he most likely had access to the house. Probably knew how to turn off the alarm when he entered. Probably had his own key. Agreed?"

"Yes. More than likely."

"When he replaced copy number one with copy number two, he had already stolen the genuine painting, which he had quickly fenced, so that he got out of that transaction completely. That's usually the way. So whoever is offering it now got it from Wilbur. And it may have already passed through several other hands, thereby blurring the trail of evidence."

"But again—why bother making the switch from one to two? Charles Watson wouldn't know the difference."

"Difficult to say. Maybe he thought he could fool Mrs. Watson by telling her he had returned the original, at which point he intended to ask for her forgiveness and take up where he'd left off with her, while secretly enjoying the proceeds of the original's sale. I can't see any other reason for exchanging forgery two for forgery one. That assumes that Emily Watson recognized forgery number one as a fake."

"Which she did. And at that point, she hired me to get back the original."

"Yes, that fits."

"As for the original, what about bills of sale and that sort of thing?"

"Easily forged, my friend. No trouble whatsoever there. But the point is—the person offering the genuine Monet now may be completely innocent of any wrongdoing and may believe he acquired the painting legitimately. Meanwhile, the new and improved second forgery is hanging above Charles Watson's mantel."

"You'd think Watson would want to know, one way or the other—whether the thing he has now is legitimate."

"Yes. You would think that, wouldn't you. Perhaps he took it to another expert."

"Maybe. But he knows nothing about art. Why would he not take the simplest route and bring it to you?"

"Why, indeed? Perhaps he doesn't need to have it evaluated, because he already knows."

"That's occurred to me, too, because I'm pretty sure Charles Watson knew Wilbur Hanson."

"Really! What makes you think so?"

"There was a painting in Hanson's apartment. A nude. One of many. All men, by the way. And one in particular looked an awful lot like Charles Watson."

Bunny raised his eyebrows. "Well, well. Naughty boy."

"There's more. I noticed the nude the first time I searched Wilbur's apartment and then made the connection when I met Watson. But I couldn't be positive, so I went back to Wilbur's apartment to double-check—to make sure it was really Watson. And the painting was gone."

"Hmmm. And what does that suggest to you?"

"Nothing I can be sure about. But—if it really was a painting of Watson in his birthday suit—it suggests the possibility that Watson was in cahoots with Wilbur, somehow. Maybe he was involved in the theft of his own Monet and is now selling it privately and secretly—which would then allow him to put in an insurance claim and essentially double his money."

"I see. It's possible, I suppose. For that to work, the secrecy of the private placement would of course have to be ironclad, for surely the insurance company would investigate the theft and try to recover the painting before paying out. If anyone in the daisy chain, as you call it, talked, the insurance company would unravel the whole scheme, if you'll forgive me for mixing metaphors."

"I see what you mean. Secrecy would be paramount. But if there were one or two buyers who didn't care about anything except acquiring a Monet, didn't care whether it was stolen or not, and in fact even knew it was stolen, they'd have every incentive to keep things completely quiet."

"And, as I said, such an *avis* is not all that *rara*."

"All of which says that the key to this little mystery is the painting now hanging in Watson's house. If it's genuine, then—"

"Which is unlikely, because Emily Watson told you Wilbur stole it."

"Yes, but he returned to the house the night he was shot. Maybe he had second thoughts and replaced the original just before she discovered him and shot him."

"In that case, what did Wilbur do with the forged painting he replaced?"

"Forgery number two? I don't know. Maybe he replaced the original some time before the fatal evening. He did have access, as we've said. But why did he come to the house that night?"

"That is the question. Perhaps he was overcome by passion for Mrs. Watson."

"I met her. I doubt it."

"Don't be so sure. It doesn't do to underestimate the potential charms or passions of a woman on the cusp of hysterical middle age. Remember what the poet said: 'What is our life? A play of passion.'"

"Shakespeare, I suppose."

"Walter Raleigh, actually."

He examined his pipe lovingly. It was a highly polished, well-used, straight-stemmed briar.

"We can thank Raleigh for the blessings and curses of this aromatic weed. I think of him every time I light up. In those days, though, they thought it was good for you physically, not just psychologically. And they used clay pipes. They missed out entirely on the added pleasures of briar." He smiled a little diabolically.

Well, the next steps were obvious. "I think we have to find out whether the thing that's on the wall now is real or a fake," I said.

"That would be useful, I agree."

"I don't suppose you'd be interested in a little breaking-and-entering."

He smiled benignly. "Not in my line, I'm afraid."

"I didn't think so."

I suppose it was in my line, more or less. But I didn't like it. There had to be some way to get into Watson's house and switch forgery number one, the painting I had, for whatever was hanging above the mantel now, with the hope that Watson wouldn't notice the difference. There had to be some way that did not involve burglary, that is.

Maybe the simplest was to do it legally. Odd that I didn't think of that first, I suppose.

I went back to the office and called Kowalski. I ran through the various theories and explained that we had to get ahold of that painting above the mantel—and switch it for forgery number one. Could a search warrant work?

"It could work, but I don't think the court would issue one—not on the basis of your theories. We'd need a lot more than just your suspicions. A man's home is still his castle, you know."

"Even the scene of a murder/suicide?"

"As far as we're concerned, that's all there was. Plain and simple. The court would see it that way, too. We'd need evidence connecting the artwork to the shootings. At this point, all we got is your quarter-baked idea. Besides, what you're asking me to do is commit theft under the guise of a search warrant. I may bash the occasional bad guy to get a confession, but I try like hell to play it straight. We got a new guy in Internal Affairs who's got a hard-on for the working cop."

Swell. That was the real point, I realized. Kowalski probably could have talked the court into issuing a search warrant, but he didn't want to get involved in a switcheroo that could cost him his badge if word got out.

"What would happen if a certain dashing young private dick snuck in there and made the switch?"

"I don't know anybody who answers to that description, but if there was such a dashing young dumbass, he'd go straight to the slammer if he got caught. And let me also advise you that the house has extensive burglar alarms, to say nothing of a twenty-four-hour Jap houseboy who is proficient in various forms of oriental hand-to-hand combat. They say he's well versed in the art of causing pain."

"What, no dogs?"

"Just one. A Rottweiler. A hundred pounds plus. Wears a spiked collar. Name's Ming."

"Ming?"

"Yeah, after Ming the Merciless in *Flash Gordon*. There used to be a toy poodle—Mrs. Watson's dog—but he got run over by a garbage truck, so there's just Ming. But he's more than enough. Still feel like a midnight adventure?"

"Not really."

"Sorry I can't help you on this. The law's a bitch sometimes."

"You mean 'the law's an ass.'"

"Eh?"

"It's from Dickens."

"Him again?"

"Yeah. Well, thanks for the info and advice. I'll think of something."

"Don't tell me about it until afterwards. Just between us girls, it sounds like you may be on to something, so keep me informed."

"All right." He was perfectly willing to let me do the job for him, but that was as far as he'd go.

So much for the legal route.

I sat and thought about it for a while. The idea of breaking into a house guarded by a Rottweiler and a Jap judo expert had no appeal. Plus, there were the burglar alarms, and in that neighborhood the cops would be quick to respond. The swankier the district, the faster they came. Live in the slums and you might as well send for the cops by postcard. But the Bel Air cops knew who paid their salaries.

No, what I needed was a story, not a jimmy and a black mask.

The more I thought about it, the more it seemed that the two keys to this case were the private-placement market on the one hand, and the insurance business on the other. I needed to know more about how the insurance side of things worked.

I called Bunny back and asked him. This time he didn't seem reluctant to talk on the phone.

"Ah, as it happens my cousin Jimmy Fairchild is one of the 'names' at Lloyd's, so I know a bit about how it all works."

"'Names'?"

"Yes. That's what they call the investors who get together and underwrite a certain risk, like a merchant ship or a footballer's legs. When the sum is large, no one wants to take on the entire underwriting, so they get a syndicate together and each 'name' takes a piece of the risk and receives a corresponding piece of the premium. Insurance is all about evaluating and spreading the risk—whether you're talking about oceangoing vessels or paintings of flowers in a pot. If the ship sinks or the painting is stolen, the names all get together again and put in their share of the claim—after a thorough investigation, of course."

"I see. Is that how it works here?"

"Well, in principle, yes. But not in practice. You see, there are certain insurance companies that like to underwrite works of art, but they also like to hedge their bets now and then, so they sell off a portion of the underwriting to what's called a re-insurance company—which as the name suggests is a company that insures the insurer—to some degree or other. Unlike Lloyd's, the two companies are separate, not a collection of individual investors, or names. You see?"

"More or less."

"Why do you ask?"

"I thought it might be a way of getting into the Watson house without breaking a window or getting eaten by a Rottweiler."

He paused, and I could hear him sucking on his pipe.

"I think I see where this is heading. You're going to start a ferret in the form of an insurance agent into the house in Bel Air and see what comes running out."

"Start a ferret?"

"Useful animals, ferrets. They go down into a rabbit hole and chase the unfortunate creatures out into the waiting nets of the hunters. Do you know anyone who can play one?"

"This is Hollywood, Bunny. Ferrets are a dime a dozen."

But of course I had access to a particularly beautiful ferret who happened to owe me a favor. And even if she didn't, I figured she'd sign up, just for love. Or half love.

CHAPTER ELEVEN

The next morning I called my FBI friend, Marion Mott. I wanted to know if he could help me set up a cover story with a re-insurance company. We had gone through this routine before, when I was helping him with a sting against the local mob in Youngstown. We'd set up a plant in the New York office of First National City Bank who would verify my bona fides as a banker in case anyone from the mob tried to check up on me, which of course they did. I needed the same kind of arrangement for Myrtle, and I explained what we were going to try to do.

"Seems pretty straightforward," he said. "Can she pull it off, do you think?"

"She's an actress."

"Oh, well, that's perfect. What's her cover name?"

"Elizabeth Bennett."

"Sounds familiar."

"It's from *Pride and Prejudice*."

"Radio drama, isn't it? That could be risky."

"No, it's an eighteenth-century novel."

"Oh. That's all right, then. Nobody reads that stuff."

Marion didn't know anyone offhand who could fill the bill, but he promised to look into it and get back to me. I was sure he'd come up with something.

"You run into many Reds out there in Lotus Land?" he asked, as we were about to hang up.

"Not that I know of."

"Well, if you do, let me know. Tit for tat. Word is, the place is rotten with them, especially the unions and the writers. I can pass anything you dig up along to our local office. Feather in my cap."

Well, I figured the local Feds had a pretty good handle on the area subversives and fellow travelers, so I wasn't going to worry about that. And all the writers I knew from the Garden of Allah were usually too soaked in gin to worry much about the proletariat, even though they would all most likely give lip service to the cause, if only as a kind of middle finger to the producers. But to make Marion happy, I said I'd keep my eyes open.

You might wonder how someone with Myrtle's charming but quite noticeable accent could pass as an Anglo-American insurance investigator named Elizabeth

Bennett, but our backstory included her marriage to a doctor back east and, to awaken Watson's potential appetite, her divorce. That was assuming that Watson had that kind of appetite. Of course there was the distant problem that if and when Myrtle appeared on the silver screen, Watson might notice and realize he'd been set up. But that seemed a slim chance and a long time away. By the time Myrtle had her name, Yvonne Adore, up in lights, this case would be long over.

Later that afternoon as I sat at my desk tossing cards into my hat, Marion called back.

"You're a fast worker," I said.

"Your tax dollars at work. I got an answer for you. Yankee Re-Insurance. It's a mid-sized outfit in Boston. Our contact there is the vice president for security. We do each other favors now and then. Not me personally, but the Bureau."

"What's his name?"

"George Eliot."

"Really?"

"Yep. Anyway, we've worked with him before, and he agreed to be the beard for Elizabeth Bennett, who it seems is one of their top fraud investigators. I gave him a description of her, based on what you've told me. So if anyone wants to check, she's covered."

"Great! What's their address? I'll have some business cards made for her."

He told me, and I thanked him once again.

"Happy to be of service. Just keep your eyes open out there. Reds under the beds and all that."

"You got it. How's the local sting going?" I was referring to "our" case against Youngstown's finest Mafiosi.

"Still building."

That was fine by me, although it did seem that Marion was taking his own sweet time about it.

❧

The phone rang just as I was about to leave the office.

"Hiya, Sparky."

"Ah! 'Her voice was ever soft, gentle and low, an excellent thing in a woman.'"

"Smooth talker," she purred. "One of yours?"

"Sure, what did you think?"

"Cute. Well, I got something for you."

"Will it cost me dinner?"

"It's not that kind of something. Besides these days it takes more than dinner. I found out some stuff. Are you going to be at the Garden tonight? I am."

"I wasn't planning on it."

"Got a date, huh? Well, you can tell her this is all business. It'll stay warm."

"'It'?"

"You know. I'll be there at eight. It'll be worth your while."

"'It'?"

"You know," she laughed.

"Deal. See you then."

I called Myrtle's answering service and left a message that I wouldn't be able to come to Malibu that night. It was business, I said, and more or less believed it.

I got to the Garden about halfway through the cocktail hour. The writers, most of them, were gathered around the pool, and the dumpy brunette was trying to teach the rest of them the basics of the Mexican hat dance. The combination of gin and general physical collapse was not a good foundation for this kind of thing, and most of their steps looked less like dancing and more like someone half-heartedly crushing a cigarette or a caterpillar. But they didn't seem to mind. The dumpy brunette had brought along three fifths of a mariachi band to supply the music. I learned later that she'd found the Mexicans in a diner on Sepulveda, and I wondered whether it was the same one Rita Lovelace had worked in before being discovered. The Mexicans had stopped there after doing an afternoon wedding and were happy to pick up a few extra dollars playing for a pathetic bunch of drunken gringos.

Not everybody was dancing, though. Sitting over to the side, by himself, was my friend Hobey. He was holding the inevitable glass in his hand and staring at it, as usual, looking for answers that he knew weren't there. He looked profoundly discouraged and more than a little seedy. He was wearing an unlikely-looking tweed jacket—unlikely for Hollywood, that is—and a button-down white shirt with an orange-and-black knit tie that didn't extend past the third button of his shirt. He looked more like a prep-school classics teacher than a writer of screenplays. I decided I shouldn't interrupt his gloomy reveries, but he looked up and saw me and smiled wanly and beckoned me over to his table.

"Not interested in the Mexican hat dance?" I asked.

"I got over dancing in the Twenties. Danced from New York to Paris and on the boat in between, practically nonstop. My wife liked—or I should say likes—to dance. She's studying to be a ballerina, if you can believe it. How many thirty-five-year-old beginning ballerinas do you know?"

I knew there was some sort of mystery about her, something like Mr. Rochester's first wife, though not that dramatic, so I didn't follow up that line of conversation.

"Have a drink," he said. There was a bottle of gin and another of tonic, a bucket of ice, and several unused glasses.

"Thanks. Expecting a party?" I asked, indicating the clean glasses.

"Always expect a party. That's my motto. Usually it doesn't happen. Usually you're disappointed. But to expect anything less is to surrender."

"Surrender to what?"

"Things."

"Oh."

"You've got to combat things, even when you know you're going to lose."

"Sounds pessimistic."

"No, romantic."

I knew him well enough by now to understand that when he said "romantic," he wasn't talking about women. Not entirely, anyway.

"I've been sitting here thinking deep thoughts," he said.

He looked it. I merely nodded, knowing I was about to hear these deep thoughts whether I was interested or not.

"I've been thinking about the difference between a romantic and everybody else—and especially your basic garden-variety sentimentalists."

"Yes?" I wondered if I really needed this.

"Yes. Here's the difference. A romantic knows he will always be disappointed, that nothing is permanent or reliable, that the last party might very well *be* the last, even while he looks forward to the next. A sentimentalist thinks things will go on, love will never end, the sun will come up tomorrow, and the weather will always be fair. A romantic is always a tragic hero, a sentimentalist is always a . . . Rotarian. Or should I say Optimist? Ha!"

"You don't expect the sun tomorrow?"

"I think it's likely. But it was Hume who said that that expectation is merely the result of habit or custom. There's no *reason* to think it will. No reasonable foundation for believing it. Not that Hume was a romantic, you understand."

"I never thought he was," I said.

I don't think he heard me; or if he did, he paid no attention.

"But you see, the romantic has an advantage," he said, "because he expects disappointment. Knows it is lurking in the shadows or around the corner. Maybe over there in the oleanders. The sentimentalist never sees it coming and is shattered when it does. I feel sorry for them, now and then."

From where I was sitting, I could see what was actually happening in the oleanders. Oh, those naughty writers.

"But, you know," he continued, "that's what makes 'Ode on a Grecian Urn' so perfect—the permanence of the lovers' passion is such a contrast to the impermanence and disappointment the rest of us have to endure."

"You speak from experience."

"Brother, do I."

I nodded, sagely, and fixed my drink. I wondered why he was feeling low this particular evening. Maybe he'd gotten fired again or had had another screenplay rejected. Or maybe he was still stuck trying to finish the novel he was working on, the one about a man with a difficult wife. Or maybe he was between love affairs. Or he'd gotten a letter from his kid asking for money. Maybe all of that, and a few other things too. One thing was certain, though—he was pretty drunk. And his tedious philosophizing was one more reminder to me of why it's always better to be alone when you want to have more than one or two drinks—assuming you have any regard for the feelings of your fellow man.

We sat there in silence, him brooding, me pretending to brood sympathetically.

But I'll say this for him—he wasn't the kind of person who stayed morose for long, drunk or not. He took a few long drinks, refilled his glass, lighted a Camel with a match from a Trocadero matchbook. Then he looked over at me, brightened up, and asked what I was working on now.

"Anything juicy?" he asked.

My first instinct was to fall back on client confidentiality. But then I remembered I didn't really have a client. I'd been paid off and dismissed by Charles Watson. If I was working for anyone, it was for the cops, and they didn't pay. They regarded that sort of thing as money going in the wrong direction. Not for the first time, I wondered what I expected to get out of this case. Maybe I was just trying to satisfy my own curiosity. Maybe helping the cops was in my long-term, if not immediate, interest. Or maybe it was something else. But whatever the reason, I was still involved, and it occurred to me that my friend Hobey was a writer; his stock in trade was figuring out plots. So maybe he could shed some useful light. Also, I had an hour or so before Catherine was due, and I'd far rather hear his angle on the story than listen to more theorizing about romantics.

"How much time have you got?" I asked.

"Ah. That is the question. Are you speaking existentially or practically?"

"Practically."

"I have until this bottle is empty, at which point I will have to get another one, and at that point I will be available until that bottle is empty, but I make no guarantees of perfect sobriety beyond the second bottle. Why? Is it a long story?"

"Kind of."

"Good. I like long stories. Tolstoy, for example. He wrote some shorter pieces, but his best work is long. Very long. I think *Anna Karenina* is better than *War and Peace*, although both are long stories. Maybe just a touch longer than they need to be."

"I agree."

"There's talk of making a movie of *Anna Karenina*. Who do you think should play her?"

"Garbo, I suppose. She seems the logical choice."

"Bah. I think they should use Mae West. That would make it a comedy. We all need a good laugh these days, and incongruity is the soul of comedy. Everyone knows that. They'd have to change the ending, of course. No one would believe Mae West would kill herself over a man. Most likely she'd throw Vronsky under the train after slapping him around a little. Then she'd go and find someone else. Dime a dozen. Men, I mean."

"That would mean changing the story, a little."

"Who cares? The great unwashed mass of moviegoers out there don't know any better. They don't know *Anna Karenina* from *Little Orphan Annie*. And the studios certainly don't care about creative integrity. They don't have any trouble changing a writer's endings—or beginnings or middles, for that matter. No problem. Presto, change-o. Believe me, I know. Buy a title and then write a whole new story, and I use the word 'write' in the broadest possible sense. They could turn *Anna Karenina* into a musical with Busby Berkeley choreographing the dance numbers and Irving Berlin providing the songs. Eddie Cantor as Vronsky. Harpo Marx as Karenin, the husband who suffers in silence. What do you think?"

"I could see that," I said.

"Me, too. Speaking of length, do you know what Doctor Johnson said about *Paradise Lost*?"

"No."

"He said 'None wished it longer.' Ha. But we seem to be wandering off course."

"Maybe a little."

"We were talking about the case you are working on. Tell me the long version, omitting no details, pertinent or otherwise."

So I did. It took a while. In the middle, he called a timeout to get a fresh bottle of gin.

"What do you think?" I asked, when I was finished. "Kind of confusing, isn't it?"

"Confusing?" he asked. "Not at all. It's as plain as the nose on Jimmy Durante's face. Watson's your man."

"How do you figure that?" Of course, Watson was a suspect, but I didn't see that there was enough clear evidence of anything for Hobey to be so positive.

"I'll tell you," he said. But instead of launching into his theory, he paused for several seconds, looking at me with a kind of glassy, otherworldly expression, his face suddenly pale, his skin seeming to grow tighter over his face. Then he yawned, closed his eyes, and passed out. I felt his wrist, just to make sure there was still a pulse. There was. And he was taking easy, although shallow, breaths. What's more, he was smiling, so I figured he wasn't having a heart attack. I also figured this wasn't the first time this had happened, so I didn't feel bad about not sending for an ambulance. He'd wake up sooner or later, and the stairs to his upper-floor bungalow apartment were only a few feet away. Besides, I noticed Catherine Moore coming into the pool area from the front of the hotel. She saw me and waved.

"Hiya, Sparky," she yelled. The Mexican hat dancers didn't notice. The noise of the band drowned out her all-purpose greeting.

She was wearing a dress made out of silver sequins, as far as I could judge, and her hair had been recently re-platinum'd to match. Somehow the silver motif accented her flawless complexion. For a woman with a few miles under her keel, she remained astonishingly youthful and vibrant looking. I felt the stirrings of impure thoughts.

She came bouncing over to the table, smiling flirtatiously, innocent of underwear.

"You look lovely," I said, truthfully. A little gaudy, maybe, but lovely nonetheless.

"Thanks. Who's your friend?" she asked as she sat down and poured herself a drink. "Is he alive?"

"In a sense. He's a writer."

"Too bad for him. I hear those guys make decent money, but they get fired all the time. Makes 'em nervous."

"I've heard that too."

"And when it comes to getting a little action, writers are way down on the totem pole. Even producers' nephews have more pull with the girls, you know? Nobody jumps in the sack with a writer except the girls who just got here from Akron, or some place in Ohio. They're still dumb enough to believe everything people tell them. It doesn't take them long to get wise, though. Personally, I'd rather sleep with a private dick than a writer any day." She winked elaborately and patted me on the knee. "I speak from experience, too."

"Thank you."

"You're welcome." She examined the sleeping Hobey with a critical eye. "He's not bad-looking, though, in a faded sort of way."

I had a feeling Hobey would have appreciated that. He was at the stage of life and career when even halfhearted compliments were welcome. What's more, I also had the feeling that he was reveling a little bit in his failures. Or maybe wallowing was a better word. His alter ego, Hobey Baker, was an "athlete dying young" as well as a war hero, and so appealed strongly to this Hobey, who was neither an athlete nor a dead hero, but who was feeling the clammy hand of creative failure, which to him was another kind of death. This wasn't amateur psychology on my part; he'd told me as much one night as we split a bottle of gin.

"How's the screen test coming?" I asked Catherine. "Scheduled yet?"

"No. We decided it wasn't necessary. You know?" She smiled slyly. "I mean why bother? We both knew I'd pass. You think Marion Davies had to take a screen test? Not hardly. I'll say this for Manny, though. He didn't take much convincing to see that light. Not after last time. He knew it was either the green light for Catherine or the highway for Shorty."

"Well, that's a step in the right direction."

"You said it. Tomorrow I'm going to start electrocution lessons. Ha, ha! That was his word. He meant elocution, of course. Manny don't always get his English straight. I think he thinks in

Jewish and then translates it in his head before he talks English. Sometimes it comes out somewhere in the middle, especially when he's talking fast."

"I've noticed."

"And speaking of English, there's this guy from London who says he's a lord somebody. Lord Helpus, most likely. He's going to be my teacher, but if you ask me he's probably a phony. I mean, if he's such a high-and-mighty lord, why is he giving 'electrocution' lessons to anyone, let alone someone like me, just starting out?"

"It does make you wonder," I said. And she was probably right. The town had more than its share of "aristocrats" who began life selling vegetables in Covent Garden and picked up their accents listening to the BBC, before coming to sunny California where no one minded a phony as long as he had a plausible story. "But I'm sure you'll do well with your lessons."

"I think so too. But if it don't work out, I guess I can always be a private dick's girl Friday. I can chew gum, sit on your lap, and crack wise with the best of them. Whaddayah think, huh?"

"Can you type and take shorthand?"

"No. Does it matter?"

"Not a bit. The job'll be there if you need it, but I don't think you will."

"Me neither. If I flop as an actress, I'll probably marry Manny. It'd just be another kind of acting, and I won't need lessons for that."

"Since you mentioned it, what exactly does this private dick's brand-new ace assistant have to report?"

"The things I do for love," she sighed, insincerely. "For example. To get anywhere at all, I had to spend the afternoon in bed with Tony."

"Nice for him."

"I know. But not so great for me. I told myself what I was doing was a little bridge maintenance. You know, keeping that bridge open in case this deal with Manny falls apart, which I don't think it will, but you never know. But that was a pretty big pothole I filled up, let me tell you. Tony must've spent the morning eating oysters."

"I've heard they do work."

"They work for him, that's for sure. But after a couple of hours the oysters wore off and he passed out, which was just a little too convenient, if you ask me, because he didn't have to explain why there wasn't something sparkly in a velvet box for me as a present in exchange for what had just happened. Not that he was expecting me that day or anything, but you'd think a guy like Tony would have a stash of sparklers set aside for just this kind of last-minute thank-you. Maybe dip into that safe where he keeps all the jewelry people leave behind when they can't pay their gambling debts. You'd think he'd unbuckle a bit, and I'm not talking about his pants, which he unbuckles PDQ, like everything else he does when it comes to the bedroom.

"But no dice. No ice. I'm beginning to think he's as cheap as Manny Part One. So I listen to him snore for a minute or two and then get up and get dressed and go into the casino to find this guy Al Cohen, who was off duty just then and standing at the bar drinking straight gin with an olive in it. They call it a martini so people won't think you're a lowlife drinking straight gin, but that's all it is. So I go up to him and say 'Hiya, Sparky. How's tricks?' and he brightens up and smiles real wide because he's always had the hots for me, you know?"

"Who could blame him?"

"I know. Well, anyway, he offers to buy me a drink and I ask for a Manhattan on the rocks, which is not straight bourbon because you mix in sweet vermouth which makes it elegant, along with the cherry. So we get to talking, and sooner or later the subject comes around to the high-rollers table, which is where Al almost always works. So I ask him about the guys who are regulars there. Turns out it's usually the same crew—a couple of producers, a pansy director, and this guy Watson. And Tony, of course, although he don't always sit in, but he's there regular enough, because these other mugs lose money like it's going out of style.

"And, to make a long story short, it turns out that this guy Watson is the biggest mug of them all and is into Tony for over a hundred grand, which doesn't sound like much in Hollywood but turns out to be a big number for this guy who is living ahead of his means. Seems like the real estate business ain't what it used to be."

"What *is*?"

"You should know better than to ask that one, Sparky."

"I take it back. But you're the exception that proves the rule."

"You said it. Anyway, Tony's been stringing him along for a few weeks now, but Tony ain't what you call a patient guy—don't I know it—and lately when he greets this guy Watson he's not so friendly like he used to be when Watson was paying up for his losses with real money, not markers. Even said something one time having to do with knees. Tony, I mean."

"As in the breaking thereof?"

"Sure. What else could he mean? I mean he likes *my* knees, and the less said about that the better. Anyway, Al said the last time Watson came out to the boat and lost big was when Tony mentioned knees, and Al said Watson turned whiter than gefilte fish and said he'd come up with the money in a couple of days, but that was more than a week ago and Al said they hadn't seen Watson since then and he was pretty sure Tony hadn't seen the money either."

"Interesting. I wonder if Watson owes money to the other regular players."

"I don't know, but I wouldn't be surprised." She fired up a Lucky Strike and then smiled at me in a way that reminded me of the old expression "butter wouldn't melt in her mouth." "So, did I do good, or what?"

"You did good. Thanks." I'd leave explaining the difference between adjectives and adverbs to her speech teachers. Besides, I liked the way she talked, her husky voice always tinged with teasing or innuendo. I could live with a few grammatical errors.

"You're welcome. And the way I see it, you owe me dinner."

"You're on. What would you say to a little lobster?"

"I'd say 'Hello, Pee Wee, where's your big brother?' But if you throw in some caviar and champagne, I guess I'll get by. But I wouldn't count on hanky-panky afterwards. I should give it a rest, after this afternoon."

"I understand."

She affected a pout. It was nicely done.

"Don't be *too* understanding, Sparky. It hurts a girl's feelings. Besides, I bounce back quick, so you never know."

Just then Hobey gave a little lurch and opened his bleary eyes. He looked at Catherine and, after focusing, smiled sweetly.

"Hello," he said.

She evaluated him for a second. "You know, for a writer, he's pretty cute." This as an aside to me.

"Am I in heaven?" he asked, blinking.

"Not yet, Sparky, but if you play your cards right, you never know." Apparently, she was starting to bounce back already. Or, more likely, she was just being herself; she couldn't really turn it off. Anyone in pants, not counting girls in slacks, was a conquest needing to be made, if only for the sport of it.

Hobey stared at her like a spotty freshman gazing at the prom queen.

"Hello," he said again.

"Kind of short on vocabulary for a writer," she said.

"He gets better," I said.

By way of proof, he stood up a little shakily and smoothed his hair.

"Allow me to introduce myself," he said. "I'm Hobey Baker. I'm an all-American football player. I play for the Princeton Tigers. We are undefeated."

"Pleased to meet you, Hobey. I'm Catherine Moore, the actress. And for your next game, I think you should wear a helmet."

"For you, I will. Would you like to hear the Princeton fight song?"

"Not particularly."

"As you wish." He stared at her for a few moments, trying to think of what to say next. "Then perhaps a line of poetry, something appropriate to your loveliness."

"That'd work better. As long as it doesn't start 'There was an old hermit named Dave.'"

"As a matter of fact, I know that one, or one like it. But it would hardly be appropriate to your loveliness."

"You got that right," she said.

With a drunk's natural lack of self-consciousness, he put one hand over his heart, extended his other arm, and reached back into his store of memories for an appropriate line.

"'Away! Away! For I will fly to thee, not charioted by Bacchus and his pards, but on the viewless wings of poesy, though the dull brain perplexes and retards; Already with thee! Tender is the night.'"

"That's good, though it doesn't make much sense," she said. "The way he talks, he could teach electrocution," she said to me, grinning. But I could see that she kind of liked him. Well, he could be charming when he tried. As for her earlier remarks about Hollywood girls not going to bed with writers, I knew Catherine better than to put much stock in that. It also occurred to me that a night spent with Catherine might do Hobey a world of good, maybe dispel some of the blue devils he was half courting, half hating.

Having finished his opening number, he gaped at her with an expression that signaled devotion mixed with shyness and lust.

"Is it a vision, or a waking dream?" he asked, taking her hand and kissing it in the approved continental manner. "Fled is the music," he said, gesturing to the mariachi band, who had finished "La Cucaracha" and were taking a break. "Do I wake or sleep?"

I couldn't be sure, but I think she actually blushed. Of course, it could have been the gin.

"Smooth talker," she said, looking at him through lowered lashes that looked almost real in the soft glow of the pool lights.

⚜

So the three of us had dinner together. Although we were having lobster, Catherine refused her bib, no doubt because it interfered with our view of her breasts. Hobey refused one also, which he later regretted when he spotted his shirt and knitted tie with lobster juice and melted butter.

I was eager to hear the finish to Hobey's reasoning for suspecting Charles Watson, but he was too busy admiring Catherine to be much interested in art theft. Obviously, Catherine's information about Watson's poker losses strengthened his possible motive for stealing the Monet and selling it. What better way to raise six figures in a hurry? But Hobey was more interested in Catherine than in mystery plots, and I can't say I blamed him. They were chatting gaily and apparently had more or less forgotten I was there.

"So, tell me, Hobey. What kind of name is Hobey?" asked Catherine. "I never knew anyone called Hobey before."

"Well, formally it's Hobart, but everyone calls me Hobey. My middle name is Amory."

"Fancy!"

"Yes, isn't it? I come from a long line of Bakers."

"That's funny. So do I."

"Charming," he said, sincerely.

"Yeah, but is that your real name?"

"In a very real sense, yes, it is. It is the name of my secret self. My nom de guerre romantique, so to speak. You know what Yeats said."

"Not offhand, but I bet *you* do."

"I will tell you. He said 'there is for every man some one scene, some one adventure, some one picture that is the image of his secret life.' For me, it is Hobey Baker."

"I get it. Your stage name."

"In a way, yes."

"I've been trying to come up with a stage name for me, too," she said. "I mean 'Catherine Moore' is all right for everyday life like going to the supermarket or the Brown Derby, but it doesn't jump off a billboard or a theater marquee, you know? I need something a little snappier, something that'll look good in lights."

"Yes, I see what you mean. Well, we shall have to solve this problem. As an author, I am an expert at creating character names, if I do say so. So you have come to the right shop."

"Good. I could use some ideas. I don't have any—when it comes to names, that is."

He stared at her for a few moments, like the proverbial boy with his nose pressed against the bakery window. She did nothing to discourage him and in fact crossed her legs slowly and meaningfully, making the silky swishing sound that was guaranteed to arouse impure thoughts in Boy Scouts, parsons, and the rest of the male race, with some exceptions, though not many.

Then Hobey suddenly emerged from his sinful meditations.

"I think I have it!"

"Is it catching?" she asked, giggling, for she too had indulged deeply in the Veuve Clicquot.

"No. I'm talking about the name. 'Diana Hunt!' What do you think? I think it's very attractive. Very alluring. And allusive."

"Not when you remember what rhymes with Hunt."

"A baseball allusion?" he asked, playfully.

"Or something."

They went on discussing the merits of various names, with Hobey suggesting and Catherine rejecting, for good and solid reasons, I thought. I stayed out of it while we finished the lobster and three bottles of champagne, and it was obvious to me that I was not going to get anything useful out of Hobey, especially after Catherine asked him whether he ever wrote books and not just movie scripts. I knew by now that the chance to talk about his writing was like the real Hobey Baker spotting a gaping hole in the middle of the Yale line. His eyes lit up, and it would obviously be full speed ahead until the champagne was gone.

So I drained my glass and excused myself.

"You leaving, Sparky?"

"I'm a little tired," I said. I glanced at Hobey, and he gave me a lopsided, grateful smile. It was the smile of a fraternity brother, which made me wonder which fraternity we were in. Well, I saw the tie on the doorknob and knew not to interrupt.

"'Goodnight, sweet prince, and flights of angels sing thee to thy rest,'" he said as I started toward the Garden of Allah.

"That's pretty," said Catherine, smiling sweetly and yet seductively at Hobey. "A little something of your own?"

The next morning, I was sitting around the pool drinking coffee. I was the only one there, because it was still only nine o'clock. I was about halfway through my second cup when Catherine came bounding down the steps from Hobey's second-floor bungalow.

"Hiya, Sparky," she said, gaily.

She looked as fresh as the morning, and I told her so.

"Thanks," she said. "Nothing like putting a smile on another human being's face to make you feel good all over, like you've done something worthwhile. You know?"

"I'll take your word for it."

"You don't have to. Just ask Hobey. Did you ever see someone sleeping and grinning at the same time? Well, I'm off to electrocution. Call me if you get lonely or you need me to do a little more private detecting. I'm available." She laughed and made her exit with a fine silver-sequined sashay, her high heels clicking on the flagstones. It wouldn't be long before she was a star; I was pretty sure of that. One way or the other, she was going to make it.

CHAPTER TWELVE

Later that morning, I went to the office and had Della place a phony long-distance call to Charles Watson. She called him at his office.

"Mr. Watson?" she asked, as I listened on the other line.

"Yes."

"I'm calling from the Yankee Re-Insurance Company in Boston." Della's scratchy smoker's voice made it sound like a scratchy long-distance call all right.

"I got all the coverage I need right now," he said, gruffly. I didn't blame him; no one likes getting those calls.

"Oh, I'm not calling about additional insurance."

"Well, what, then?" he growled.

Della went on, professionally unfazed. "As you may or may not know, we have been approached by your existing insurance company, Prudential, to underwrite a portion of the risk on your Monet painting."

"Really? I had no idea."

"Well, that's not at all surprising. These transactions are always between companies, and the risks generally get sold off on a regular basis without the client's knowledge. Perfectly normal and standard procedure. It's a matter of hedging, so to speak. The painting is insured for one hundred thousand dollars, and we are being asked to reinsure Prudential for exactly half that amount. Prudential will retain the balance. Your coverage is not in the least affected. In the event of a loss, Prudential would pay you the full amount and we would reimburse Prudential for our half. Do you see?"

"So what do you want with me?"

"Well, before we agree to any underwriting of art in a private residence, we need to have one of our inspectors evaluate the security system. Of course, Prudential did an inspection when they wrote the initial policy, but we have to do our own evaluation to satisfy our underwriters. Different companies have different security standards. You can understand that, I'm sure."

"I guess so. You want to have someone come out and look at my burglar alarms?"

"Yes. If it would be convenient."

"What happens if you don't approve my system? Am I still covered?"

"I'm sure everything will check out properly," said Della, smoothly. "Prudential's security standards are extremely high and will satisfy our own, I'm sure. It's more or less a formality. But necessary. Our representative, Miss Bennett, is in Los Angeles this week and would be available to stop by at your convenience. It won't take very long, I assure you. An hour or so. Would tomorrow suit you? Just after lunch, say?"

"I suppose so."

"That's splendid."

"But I assume you wouldn't mind if I call my insurance agent to make sure this is on the . . . that this is standard procedure."

"Oh, of course. I don't blame you in the least. Our records show that Michael Chomsky is your agent at Prudential. I'm sure he'll be happy to verify everything. Shall we say one o'clock tomorrow?"

"Yes, all right, unless you hear from me to the contrary. What's your number there?"

Della gave him George Eliot's private number in Boston, and then bade him a cheery good-bye.

"Nicely done, loyal employee," I said.

"Piece of cake, chief."

The more I thought about it, the less I liked the idea of having Myrtle pose as Elizabeth Bennett. It would be far better in some ways to use Della. She would be able to improvise the role of a security expert, whereas I had my doubts about Myrtle no matter how thoroughly I briefed her. Not that Myrtle was any shrinking violet. To my knowledge, she had already sent two rapists to the infernal regions, and who knew what other skeletons were tucked in the corner of her closet. Plus there was her unquestionable beauty, of a quality to distract any man, even one who now and then liked to romp in the nude for an effeminate painter. Watson after all had been married, so I had to assume he had some level of susceptibility to a beautiful woman, regardless of what other fantasies he enjoyed. So I was torn about which gal would be the better insurance agent.

Maybe the best idea would be to send them both. I asked Della what she thought and she agreed.

"Myrtle can distract him while I make the switch."

"You sure you're. . . ."

"Up to it? No sweat, chief. How tough can it be? Besides, if it seems like there's a problem for some reason, we'll abort the mission and think of something else."

We agreed to meet that evening to go over the plan, but until then I had a few errands to run. First I stopped at a frame shop and had the painting we called forgery number one tacked on to what the frame guy called a stretcher—basically a wooden frame that holds the canvas and fits inside the fancy frame. Fortunately, even when it was tacked to the stretcher, the painting was small enough to slide inside a regulation-size briefcase, so either Myrtle or Della would have no trouble smuggling it into the house.

Then I went to a local print shop and had some business cards made, a set for Della under the name "Elizabeth Bennett," and one for Myrtle as "Magda Kowalski"—a nod to my cop friend and an exotic-enough-sounding name to account for her accent.

That evening, Perry and Della came out to the house in Malibu, where the four of us went over the plans for the next day. When I finished going over what I thought we should do and how we should do it, the two women were on board, but Perry was skeptical.

"If you ask me," said Perry, "you're going about this the Chinese way."

"Meaning?"

"Well, when I was in the Navy, we stopped a few times in China and I got to see how they do things over there. One time they were trying to move a freight barge upstream in the Yangtze, which is their excuse for a river though you wouldn't want to swim in it or eat any fish that came out of it. Anyway, they had to move this barge, so they got about ten thousand barefoot coolies together and attached them to ropes and dragged the thing upstream an inch at a time. Looked like something Cecil B. DeMille would direct. Seemed to me it'd have been a lot easier to push the barge with a tug."

"Maybe they didn't have a tugboat, but they did have ten thousand coolies."

"Maybe. But it still struck me that they made things harder than they needed to be."

"So you're saying we're going about this the hard way."

"Well, maybe not the hard way, but certainly the complicated way."

"Do you have a better idea?"

"Wait till the guy goes out one evening, knock the Nip on the head, poison the dog, snip the burglar-alarm wires, make the switch, and bob's your uncle." Perry had also spent time in England, which is where he picked up some British expressions and where, as a matter of fact, he had also picked up Della.

"Bit messy," I said. "Besides, the whole idea is to make the switch without Watson suspecting anything at all, anything out of the ordinary. Various canine and oriental bodies scattered around are mighty suspicious, to put it mildly."

"That's easy. Steal a few things to make it look like a burglary. Something nice."

"I could use some silverware," said Della. "I mean the kind where the silver doesn't rub off." She looked at Perry in a meaningful way, a look that said she had brought this up with him before—real silverware, I mean.

"It would be wrong to poison the dog," said Myrtle. "I don't like that idea."

"Well," said Perry. "I didn't mean poison, exactly. Just a mickey. A hot dog loaded with sleeping pills. Just something to make him pass out for a while. No harm done. They say there's not even any hangover from those things. It was on the radio."

"You gotta admit," said Della, "Perry's got a point."

"What about the cops? As soon as that burglar alarm wire gets cut, they'll be there in no time."

"Maybe. But that's a problem for real burglars who are thrashing around trying to find the good stuff. That takes a little time. You already know what you're looking to do. In and out, no problem. A minute or two. No more. A cop with a rocket on his back wouldn't get there in time."

"It sounds all right," said Della, after smiling sweetly at Perry and firing up a Pall Mall. "There's just one possible hitch. Won't it seem like too big a coincidence that someone robs the house so soon after someone checked the security system?"

"It's a thought," said Perry.

"I agree," I said. "But we've got a pretty iron-clad story set up with the Yankee Re-Insurance company. Besides, the silverware is the only thing anyone will notice is missing. After we switch the paintings, we have to assume that no one will see the difference."

"You got a point there," said Perry. "Which means it's all the more important to take the silver." He smiled, beatifically, at Della.

"So, I think it's a risk we can afford to take," I said. "And if we find what I think we'll find when we get the painting, Watson will be too busy explaining his own actions to worry about who put his shorts in the wringer and how they did it."

That sounded good, I thought. But I knew the risk was real.

"I have one last question," said Myrtle. "We're all assuming that the painting is a forgery and that Watson knows that, because he has sold the real one. But what if we're wrong? What if the painting is genuine? What do we do with it then?"

"Well, as my friend Manny Stairs once said, we'll jump off that bridge when we come to it."

Deep down, though, I knew she had a real point. If the thing turned out to be real, we'd be quite literally guilty of grand larceny along with burglary, kidnapping of a Jap houseboy, and assault with a loaded wiener. That was a pretty heavy downside. The upside was, we'd have a painting worth a hundred grand. Maybe more. And no one the wiser, except, of course, for our friend Bunny Finch-Hayden. And there was something about Bunny that made me pretty sure he'd be willing to take a cut in exchange for his services. At least, he'd be approachable. And if he felt like playing ball, split five ways, there'd be plenty to go around. It was a very tempting scenario.

But Myrtle brought me back to earth.

"If it's real," she said, "we will have to put it back."

She didn't phrase it as a question.

Della nodded in agreement.

"Just remember, chief," she said. "We're detectives, not art thieves. Silverware is one thing. Art is something else."

Was it?

Perry scowled and looked disappointed.

"Women," he said.

"Cheer up, Perry," said Della. "A little honesty wouldn't hurt you. And, while you're in there, if you have the time, I wouldn't mind a chafing dish."

CHAPTER THIRTEEN

We met at the house in Malibu the following night so that Myrtle and Della could give us a briefing on their visit to Chez Watson.

They weren't able to switch the paintings.

"He hovered around us the entire time we were there," said Della. "And you know who was to blame for that," she said, with a sly glance at Myrtle. Well, that at least showed Watson was susceptible to female beauty, something that had not been a foregone conclusion by any means, given his antics as a male model. "If he'd have gotten any closer, we'd have had to exchange vaccination records."

"I'm sorry, miljenik," said Myrtle.

"No problem, honey. I always figured making the switch was a long shot."

"Question is," said Perry, "did you get the layout? 'Cause it looks like we're gonna have to sneak in there and make the switch."

Della fired up a Pall Mall with her Zippo. Della was a master at the satisfying thumb flick that only a Zippo can provide.

"Yep. As soon as he got a look at Myrtle, he lost the 'This whole thing is a pain in the ass' expression and turned on his 'I think I'm in love' look. He gave us the grand tour of the whole house, and wasn't in any hurry about it either."

"So you located the painting."

"Yep. It's hanging above the mantel in what he called the drawing room, which is in the back of the house. You can get in there by some French doors that lead in from the patio and swimming pool."

"Did he show you how the burglar alarm is set up?"

"Oh, yes. He was very proud of that. Very sophisticated. He was a smug SOB, wasn't he, Myrtle?"

"Yes. That is the word."

"What sets off the alarm? Are there cameras?"

"He didn't mention any cameras, and we didn't see any. He turns the alarm on whenever he leaves the house or when he goes to bed for the night. Once it's on, the alarm sounds if any of the windows or doors are opened for any reason. Or if any of the wires are cut or damaged. The alarm is tied in with the local cops, and when they hear it, they get there faster than the Green Hornet. That's how he put it, anyway."

"Did he say what that meant, exactly?"

"Three minutes. They've run some tests. Apparently this guy pulls some weight in Bel Air."

"Where's the alarm's on/off switch?"

"By the front door, at the other end of the house. But he said there was a secret code you had to enter to activate the thing or turn it on or off."

"Hmm."

"I agree," said Perry. "All that to protect a painting of flowers."

"Don't forget the silver, Perry."

"How could I?"

"How about the Rottweiler?"

"He's big," said Della.

"He seemed pretty sweet, though," said Myrtle. "I have seen many worse-looking dogs."

"I'll tell him you said so while he's chewing on my leg," said Perry. "Looks like there's a loaded wiener in his future."

"Are you sure it won't hurt him?" said Myrtle.

"Pretty sure."

"And last but not least—Hirohito," I said. "Did you learn anything about him?"

"Yes. He's not married and lives alone in the guest house beside the pool. We met him. He was very small. Watson rang for him and introduced us. I guess because he's part of the security system."

"Small, eh?" asked Perry. "Those wiry types can be tricky. On the other hand, if he's small, it'll make it easier to stuff him in a burlap bag for shipment to Borneo."

"Oh, I hope that won't be necessary," said Myrtle. "He seemed so helpless."

"They all do, just before they stick a samurai sword in your back," said Perry.

Perry didn't care for the Japanese.

"It was strange, though," said Myrtle. "Something was odd about the houseboy. He seemed nervous. Ill at ease."

"Any idea why?"

"Not really."

"Makes you wonder," I said. "Maybe he's an illegal. That would make him nervous around strangers who look semi-official."

"Where is he when Watson's out? Is he inside the main house?"

"Yes. Watson goes to the office every day and out most every night, and the houseboy stays in the main house until Watson comes back. Along with the dog. And an automatic pistol. Name's Ming, by the way. The dog, not the Jap."

"How was his English?"

"Can't say. He only barked once or twice."

"Very funny. The houseboy."

"He didn't talk much," said Della. "Just did a lot of bowing."

"I suppose there's a wall around the estate," I said.

"Yes," said Della, "but it's not over ten feet high." She smiled ironically. "And when you're climbing over, be sure to mind the shards of glass that are stuck in the top. Don't drag any parts you're fond of." She looked at Perry. "Wear your jockey shorts, dearie. Don't go like usual."

"Swell," said Perry. "And you want me to worry about finding a chafing dish."

"Well," I said, "I guess it's not impossible. Breaking in there. But it's not going to be easy. We're going to have to come up with something better than loaded wieners."

"There is one good thing, though," said Myrtle. "When we were finished, Watson asked me to go gambling with him. Out on the *Lucky Lady*."

I didn't like the sound of that. "When?"

"Tomorrow night. He asked me where I was staying, but I didn't say. I acted shy, and he seemed to understand about that."

"Don't kid yourself," said Perry. "He didn't want to come on too strong and queer the pitch."

"But I told him I would meet him out there. On the ship. He seemed pleased."

"Pleased?" asked Della with a snort. "He was happier than a two-peckered puppy."

"You can't go," I said. "It is way too dangerous."

"I know. Of course I won't go. But he doesn't know that, does he?" Myrtle said this with a mischievous grin, showing her one slightly crooked eyetooth. God, I hoped the Hollywood rag merchants wouldn't make her straighten that.

"What time did you arrange to meet?"

"Ten o'clock. That will give you time to get into the house, won't it?"

"Easily. And more importantly, time enough to get out."

The way we figured it, Watson would leave his house around eight. We'd be watching from across the street to make sure he left and stayed gone. He'd drive to Santa Monica and catch the water taxi, get to the *Lucky Lady*, and cool his heels waiting for Myrtle. He wouldn't be back until at least midnight. And he'd be in a bad mood. But by then we'd be gone, one way or the other.

I woke up in the middle of the night. The clock said three A.M. I half remembered something my friend Hobey had said about three A.M. being something or other, something that wasn't any good. I knew what he meant.

Myrtle was talking in her sleep, in Croatian, as usual. It sounded like someone emptying a tray of ice cubes. But she looked wonderful saying it, whatever it meant, although her occasional whimpering let me know that her dreams troubled her, sometimes deeply. She still had bad ones more often than was good for her, or for anyone, for that matter—images and memories that she could repress during the day but not at night. It made me feel a little easier about dumping Rex Lockwood out with the marine life. I couldn't blame him for wanting her, but I couldn't blame her for killing him, not after what he did. And I really couldn't blame myself for protecting her. That had been a promise I'd made to myself. I wondered what Rex looked like, now that the fish and crabs had spent some quality time with him. It's the kind of thing you think of at three A.M., which, I suppose, is what Hobey was talking about.

Anyway, as I lay there for a while listening to Myrtle and wondering what she was saying, I started worrying about what the next day might bring. The thought of breaking into Watson's house had all sorts of unpleasant knobs and sharp edges on it. The more I thought about it, the less I liked any part of it.

And then, like the sudden feeling of well-being you get with that first gin and tonic, the understanding came to me— our plan to break into Watson's house was just plain stupid. For one thing, it had next to no chance of succeeding. And even if it did—have a chance, that is—what was I going to get out of it? What the hell did I care about any of it? What difference did it make to me whether the painting was real or not? The principal beneficiary of the knowledge was Watson, a man I didn't give a damn for and didn't particularly like. The hell with him. He could look after his own business; he had told me that in no uncertain terms. If he had removed his own painting, sold it, and replaced it with a copy made by his wife's lover—and maybe *his* lover, too—there was nothing illegal about that. Of course, insurance fraud was something else. If he put in a claim to try to double his money, I could do the Boy Scout routine and alert the insurance company. And I would, too, not because I was a real Boy Scout, but because I didn't like the guy.

So, the whole breaking-and-entering idea made no sense—which seemed so suddenly obvious, I had to wonder why I had even considered it in the first place. There was only one answer, and when I looked in my imaginary mirror, what I saw disturbed me a little. Looking back at me was a guy who all along had been half planning to acquire a valuable piece of art for his own collection—and only a temporary acquisition, at that, just until it could be sold for six figures to someone who just had to have something signed by "Monet."

At that moment, I wasn't all that sure I liked the guy in my imaginary mirror—which is another thing that happens to you at three A.M.

On the other hand, I could tell myself that I was really only "half planning" the caper, while the other half of me was sincerely wondering how to account for those two bodies, not counting Lockwood. Had Emily Watson really shot her lover and then committed suicide? It looked that way, but did it make sense? Emily Watson had been my client, admittedly a brief encounter, but still there was a part of me that would like to get to the bottom of that story—if there was a bottom. I mean, if there was anything more to it than what there seemed to be on the surface. Call it professional curiosity. That's not the kind that killed the cat, is it?

So I was back to the proverbial square one. The key to the mystery was still whether the painting over Watson's mantel was real or not. And making the switch was the only way to find out one way or the other. If I switched the pictures and the one I got was real, I could figure some way of returning it and letting Watson go on his merry way, ignorant and ignorantly. If it was a phony, then I could get Kowalski or maybe the Feds and probably the insurance company involved. I could walk away with a clear conscience.

So by three fifteen I had decided that making the switch was still worth doing. But not for potential profit, probably, and definitely not the way we had planned. That way still looked like amateur burglary, and what was it Perry had said? Only amateurs get caught.

Just then, Myrtle rolled over and opened her flawless eyes.

"Are you awake?" she whispered.

"Yes."

"I have been thinking. I don't want you to break into Watson's house. It seems wrong to me. And too dangerous."

"I've come to the same conclusion, honey. I'm not going to do it." Truthfully, I didn't care all that much whether it was right or wrong; I just didn't think it made any sense. Do those two things go together? Sometimes, maybe.

"I'm glad," she said and smiled and sighed and came close and cuddled in my arms. Even at that hour of the night, she smelled like springtime. And her body felt like nothing I could put into words, even though, as I've said before, I read a lot.

I called Perry first thing in the morning and told him the deal was off and that I had the beginnings of an idea about how to achieve the same results with much less risk.

"Lemme know if I can help," he said.

"Count on it."

"The old girl's not gonna be happy about the silver, you know."

"Life's not all beer and skittles."

"Brother, don't I know it."

Next, I called my FBI friend back in Youngstown. "Marion. It's Riley."

"Riley! Good to hear from you. How's California?"

"Sunny. Same as last time you asked."

"Does it ever rain there?"

"Only when necessary."

"Nice duty. Well, what's up?"

"Just a question. Who in the government watches out for illegal aliens? You know, like Mexicans crossing the border in the desert so that they can come up here and pick tomatoes."

"I forget which agency used to do that, but in the last couple of years we established the Immigration and Naturalization Service. That's their pigeon, as the Brits say. I've been reading English spy novels."

"Good for you," I said sincerely. I liked that stuff too. "I assume they have an office in L.A.—the Immigration and what-do-you-call-it?"

"INS for short. L.A.? Are you kidding? Sure."

"Know anyone there?"

"No. But I can make some calls."

"I'd appreciate it."

Something Perry had said triggered that call. The girls, and I use that term loosely when it came to Della, had said the Japanese houseboy seemed ill at ease and nervous, and Perry had suggested he might be an illegal. Maybe he was, maybe he wasn't. But he was at least a foreign national, which meant that the Feds could have some legitimate interest in questioning him. Checking his visa and that sort of thing. So if I somehow made a connection with the local INS boys, maybe we could pay a visit to the Watson place when Watson was at the office. While the INS guys were sweating Hirohito, I could slide into the drawing room and make the switch.

It was a decent plan, but it had a flaw—I'd need to get friendly fast with the INS, friendly enough to have them do me a slightly irregular favor. True, they might bag an illegal, but that was a long shot. Marion would have done it. Kowalski might have done it. But I was new to the INS. I doubted they'd do it.

No. It was a bad idea, what Perry called The Chinese Way.

But pretty soon a good, or at least better, idea pulled into the station, right on schedule. Perry and I could pose as INS. All we needed was a couple of believable ID cards. That way, Perry could have the pleasure of terrifying the poor houseboy while I made the switch. No complications with the Feds, no time wasted.

I called Perry back.

"You remember when you said ninety percent of the Japanese coming up from Mexico were illegals?"

"Sure. That figure may be low."

"How do they get jobs then?"

"Phony visas, of course."

"That's what I thought. You wouldn't happen to know anyone who puts these phony papers together, would you?"

"What do you think?" He sounded mildly insulted. I suppose it was like asking an English professor if he'd heard of Shakespeare.

"Sorry."

"There's a guy in Pedro named Blinky Malone who specializes in that sort of thing." Like many Angelenos, he pronounced it "Peedro."

"Friend of yours?"

"We've done business. Leave it at that."

"Why do they call him Blinky?" I figured Perry would appreciate being fed a straight line.

"I don't know, but if I were you I wouldn't ask him."

"I'll remember that. Could you arrange to have Blinky whip up a couple of government ID cards?"

"Sure. What would you like? FBI? U.S. Navy? Driver's License? Girl Scout merit badge?"

"Immigration and Naturalization Service."

"How soon do you need them?"

"Soon as possible."

"Like today?"

"Today would be good."

"Might cost a little extra, for the rush job."

"That's okay."

"One for me and one for you?"

"That's right."

"Okay. What names?"

"Anything but ours."

That afternoon, Perry came by with two ID cards, each showing an impressive seal of the United States and the words "Immigration and Naturalization Service" embossed on a green background that featured an eagle with a wide wing-spread. It was, as usual, fast service from Perry and his network of shadowy characters. Whether the cards were copies of actual INS ID's or just the creation of Blinky's fertile imagination didn't really matter. They only had to fool one rather nervous Japanese houseboy. Which should be easy enough. Each card featured a picture of some guy who might have been me and Perry. The pictures were intentionally blurry, and the likenesses were close enough. The name on my card was Herman Clapsaddle. Perry's said Emile Phengfisch.

"I always liked the name Emile," he said.

"Yes, but what about these last names?"

"Well, that's kind of an inside joke. I knew a guy in the Navy name of Herman Clapsaddle. Pennsylvania Dutchman from around Lancaster. He married a girl named Ethel Phengfisch from Blue Ball, and I used to tell him he married the only girl in the world who was happy to change her name to Clapsaddle."

"I see."

"You said not to use our real names."

"Right."

"So, Agent Clapsaddle, what's the plan?"

That night around eight o'clock, we were parked on the street opposite the gate of Charles Watson's house. Perry was dressed in his only suit, a garment that had been stylish at some point but now looked a little small on him. And shiny. His hand-painted tie looked like something Monet might have produced on a bad day, but in a sense it was appropriate, given our mission. Taken all together, Perry looked like just the kind of low-level G-man who'd love to roust a foreigner.

Looking at the wall from where we were parked, I was glad we weren't going to try to scale that thing. It was smooth plaster over brick, and the top was rounded-off concrete, and you could see the glass shards glistening in the light of the streetlamp. There was an iron gate closing off the entrance.

Around eight fifteen, Watson's car came down the driveway and pulled up to the gate, which swung open when Watson activated a switch from his car. He was driving a freshly polished Cadillac convertible, and you could almost see the cloud of cologne trailing behind as he pulled out and sped off down the road. The gate swung shut behind him. I almost felt sorry for the poor sap—going to meet his dream girl, who, like most dream girls, wouldn't be there when he arrived. "Fled is that music . . ." and so on.

We waited another fifteen minutes or so just to make sure Watson didn't come back for some reason. It was unlikely. The way he'd peeled out of his driveway showed he was in a hurry.

When we figured the coast was clear, we got out and walked to the gate. There was a small box mounted on the wall with a telephone inside. I picked it up.

"Yes, please?" said the voice. It was obviously Hirohito. I won't try to imitate his way of speaking. Reading dialectic has always seemed to me to be pretty tedious, except in Mark Twain or Charles Dickens. They can pull it off. I won't try.

"Federal officers. Open the gate."

There was a long pause.

"Mr. Watson no home," he said, finally.

"It's not Watson we want to talk to. It's you. Your name's Satchiko, isn't it?" The girls had pulled that out of him.

"I am Satchiko, yes."

"Well, then, open the gate."

There was another pause.

"You wish to speak to me?" he said, just to be sure, or maybe buying time.

"That's right. We're from the Immigration and Naturalization Service. It's a routine check. Nothing to worry about."

More silence.

"Come back tomorrow. Too late now."

"Listen, pal. Either open this gate and let us in or we call for backup, and you'll have to explain to your boss why his gate got smashed in."

"I do nothing wrong. My papers good."

"Maybe. But we're here to check, and we're going to do it one way or the other. You can cooperate, or you can go downtown in handcuffs. Believe me, you won't like it downtown. You may be a gardener, but downtown you'll learn there are other ways to use a rubber hose. So it's either the easy way or the hard way. We don't care which."

He digested this.

"Not in trouble?"

"Not unless you don't open this gate. I'll give you ten seconds."

He thought it over some more.

"Wait, please."

We heard the buzzer sound on the gate, and it swung slowly open. We walked up the driveway to the house.

"Nice work, chief," said Perry. "I liked the part about the rubber hose."

That didn't surprise me.

The front door was one of those heavy imitation Spanish numbers. As a matter of fact, the whole house was imitation Spanish. Of course, most of the houses were imitation something or other. The bigger the house, the better the imitation, usually, although there were some godawful-looking mansions here and there. You wouldn't be surprised to see something with a gothic tower attached to a half-timbered "Jolly Olde England" cottage. As often as not, these things sprouted up because some producer had given carte blanche to a wife just to get her off his back.

You can say that money can't buy taste; most of the people who say that don't have any—money, that is. But there's no denying that it can buy you a scared-looking Japanese houseboy-cum-gardener like the one peeking cautiously from behind a crack in the front door after we rang the bell. We flashed him our INS ID cards and pushed on in.

The Rottweiler was lying next to a fireplace in the main hall just beyond the entrance. He lifted his head and growled a little, but then went back to sleep. I guess he figured it was all right as long as Satchiko let us in. In the fireplace, gas flames flickered around ceramic logs; the fire was for atmosphere, not heat. There was a stuffed moose head above the mantel. He looked serene and indifferent to his fate. I had a quick mental image of the argument between Watson and his wife when he brought that thing home. It wasn't the kind of thing she'd have liked. I imagine that like most married couples, they had made arrangements. In this case, the arrangement allowed hubby to decorate the main entrance hall like something out of Teddy Roosevelt's game room, while she spent thousands on French paintings and hung them in what they called the drawing room.

Satchiko bowed low in the approved fashion and smiled nervously.

"Not in trouble?" he asked.

"Probably not. We just want to see your visa."

"Have here," he said and dug in his pocket to find a wrinkled bit of paper. Apparently he kept it with him like some sort of talisman.

Perry took one look at it and winked.

"One of Blinky's better efforts," he said to me.

Well, that figured. Of course, we didn't care whether it was legitimate or not.

"Well, Satchiko," I said. "This *looks* real, but we still need to ask you some questions. Agent Phengfisch here will conduct the interview. Where can we have some privacy?"

"Here. In main hall. By fire. Please."

"Is there anyone else in the house?"

"No. Just me."

"Well, we'll see about that."

He bowed again and led us to some overstuffed chairs near the fire.

"Now here's how this is going to work, Satchiko. Agent Phengfisch will ask you some questions. Meanwhile, I have to have a look around the rest of the house to make sure there are no illegal aliens living here."

"No one but me," he said, a little alarmed. "Like I say."

"I'm sure you're telling the truth, but we have to look anyway. It's routine. Sit there with Agent Phengfisch and answer his questions, unless you'd like to go downtown and answer them there."

"No. No, thank you. Here better."

"You got that right," said Perry.

Perry sat down in a chair opposite Satchiko, who perched on the edge of his seat like a bird contemplating flight. He was sweating and looked terrified. Well, given Perry's evil grin and the fact that his papers were phony, some nervousness was understandable. I felt a little sorry for him, but we wouldn't be there very long, with luck, so his ordeal would be short.

"Agent Phengfisch, I'm going to check the rest of the house."

"Yes, sir," said Perry.

I headed down the hall toward the rear of the house. I could hear Perry saying "Now see here, Tojo," but pretty soon I was poking my head into the rooms that led off the main hall. There was a library impressively stocked with leather-bound volumes and one of those curving library ladders that made me green with envy. The whole room did, in fact. I wondered whether either of the Watsons had read any of these books, or whether their decorator had simply bought them by the yard. I had been in one Hollywood mansion where the library was actually a bar, with the booze and all the fixings hidden behind the bookshelves. Of course, that had been during the recent unlamented period known as Prohibition.

Next in the hallway was Watson's office—a standard affair with leather furniture and a French Empire-style desk all filigreed and carved and obviously expensive, but too ornate for my taste. I went in for a moment and looked through the papers on the desk, but there was nothing of any interest to me. I didn't know what I was looking for, but whatever it was, I didn't find it.

Finally I came to the drawing room, the scene of the murder and suicide. Just in case there were cameras, I slipped a silk stocking over my head before I went in. The stocking had Myrtle's scent on it, which made something in my abdomen do a happy turnover. I switched on the lights and looked at the carpet for traces of the killings, but of course there weren't any. Watson had no doubt replaced the bloody rug. Still, it gave me a queer feeling to see the place, knowing that the woman who had been in my office not very long ago had been stretched out on this very floor with a bullet in her brain. Had she really killed herself? For love? If so, what a waste. As for Wilbur, well, I hadn't known him.

As advertised, the Monet was above the mantel. I put on a pair of surgeon's rubber gloves and then carefully checked for wires that might be connected to the picture frame—wires that might be part of the security system. I couldn't see any. Thankfully, I didn't see any cameras, but that was no excuse for dawdling about making the switch.

I stood on a stool and removed the painting from above the mantel. I had the other copy in my briefcase. I fumbled a little getting the picture out of the frame, and when I replaced it with the one I'd brought, I didn't worry too much about getting all the fastenings secure in the back. One or two would hold the thing. Even so, it took a few minutes to get the painting straight and secure. While I was at it, I compared the two pictures, and for the life of me I couldn't see much, if any, difference. Well, that was all to the good. If I couldn't tell them apart, Watson probably wouldn't notice the exchange. It would take someone like Bunny to see what made one better than the other, or at least different. It did occur to me, though, that this picture in my hand might actually be the real thing—something worth a hundred grand. And I was reminded of something Sergeant Kowalski had said—the human race seemed to be getting dumber by the year.

Finally I finished making the switch. I put the new painting in my briefcase, along with the rubber gloves and silk stocking, and then hustled back to the main hall. I was surprised to see Satchiko leaning back in his chair and smiling. Perry was also apparently in a jovial mood. Satchiko shot to his feet and bowed when he saw me, but he didn't lose his much more relaxed expression and manner. He stuck out his hand to show me his visa. At the top Perry had written: "This guy's OK. Emile Phengfisch, INS."

"Paper good now," said Satchiko.

"Yes. Congratulations. Welcome to America."

"Thank you." Another bow.

"Well, that about finishes our business here," I said. "Now, one word of warning, Satchiko—don't mention this to anyone. The INS is a secret organization. You could get in real trouble if you tell anyone about our visit tonight. And I do mean *anyone*. Understand?"

"Yes. No tell no one."

"Including your boss."

"Him especially," he said. There was something strange about the way he said that, but I couldn't put my finger on it.

"Good. Now if you'll open the gate for us, we'll be on our way."

We shook hands and he bowed some more. And we left.

"I assume you got it," Perry said as we were walking back to the car.

"Yep. No problem. Thanks for your help."

"Glad to do it."

"Seems like you and Satchiko got pretty chummy there. I'm surprised."

"Oh, well, he seemed harmless enough. I spent a minute or so pretending to study his visa, and when I signed it, he relaxed."

"What a nice guy you are."

"That's what everybody says. I tell you what, though. There's something fishy going on in that house."

"What do you mean?"

"Well, after I signed his visa and he relaxed, I kind of casually brought up the question of the killings. Sort of asked if it was spooky living there. That kind of thing."

"And?"

"He got funny and nervous again. Said 'Know nothing,' in a way that made me think he really did know something."

"About the shootings?"

"Who knows? But these guys are sneaky little bastards. They're good at hiding and watching. Maybe he saw something."

"But he clammed up when you mentioned it."

"Right. So I changed the subject. Didn't want to scare him off. If he does know something useful, we'll want to be able to find him when the time comes."

"Interesting. Sounds like *you* should be the private dick, and I should be running boats."

"No, thanks. Private dicks don't make squat."

I wondered what Satchiko knew—and why it scared him.

CHAPTER FOURTEEN

First thing in the morning, I called Bunny and told him I had the other Monet.

"Well done, Thomas!" he said. I had to remember that, to Bunny, I was Thomas Parke D'Invilliers, although he knew that wasn't quite my real name. "How did you manage it?"

"Professional secret," I said.

"I understand. Some things are better left unspoken. I have to remind myself of that, now and then. Bring it over any time this morning. I have a conference with a lady who is interested in the arts, but that will be over lunch. Under normal circumstances I would ask you to join us, but our business is rather delicate."

"To un-speak something that was better left unspoken?"

"Something like that."

"I suppose a suspicious husband is involved in some way."

"Well, as it happens the 'maritus cuckoldus' is not always so asleep at the switch as one would like. Well, see you soon."

An hour later, I was in Bunny's office, and he was bent over his desk, examining the painting with a magnifying glass.

"Hmmm. This *is* rather good. *Much* better than the first one."

"But still a fake?"

"Truth to tell, I don't know yet. Can't tell at first glance this time. That in itself says a lot."

He stood up and polished his glass with a handkerchief that he pulled from the pocket of his tweed jacket.

"Our boy had talent," he said.

"Our boy?"

"Either the forger . . . or Claude Monet."

"That good, eh?"

"In a word, yes."

"For the sake of argument, let's assume it's real. What would it be worth?"

"On the auction market, perhaps as much as two hundred thousand. On the private market, roughly half that, because the buyer would naturally assume it was stolen."

"Hmmm."

"Quite."

"What do we do now?"

"I'd like to keep it for a couple of days and run some tests. The first thing to do is analyze the stretchers, to see if the wood really is as old as it should be. That's not a foolproof test, of course, but it's often a useful clue. Same thing with the canvas. Then I want to examine the actual paint. A small chip can reveal a lot about the actual age of the piece."

"Won't that ruin the painting?"

"No. I'll take it from the side where it folds under and is hidden by the frame."

"How about the overall technique? Does it seem like the real thing?"

"I'll give that a more thorough look, of course, but at first glance I have to say that whoever did this painting understood Monet's technique perfectly."

"And who would know that better than Monet himself?"

"Who, indeed?"

As I left Bunny's office, a small voice in the back of my mind wondered whether leaving the painting with him was such a good idea. After all, he was an artist himself. He had said with all due modesty that he had talent, if not genius, and who was I to distinguish between the two? Who was anybody, when you got right down to it? Might he use the opportunity to make a new copy? That way, if the painting were genuine, he could keep it, sell it himself, and give me back the new copy. He knew the private market; he had told me that. How long would it take to slap together a small copy of a pot of blurry flowers? How long would it take the paint to dry? Was there a way of accelerating that process? Using a heat lamp or something? I was out of my depth on those questions. There was no doubt he could fool me, tell me anything he liked. Could Bunny be less than honest? The thought was probably unworthy of me, but I couldn't help thinking it. But after a while I dismissed the idea. After all, he had come recommended by the FBI. Still. . . .

I went to the office. No one was there, but it was lunchtime and I assumed Della had gone out for her usual Braunschweiger and onion on rye—washed down with a martini on the rocks. She had cast-iron digestion; it went perfectly with her personality.

A few moments later, she came into the office, not "trailing clouds of glory," but clouds of Pall Mall with a hint of onion fumes. By the looks of her, she'd had more than one martini. But you'd have to know her well to recognize the signs; she could really hold her gin.

"Hiya, chief."

"Good afternoon, loyal employee. What's the news?"

"Bugger all, except Sergeant Kowalski called and left a message to call him back."

"Did he say what he wanted?"

"He said he wanted you to call him back."

She spoke with the tolerance of a nanny for an idiot child and fired up a fresh Pall Mall.

I called, as instructed.

"Kowalski speaking."

"Ed, it's Bruno Feldspar."

"You sure about that?"

"Would I lie?"

"Of course."

"What's up?"

"I'm curious. How are you coming with the artwork angle?"

"Still checking it out. I have an expert looking at one of the paintings. He's going to test it to see if it's real or a forgery."

"Hmmm. And how, pray tell, did you come by this particular painting?"

"Some things should remain unsaid. You know what the Spanish say—what the eyes do not see, the heart does not feel."

"Un-huh. Leave it to them to come up with some bullshit saying. Cops have a saying, too, you know—what the suspect conceals, a nightstick reveals."

"And it even rhymes. Who said cops have no sense of humor? But let's just say I got ahold of the thing and no one is the wiser. What's more, I fully intend to return it, with no harm done."

"Someone should write a poem."

"Somebody did. 'Ode to Virtue.' Aristotle."

"The shipping guy?"

"Sort of. So . . . what can I do for you?"

"Well, since you're helping me, I thought you'd be interested to know that the recent Mrs. Watson was insured for fifty grand, with her loving husband the beneficiary."

"That *is* interesting."

"Isn't it. In real detective work, we call that a possible motive."

"For what? Suicide?"

"Or for a homicide made to look like suicide. It's been known to happen."

"But I thought life insurance companies didn't pay out on suicides."

"They don't, if the policy was taken out within two years of the sad demise. Otherwise, they're on the hook for it."

"How long ago did Watson take out the policy?" As if I couldn't guess.

"Two years and one month ago."

"Figures."

"Doesn't it? So I'm suddenly interested in art. Keep me informed. Anything you turn up might be useful. I wouldn't mind nailing a high-profile guy like Watson. Feather in my cap. Sounds like there could be a tie-in somewhere."

"There's something else. I just happened to have a chat with Watson's houseboy. I couldn't be sure, but there was something funny about his manner, especially when I mentioned the killings in the house."

"Yeah? That's interesting. You figure he saw something he shouldn't have?"

"It occurred to me. If it starts to look like Watson was something more than an aggrieved husband, you might want to have a talk with the houseboy. Between us, I don't think his visa is genuine, so if you hauled him downtown, he'd most likely be cooperative."

"Figure he might skip?"

"I don't think so. I didn't make a big deal out of the killings, and when I saw him getting nervous, I changed the subject."

"As my old man used to say, 'ya done good.' He wasn't so hot with the grammar, but he could beat the crap out of a suspect with the best of them."

"They don't make 'em like that anymore."

"That's what you think. Anyway, thanks for the tip."

"No charge."

I hung up. I put my feet on the desk and thought about recent developments. I started to calculate the possible haul

Watson could make by getting rid of his wife and simultaneously selling her precious Monet. There was fifty grand from life insurance, another hundred grand from selling the real Monet on the private market. What's more, right now he believed he had the second forgery, which even Bunny thought would pass most tests. Watson might be planning to sell that one too. If he could get a hundred grand for the real thing, he could plan on getting a similar number from some gullible collector for a first-rate forgery. Both buyers would hang the pictures in some safe place in their houses and gleefully pat themselves on the back, thinking how clever they had been. Only one would be right. But neither would ever say a word about how or when they had made their acquisitions. And a couple of generations from now, the heirs of the second buyer would try to sell their copy. At that point—as the French say, "quelle surprise!"

Then there was the fact that Watson was into Tony the Snail for about a hundred grand. Would Watson have the cojones to enlist Tony or his goombahs into staging a murder/suicide? And I don't think Tony would scruple at giving one of his boys the contract. They knew how to do this sort of thing. Tony would then get his money, and on top of that earn a fat fee for the job, which would still leave Watson with a tidy sum.

What's more, with Wilbur, the forger and boyfriend, out of the way, his part in painting the copies would never come to light. Then there was the element of revenge—no man likes the idea of someone else sleeping with his wife. Finally, there was that little matter of the nude portrait Wilbur had painted of Watson. Whatever had inspired that indiscretion would forever remain Watson's little secret. He might blush to remember the circumstances, but he'd never have to explain anything to anyone else. After all, most likely the only other person who knew about it was me.

So it all fit, didn't it? And I remembered something Hobey had said just before he passed out that night—"Watson's your man." Of course, Hobey was no detective, but he was good at devising plots. Was there really that much difference between a hack writer and a hack detective? Not from where I stood. On second thought, though, it wasn't right to call Hobey a hack, no matter what Hollywood thought of him these days. When it came to judging writers, Hollywood almost always got it wrong. As for me, well, I've been called worse.

But the question before the house was—had Watson already disposed of the real Monet, or was it sitting on Bunny's desk at UCLA?

And what if—against all odds—that one did turn out to be real? What then?

I had kept my rooms at the Garden of Allah. On the surface, this was a concession to the morals clause in Myrtle's contract, but in fact it was an arrangement that suited me better than living full-time in the house in Malibu. Show me a man who is living with a woman who doesn't secretly wish for a place of his own, a place to go off to now and then, just to be alone, and I will show you a man who will have changed his mind in a year or so. I can't be sure, of course, but I would bet the same thing applied to women. How could it be otherwise? We're not *that* different, men and women, I mean.

Myrtle had lost a lot of her nascent gaiety after the incident with Rex Lockwood or whatever his name was. That was not surprising, of course. Bashing someone to death with a poker is apt to take the shine off anyone's joie de vivre. She had reverted to a kind of Slavic melancholy that enhanced, rather than detracted from, her allure. She started going to the Catholic church and even asked me to go with her once, which I did. It turned out to be a solemn high mass, and the incense made me sneeze, so we didn't repeat that experiment.

She never told me whether she'd confessed that business with Rex to her priest, but if she had I had to assume the guy would keep his mouth shut about it. That was in their contract, as I understood it. And maybe that kind of confession was a good thing. After all, the priest could grant absolution, which is a lot better than what my old Presbyterian preacher could do. Under similar circumstances, he would have told you to turn yourself in, and a fat lot of good that would have done.

It occurred to us that as a White Russian princess, she should be going to the Orthodox Church, but the closest one was clear across town, and we figured no one in Hollywood would know the difference even if, in the unlikely event, someone spotted her going to Catholic mass. Besides, there are only so many sacrifices you can make for the Publicity Department, and Myrtle didn't like the Orthodox outfit. It reminded her too much of the Serbs.

Despite her mild reversion to religion, Myrtle was tough, and she carried on with her acting lessons and auditions as though nothing had happened. Her better-than-Garbo-like smoldering soon caught the attention of the big shots, and she was cast in a new sheik-of-Araby epic starring some guy named Arturo, who was going to be the next big thing in profiles, flashing eyes, and all-around masculine appeal, even though the word was he was a fairy. So she was on her way. We celebrated that deal with champagne and lobsters, and we spent the rest of the evening in a variety of delightful positions, so that when we finally slept it was in happy exhaustion. We still hadn't figured out whether we were just half in love or all the way. I suppose it didn't really matter. Those were just definitions, after all, and the nights together were more than enough definition for anybody.

Anyway, on the evening of the day I talked with Bunny, I went back to my rooms at the Garden. Myrtle was working late.

As I walked past the swimming pool on my way to my bungalow, I heard a familiar voice:

"Hiya, Sparky!"

Catherine was sitting at a table across the pool. Hobey was with her. He was wearing a lopsided grin and an old-fashioned bathing suit, the kind with the upper half that looked like an undershirt. The whole outfit was orange and black stripes—Princeton colors, as it turned out. There was a third person there—a striking brunette. Like Catherine, she was wearing a skimpy bathing suit, and it was easy to understand why Hobey was grinning. He was sitting between two beautiful women; Hollywood had at last delivered on its promise.

Catherine waved me over.

"Just in time for cocktails, Bruno," said Hobey.

"I accept." I sat down in the fourth chair.

"This is my friend Hedda," said Catherine, indicating the brunette.

"How do you do," I said.

"Pleased to meet you, I'm sure," said Hedda in an accent unheard west of the East River. Don't ask how I knew that. From the movies, I guess.

"Hedda's a journalist," said Hobey with a wry smile. "Her full name is Hedda Gabler."

"Really? It seems I've heard that name before."

"It ain't my real name," said Hedda. "My agent dreamed it up."

"She writes a column for *Hush-Hush* magazine. About what the stars are up to," said Catherine. "I thought it'd be nice for she and Hobey to get to know one another, him being in the business and all."

I saw Hobey wince at Catherine's grammatical potholes, but he took a philosophical draft of his gin and tonic, and I did the same. He was obviously the broad-minded sort when it came to women. And with women like these two, who wouldn't be?

"What did you do before you became a journalist?" I asked.

"Notions. At a shop in Flatbush. But a girl gets tired of selling needles and buttons after a while. I wanted some excitement. You know?"

"Sure. So you came to Hollywood."

"Kind of. To tell you the truth, I was brought. But the gentleman turned out to be not so much of one, so I gave him the bird and was lucky enough to meet another gentleman who said he wanted to be my agent, and he got me the job at *Hush-Hush* magazine, which is how I became a journalist."

"The American dream," said Hobey.

"Thank you," said Hedda, assuming he had meant her. She had a beautifully vacant smile, long eyelashes that looked real, and a superb figure that her bathing suit did nothing to disguise. I could almost hear Hobey's heart pounding for joy. Things were definitely looking up for him. And I had to give Catherine high marks for her thoughtfulness. She was generous in more ways than one. And I told her so when we were alone after Hobey and Hedda had gone for a swim.

"He's a nice fella," Catherine said. "I was afraid he was going to fall in love with me. He seems like the type it happens to real easy. Some guys are like that. Not like you." I don't know whether she meant that as a compliment or a criticism, but I didn't pursue it. "So I figured the best way to avoid that is bring in someone else. Hedda was sort of at loose ends; her agent would like to be simpatico, but he isn't, so I figured, why not introduce her to Hobey? He wants to be in love; she needs somebody, preferably in the business. And she's broad-minded. She don't mind that he's just a writer."

"That is broad-minded."

"I know."

"How're things with Manny?"

She rolled her eyes. "About what I expected. Like old Macdonald's farm. Here a schtup, there a schtup, everywhere a schtup-schtup. But the good news is that he softened up, no joke intended, and gave me a part in a movie he's producing."

"Congratulations. You're on your way."

"I know. It's something about sand and tents. I get to wear a harem costume. Think it'll look good on me?"

"You could wear a suit of armor and still have them howling at the moon," I said.

"Smooth talker. Well, I gotta get going. Electrocution lessons, dahling."

"Does your teacher ever talk about proper grammar?"

"Like in school? No. He don't care if we say it wrong as long as we pronounce it right, you know? It's Hollywood."

"Yes, it is."

"Tell Hobey and Hedda I said so long, and don't do anything I wouldn't do."

She winked elaborately and ironically.

"That leaves a lot of room for maneuver," I said.

"Don't it?" She laughed and clattered off in her high heels, waving at Hobey and Hedda, who were off in the deep end—in Hobey's case, an appropriate place to be.

CHAPTER FIFTEEN

For the next couple of days I found myself on the beach out in Malibu, reading the latest P. G. Wodehouse novel and wishing I could write like that. The more I thought about it, the more the idea of writing for the movies appealed to me. The detective business was all very well, and as Bunny had said I did seem to have a knack for it. But it was also a little depressing now and then. Dead bodies and all that. And the money was lousy.

I read somewhere that Wodehouse had been hired at two thousand a week plus a free house in Hollywood and that he never did anything for the studio; he just sat around his swimming pool, cashed his checks, and when his contract was up, went back to England. That sounded like something I could handle. If Myrtle really did make it big, I'd at least have a good entry point. And there was also Ethel Welkin and her cousin Manny—both of whom were in my corner, for different reasons, of course. And I knew all of those writers from the Garden of Allah. They might come in handy some day.

I hadn't heard anything from Bunny, but I assumed the tests he wanted to run would take a little time, probably involve some lab work, so I wasn't concerned. For the time being, I didn't think Watson would notice the difference in his Monet.

And, as it turned out, he didn't; nor would he ever.

The news was on the radio. They'd found him stuffed in the trunk of his car out on the top floor of the airport parking garage. I guess he'd been in there for a couple of days, baking in the sun, and someone finally noticed. He'd been shot in the back of the head with a small-caliber bullet, so his face wasn't disfigured. Not from the bullet wound, anyway. The report said he was wearing a polka-dot ascot.

I called Kowalski.

"You heard, huh?" he asked.

"Just now. Any ideas?"

"Lots of ideas. Not much in the way of leads. It was a professional job, though. Not much doubt about that. No prints on the car. Everything was clean."

"Mob hit."

"Looks that way. You know any reason why he got in Dutch with the bad boys?"

"I heard he was into Tony Scungilli for a hundred grand in gambling debts."

"Interesting, but it doesn't fit. As a general rule, the guy who's owed the money wants the other guy to stay alive long enough to pay up. He may rough the guy up a little, as a reminder, but it makes no sense to kill him."

"I see your point."

"We hauled in the Jap houseboy to see if he had anything to say."

"And?"

"He didn't know anything. Watson took off a couple of days ago and that was the last Tojo saw of him. He kept showing me his phony visa that some guy named Emile Phengfisch signed. You know anything about that?"

"Can't say I do."

"Well, turns out there's no one named Emile Phengfisch working for INS."

"It's a wicked world. What'd you do with him? The houseboy, I mean."

"Let him go. We've got enough to do."

Well, I didn't have enough to do, so I figured I'd have another talk with Satchiko.

I didn't waste any time getting myself over to Watson's house. I was afraid Satchiko might take off. After all, he didn't have a job anymore. And once he disappeared, there'd be no finding him. I was sure of that.

When I got to Watson's gate and picked up the telephone, I was relieved to hear Satchiko's voice on the other end.

"Satchiko. This is Agent Clapsaddle again. You remember me?"

"Yes. Remember."

"Good. I need to have another quick chat with you. There's no trouble."

"Not in trouble?"

"No."

"You sure?"

"I'm sure."

He buzzed the gate open, and this time I drove up the driveway.

He met me at the door and bowed.

"Mr. Watson dead," he said.

"I heard. Very sad. That's not why I'm here."

"Police talk to me."

"I know."

"Come in, please."

We sat down in the same chairs in front of the fireplace. He perched nervously on the edge of his chair.

"Satchiko, you remember that sad day when Mrs. Watson shot the burglar and then committed suicide?"

He nodded slightly.

"That was a strange thing to do, wasn't it? Almost unbelievable."

"Yes. Very strange."

"Do you really believe it happened that way?"

He adopted the inscrutability of the Orient and said nothing.

"Did you see any of what happened?"

"No see nothing."

"Maybe. But what do you think happened?"

"No think."

I paused and lit a cigarette, a Lucky Strike. I don't like to smoke, but it's a good way to inject silence into an interrogation. I looked at him for a moment, using my official government face.

"How would you like to go back home?" I asked. "Back to Japan?"

"Would like. But no money."

"Well, you're in luck. You see, the INS has a program that pays the passage of some foreign nationals. Passage home."

He brightened up considerably at that notion.

"Sound good to me. Yes, please."

"There is one condition, though. The people we select have to provide some useful service to the government."

"Me only gardener and houseboy."

"I know. But we think you may be able to provide us with some information. And if you can, you will earn the passage money. Okay?"

"I try. But can promise nothing."

"Fair enough. Let me tell you a story, and then you can tell me what you think about it afterwards. Okay?"

"Yes." He didn't sound enthusiastic.

"Here's the story. On the evening that Mrs. Watson and her friend Wilbur died, a man came to the house. He didn't come to the front door, but through the French doors into the drawing room. He was wearing gloves. And maybe a mask. When he came into the room, he hid himself behind the drapes and waited there.

"Pretty soon, Wilbur arrived. He came in the same way, through the French doors. Mrs. Watson must have been expecting him, because a moment later she came into the room with a gun in her hand. She saw Wilbur. Maybe they argued for a while. Then she shot him three times. At that point, the man behind the drapes stepped out and frightened Mrs. Watson. She dropped the gun. The man picked it up, put it to her temple, and pulled the trigger.

She dropped to the floor, and the man put the gun in her hand and left.

"Well? What do you think of that story?"

He said nothing for a minute or more. I puffed on the Lucky and watched him struggle. He wanted the money, but he hated getting involved.

"You know, Satchiko, if you can verify my story, you could have the money and be out of here this very afternoon."

"What means 'verify'?"

"Tell me whether the story is true or not."

He nodded slightly.

"Not true," he said finally.

"No?"

"Not exact."

"What do you mean?"

"Two men," he said.

"There were two men hiding in the room?"

"Yes. Saw from outside. Whole thing. Through French doors. Hide in bushes."

"But one of them did kill Mrs. Watson and then put the gun in her hand."

"Yes. Like you say."

"And she shot Wilbur? Not one of the men?"

"Yes. Like you say."

"Then the two men left."

"Yes. Climb over wall. Heard one man yell. Get caught on glass. Scratch ass."

"Why didn't you call the police?"

"Want no trouble. Visa phony. Go into guest house and hide. Police come when Mr. Watson come home. He call police."

"Did he seem upset when he found the bodies?"

"Don't know. Hiding in guest house whole time."

Hard to blame him.

"Well, Satchiko, you have been a big help."

"Earn money?"

"Yes. One hundred dollars." I counted out five twenties and handed them over.

He smiled, revealing two gold teeth. That was the last I ever saw of him.

I went back to the office and called Bunny.

"Have you heard the news?" I asked.

"About Watson? Yes. Shocking business. They say it's a mob-related assassination."

"That's the way it looks."

"I gather those kinds of crimes are rarely solved."

"You gather correctly."

"Too bad."

"Yes. Too bad. I wonder if he had any heirs. There's the matter of the Monet to consider."

"I don't think that will be a problem. The second painting is definitely a forgery."

"Really! You're sure."

"Positive. As I said, we did some tests on the wooden stretchers, the canvas, and the actual paint. Everything dates from the last year or so. The forger was very clever, of course, and very talented. But no one can fool scientific analysis."

"So it's worthless."

"Yes, I'm afraid so. Someone might want it as a copy, of course. A few dollars. Something like that."

"What should we do with it?"

"If I were you, I'd hang it in my office. As a memento."

"Do you have any idea at all of where the original might be?"

"None whatever, I'm afraid. I made a few discreet calls to my contacts in the private-placement business, but none of them had heard of a Monet being shopped around or sold. Of course, they may have been hiding something, since that is the nature of their business. But if so, we'll never know about it. The painting could be anywhere in the world even as we speak. These deals happen quickly. It may be another hundred years or so before it surfaces. If then."

"Too bad."

"Yes. Too bad. Shall I send the forgery around to your office?"

"I guess."

"It'll take a couple of days. The canvas is still a trifle damp from where we applied the analytic solutions. It's still at the laboratory." He pronounced all five syllables.

"Well, there's certainly no hurry."

"No, I suppose not. Well, why don't you stop by the office later this afternoon? We'll have a drink to mark the ending of the case."

"I'd like that."

"Good. Say around five-ish."

Next I called Kowalski and brought him up to date on the painting and, more importantly, on Satchiko's statement.

"No kidding?" he asked. "You got the Jap to talk?"

"He sang like Madame Butterfly."

"I'll send a car for him right away."

I didn't mention the hundred bucks or the very strong suspicion that Satchiko would be long gone by this time. It didn't matter to me one way or the other. He'd never be able to identify the two gunmen, so his testimony was not worth much, now that we knew what actually had happened.

"So the lady killed the boyfriend," said Kowalski, more or less to himself, "and the gangsters killed her and made it look like a suicide. It all makes sense—a hell of a lot more sense than the idea that she killed herself after plugging lover boy. She was a professional hit, of course, so that brings Watson into the picture. He must have hired the gunmen to get rid of his wife. Why? Was she that big a pain in the ass?"

"Maybe. But I think the real reason is that Watson was deep in debt to the mob for gambling. I'll bet if you check his financial records, you'll find he was pretty well tapped out. So he arranged with Wilbur to paint a copy of the last valuable—and easily sold—asset he had."

"The flower pot."

"Right. She found out about it and probably threatened him some way or other. Divorce, alimony, insurance fraud, the full catastrophe. So she had to go. There was no other way. Watson was hemmed in."

"Why'd she plug lover boy?"

"Hell hath no fury."

"Yeah, I heard that. I imagine Watson set the whole thing up by calling Wilbur and telling him to come to the house. If his wife didn't kill him, the two gangsters would have. But she saved them the trouble."

"So then the mob boys got rid of Watson because he was the only one who could put the finger on them."

"Something like that. Maybe he tried to blackmail them to get out from under his debts. Maybe he had already sold the real painting, got his money, and paid off his debts, so that he could be safely put out of the way. That way, the hit men would be protected."

"That points the finger toward Tony Scungilli."

"Looks that way. I doubt we'll ever know."

"Yeah, you're right. I'd like to haul him in and ask a few questions, but he's too well connected to the powers that be. He'd be back on the street in a second or two, and I'd be checking parking meters."

"Even with your college education?"

"Especially with my college education."

"What are you going to do about the newspaper boys? Tell them the truth?"

"Why? Right now, we got a murder/suicide between pissed-off lovers. Very simple. Then we got a mob hit on a guy who got mixed up with some bad boys he owed money to. Two separate crimes, both easy to understand and put to bed. The fact that two of the victims happen to be married is one of those coincidences out of Dickinson."

"Dickens."

"Him, too. We'll make a show of looking for the Watson hit men, but nobody expects us to come up with anything there. The moral of the Watson story is, you welsh on a gangster, you end up in a trunk. The end."

"Nice and neat."

"You got a better idea?"

"Not really."

"Good. Now don't go selling your story to one of these gossip magazines. They'd love something like this, but it would make things untidy."

"Untidy?"

"That's right. Cops like things to be tidy. Means less paperwork."

"My lips are sealed."

"Glad to hear it. Well, as my old man used to say, ya done good. I appreciate the help. You may go far in this business."

"I don't know. I'm thinking of getting out of it altogether. Maybe take up writing for the movies."

"Well, nobody ever accused you of being short on bullshit, so maybe it'll work out."

A week later I got the copy of the Monet. Bunny had it delivered to the office. As he said, there was a sheet of paper pasted firmly on the back saying that this was just a copy, worth next to nothing.

I hung it next to the Barbasol calendar and looked at it for a while, wondering.

CHAPTER SIXTEEN

The movie Myrtle was in was called *The Desert Prince.*
They shot it outside Yuma, Arizona, where all those
sand dunes are—just across the river on the California
side. It took them a couple of weeks. Manny Stairs was the
producer and Catherine Moore was one of the harem girls.
Rita Lovelace was also in the movie. Myrtle stole the show,
though. She played a White Russian princess who had been
kidnapped by a desert sheik. Or something like that. It made
no sense, but it didn't need to.

Manny was delighted with Myrtle. She smoldered on
screen like nobody's business, and the rumor was that she

was so alluring that her co-star, Arturo Lopez (né Jimmy Gardner) was almost tempted to give up trolling for sailors. Manny was considering having the two of them become the studio's latest lovers, strictly for the movie-magazine crowd. I didn't mind. Nothing real would come of that.

When the movie finished shooting, we gave a party at the beach house in Malibu. Manny and Catherine came. So did Rita Lovelace. I invited Ethel and her husband, but they had something else to do. It was just as well. I really didn't need to have four former and current lovers at one clambake. Perry and Della were there, along with Hobey and his new flame, Hedda Gabler. Hobey and Manny got along pretty well, and Hobey even managed to extract a promise of a meeting to pitch a new movie idea. Of course, the ever-generous Catherine had a lot to do with arranging that. She told me she had a soft spot for Hobey, and she said it with a straight face.

I also invited Bunny, since he was between other men's wives at the moment, and I thought he and Rita might hit it off, which of course they did.

Bunny made quite a stir when he pulled up in a shiny new Rolls-Royce. The grille alone looked like something from Cartier's window. And the interior smelled like old money.

"Nice car," I said.

"Isn't it?" He didn't seem in the least embarrassed. "Just picked it up yesterday. Of course, it is rather ostentatious for a university professor to be driving around in. But I couldn't resist. Such perfection of design. I think of it as a present from my dear recently deceased maiden aunt. She was kind enough to remember me in her will."

"Lucky you," I said.

"Yes. I agree."

"You're about to get luckier."

"Really?"

"Yep. This gal coming over here dressed in almost nothing at all is Rita Lovelace. She's by herself tonight."

Rita was drawn to the Rolls like a moth to the proverbial flame. She sashayed up, her bathing suit a mere suggestion of cloth. Impure thoughts came to me, and to Bunny, from the look of him.

"Charming name," Bunny said, as he kissed Rita's hand.

"Thank you," she positively cooed. "I've heard so much about you. From Bruno."

"Who?"

"She means me," I said. "A professional nom de guerre."

"A tautology, I think, my dear Thomas. All noms de guerre are by definition professional. But never mind."

I didn't mind the correction. When you're self-taught, you take lessons however they arrive.

"Tell me, Rita," said Bunny. "What role did you play in this excellent new movie?"

"I played Yolanda, queen of the Arabs."

"Ah. How lovely. I never knew that the Arabs had queens."

"These ones do."

"What a wonderful business."

"Is your name really Bunny?"

"I'm afraid that's what most people call me. Silly, isn't it?"

"No. I like it," she said.

"Care for a drink, my dear?"

"Yes, please. A gin and tonic." Rita glanced at me briefly and winked. I remembered our afternoon.

They walked off together, chatting amiably and flirtatiously, while I took one more look at Bunny's elegant new car, wishing that I also had such a generous maiden aunt.

While I was pondering life's inequities, Catherine came up behind me.

"Hiya, Sparky," she said.

"Hello, beautiful," I said. "Want to run away from home?"

"Smooth talker. I told you, don't go falling in love with me. I got enough on my plate."

"I promise. Besides, you've met Myrtle."

"Have I! She's going to be something special, you mark my words. Or Manny's. And if he knows anything, he knows raincoats and the movie business. He was in the raincoat business before he came out here, so he knows two things real well."

"I understand."

"She's so beautiful, I'm not even jealous."

"You don't need to take any back seats."

"I know. When you're really beautiful, you can be fair, you know? Like me. It's the ones who are not so beautiful that are bitchy."

She looked at Bunny's Rolls.

"What a pretty car. Do you know what I heard him say just now? He was talking to Manny, so the subject naturally came around to money. Money and schtupping is all Manny thinks about. Anyway, this guy Bunny—and who goes by Bunny, by the way?—he said his old English maiden aunt left him twenty thousand pounds. How much is that in real money? It sounds like a lot, but it might not be."

"It's a lot. I think the exchange rate is about five dollars to the pound."

"So you multiply five times twenty thousand?"

"Yep."

"Wow. He's lucky to have a dead aunt like that."

"Isn't he."

She looked at me beneath her astonishing eyelashes. Her green eyes were all innocence.

"Do you believe it?"

"Believe what?"

"That story."

"About the dead aunt?"

"Yes."

"Why do you ask?"

"Oh, you know, when you're schtupping a big-time producer and you got a gangster on the side, you hear things."

"I'll bet."

"Well?"

Did I believe it?

Sure. Sure I did.

ABOUT THE AUTHOR

Terry Mort is a graduate of Princeton University and the University of Michigan. After graduate school he served as an officer in the navy. He is the author of numerous books, both fiction and non-fiction, most recently *The Wrath of Cochise*. He divides his time between Arizona and Colorado.